To save her soul, he'll let her burn.

Grayce has been on the run for years. Having escaped an abusive relationship with a violent psychopath, she is trying to rebuild her life one small step at a time. Things are going well until Zander crosses her path, badass and sexy as hell. His presence awakens heated desires she long ago buried. Last thing Grayce wants is a man, and the way her body reacts to Zander scares her more than the threat of being found.

Tyr will do anything to get his little dove back. She is a Beacon, and her raw, burning energy gives him power and strength. More than the evil that already compels him. But a blond giant of a man hovers protectively around her. No matter. He'll play with him too.

When Zander rescues Grayce from Tyr's first attempt to reclaim her, he reveals his superhuman abilities. Power that Grayce also has, but is yet to understand. As predestined soul mates in a race of fallen angels, Zander must help Grace control her rage before her fire threatens to destroy everyone and everything in her path. But his true challenge is more than that—to show her it's possible to trust and love again.

Books by Krissy Daniels

Aflame
How to Kill Your Boss - An Erotic Love Story

Published by Kensington Publishing Corporation

Aflame

Apotheosis, Book One

Krissy Daniels

LYRICAL PRESS
Kensington Publishing Corp.
www.kensingtonbooks.com

Lyrical Press books are published by
Kensington Publishing Corp. 119 West 40th Street New York, NY 10018

All Kensington titles, imprints, and distributed lines are available at special quantity discounts for bulk purchases for sales promotion, premiums, fund-raising, and educational or institutional use.

Special book excerpts or customized printings can also be created to fit specific needs. For details, write or phone the office of the Kensington Special Sales Manager:
Kensington Publishing Corp.
119 West 40th Street
New York, NY 10018
Attn. Special Sales Department. Phone: 1-800-221-2647.

Kensington and the K logo Reg. U.S. Pat. & TM Off.
Lyrical Press and the L logo are trademarks of Kensington Publishing Corp.

First Electronic Edition: April 2014
eISBN-13: 978-1-61650-536-3
eISBN-10: 1-61650-536-2

First Print Edition: April 2014
ISBN-13: 978-1-61650-834-0
ISBN-10: 1-61650-834-5

Printed in the United States of America

For those dispirited, who battle demons in the shadows, too weary to cry for help, you are not alone.

Chapter 1

Two more minutes. Two more minutes of torture, then *adios amigos*. Grayce out. Tired? Not a chance.

Grayce hopped off the elliptical before it stopped, grabbed her bottled water and glanced around the massive room.

No sign of him anywhere. Thank God.

On shaky legs, she forced herself to head to the weight machines. If luck was on her side, she'd get through an entire workout without running into the obscenely attractive, gargantuan blond who tracked her every move. The beast was a sight to behold. She pretended not to notice. She'd die before ogling him like the other women. Problem was, he ignored everyone. Except her.

He was the only man who could make her blush and that pissed her off beyond measure. Rounding the corner, a familiar, heated flush pulsed through her body. The warning, however, did not come soon enough. It didn't allow her enough time to run the opposite direction before her face acquainted itself with a brick wall disguised as a chest.

"Ouch, shit." Her ass narrowly avoided a painful introduction to the floor when a pair of strong hands caught her mid-fall and set her upright. Tears threatened to surface. No need to look up. Grayce cupped her nose and forced her gaze to the far wall, painfully aware of who she freight-trained into.

"You all right?" His deep silky voice cut right through the heavily guarded walls she'd built around herself, and melted a layer, possibly two, of the hardened steel protecting her most vital organ. And that was precisely why she needed to get as far away from him as possible.

Without a word, Grayce turned on her heel and jetted the hell out of there.

* * * *

Heart in his throat, Zander watched her walk away. She hadn't uttered a word. As per her norm, she looked at the wall, his shoes, the old lady riding the recumbent bike. Everything but him.

Stunned by the energy burst searing his veins, unsteady legs refused their command to follow her. Instead, he enjoyed the view. As she huffed away, blood rushed to his cock. A baggy cotton ensemble hid her form, which made her all the more tantalizing. Large breasts, curvy hips? Small waist with a firm tight ass? Made no difference to him. When he finally had her good and naked, she'd be perfect, because she belonged to him.

Full of hellfire and fury, she marched her petite frame toward the exit, shouted an obscenity, then backtracked to the locker room. He couldn't help but chuckle. Saucy little lady.

They'd get along just fine.

Being a descendent of an ancient warrior race planted on earth by fallen angels had its perks; superhuman abilities, immunity from illness and extended life spans to name a few. But there was a downside. Males of his heritage could never reach their full potential until they'd found and bonded with their other half, or soul mate as he preferred to call it.

Zander's search spanned almost twenty years. He was one of the lucky ones, knowing his one true mate existed. Most of his kind hadn't a clue. Finding their better halves was the hard part. He'd done it. Yet, there he stood, watching her walk away again.

Moments passed before Zander realized he hadn't moved an inch. As he glanced around the gym, it was no shock that everyone stared in his direction. Ladies flashed him their brightest smiles, men straightened their backs in attempt to make themselves taller and boys simply scurried to clear a path. Common reactions. None of it mattered. What was important? After years of tireless searching, his future was within reach.

Shit. He didn't even know her name.

Fuck the taking-it-slow approach. It was time to get the girl. He forced uncooperative legs to move. At the same moment, she stormed from the locker room rubbing her nose. An impressive combination of profanities followed her through the exit, drawing gasps and sneers from anyone within earshot. With a deep breath, he straightened his shoulders and trailed a few paces behind.

"Hi, Mr. Vascos," Carrie shouted from behind the counter.

"Yeah, yeah, whatever. Leave me alone. I have a lady to claim," he grumbled under his breath, waving her off as he passed.

Carrie's deflated sigh pulled at his heart strings. He was such a sappy bastard. Abruptly, he turned toward her, forced the biggest smile he could muster and took a moment to be kind to the only other person in the gym he gave two fucks about. "Carrie. How are you today?"

Blushing violet, Carrie leaned toward him. "I'm wonderful, Mr. Vascos. I met someone." Sunshine poured from her smile. "He's tall, dark and handsome and drives a Porsche. My first time in a Porsche. Absolutely amazing." Her grin grew even wider as she stared glossy-eyed at the ceiling.

"That's great." He didn't roll his eyes, but damn it was tempting. Porsches were for pussies, or men who needed help getting pussy. "He better be good to you or he'll have me to deal with." Zander winked, jogged toward the exit, and left Carrie in her state of bliss.

* * * *

Tyr Collins leaned back, rested the heels of his A. Testoni shoes on the windowsill and plucked lint from his slacks. It became impossible to hold back a smile. Worried that the stretch of his cheeks might add wrinkles to his near flawless skin, he concentrated on relaxing the major muscles in his face.

Grayce, his little dove, was finally coming back to him. The wait had been torture, but he'd set the wheels in motion, and soon her addictive energy would be his again. Unable to ignore the annoying erection that strained painfully against his trousers, he reached down for a quick rub and adjust.

Three years had passed. Slippery little slut. His spine tingled with anticipation at the imagined look of horror on her face when she'd realize he'd claimed her once again.

God, she was going to pay. Dearly.

Binoculars raised and focused, he scanned the gym parking lot to make sure his latest game piece was in place. This was going to be fun. It would've been much easier to grab her himself. But why? There was much more pleasure to be gained in toying with prey before you strike. And the fear, oh yes, the fear made it so much more satisfying in the end.

* * * *

Certain the steam screaming from her ears was visible to everyone, Grayce stormed toward the exit doors. Distance is what she needed, and mere miles wouldn't be enough. The familiar ache ignited by his presence consumed every inch of flesh. Intense attraction, need, lust. Emotions not welcome in her world forced their way through an obsessively guarded wall.

Her long lost libido had come back with vengeance and completely betrayed the memory of the hell she'd lived through at the hands of men.

With temper rising to near nuclear proportions, she struggled against shaky fingers to unlock the door to her rundown VW Rabbit.

"Don't turn around." A sour stench filled her nostrils before the words registered. Tobacco and skunk. A heavy hand weighted her shoulder. "Get in the car and slide over." The raspy voice and wheeze with each breath were a dead giveaway the man had held a thousand too many coffin nails between his lips over the course of his lifetime.

Oh hell no. Bravery, fueled by intense anger, filled Grayce with an unexpected sense of power. With a quick turn she swung her right arm at the man. Damn gym bag. Its weight slowed her momentum, and the strike barely fazed him. No way in hell was she going to allow the fat bastard to bully her into the car.

Before her bag hit the ground, her foot met his shin with force enough to evoke profanities. Freak may as well have been Superman and she a toddler for all the good it did. Putrid stench brought the sting of tears to her eyes as he grabbed both shoulders and shoved her into the front seat.

Scream damn you, scream. "You fucking bastard, get off me!" The strength in her voice came as a surprise, as did the new wave of adrenaline that pumped through her veins. Desperation guided her movements as she batted, kicked and successfully thwarted his efforts at getting a solid hold on anything other than her clothing. What had the self-defense class taught her? Crap, who could remember? Should've paid better attention.

Frenzied attempts at kneeing his groin had her awkwardly positioned, half in, half out of the car. Four kicks in, she found her target. The man wore a fearsome grimace as he doubled over, spit, and stumbled backwards in pain.

Pure evil flooded his bloodshot eyes.

Seizing the opportunity, Grayce lifted her legs at a feeble attempt to strike again. Her butt slid down the edge of the car seat and landed with a thud on unforgiving pavement, knocking the wind clean out of her lungs. Stunned and struggling to regain her bearings, she looked up in time to see a dirty, hairy-knuckled fist shoot straight for her nose. Except, it didn't make contact.

Playing out like a slow motion scene from an action movie, the perp was violently jerked back by the nape of his neck. Arms and legs flailed in front of him as he was lifted off the ground, eyes wide with disbelief. Tossed like a rag doll across the parking lot, he bounced off the chain link fence, wrapped around a street lamp and landed with a thud. His body twitched, then lay ragged and motionless, slumped in a heap on the cement.

Grayce fought to draw breath as her gaze traced the length of the figure towering with protective intent. Hmm, muscles and more muscles. Horrified and dazzled simultaneously, she stared into the face of the man she'd tried so hard to avoid.

Chapter 2

Well Z, helluva way to make a first impression. Nothing like bringing out the big guns on a first date.

Acting on instinct, he squatted to brush tangled hair from his woman's face. Intense, powerful vibrations passed between their flesh. He didn't flinch. Knew it was coming. She however, did not.

Holy hell, she felt it.

Wild eyed and bewildered, she cowered and backed away. Definitely an inappropriate time to smile, but shit. What else could he do? For years he'd waited for this moment. "Did he hurt you? Can you move?"

"Yeah. I mean, no. I mean, I think I'm okay." Liar. Attempts at pushing herself up had her wincing in pain. "Fucking bastard."

"I love a girl with a potty mouth." God, did he ever. In fact, it hadn't dawned on him until right then and there how much he loved it.

"I'm sorry, I'm pissed right now."

Palpitations, rapid breaths, sweaty palms. Every cliché hit him at the same time. As he bent to help her up, vanilla scented hair ticked his nose.

Reminded him of home.

Lifting her wasn't such a good idea. Blood rushed to his sex and he'd never been more thankful for an oversized hoodie. "Can you stand?"

She nodded. A hazel-eyed glare traveled the length of his torso and width of his chest.

Pleasured by her perusal, excited by the red glow dusting her cheeks, he bit hard on his lower lip. The urge to taste her, the need to claim her fleshy pink mouth nearly short-circuited his brain.

"Wow. Workout much?" Cringing, Grayce placed shaky hands on his forearms. With all the tenderness he could muster, Zander attempted to set her upright, straighten her clothing, offer some comfort.

Big mistake.

With a sharp intake of breath, her body tensed and terror filled her eyes.

Fear was not the reaction he'd expected. Sure, he was huge and most people stayed the hell out of his way, but she wasn't most people. This woman was his missing half, created by the heavens for him alone. If anything, his presence should calm her. She should crave his touch, not recoil from it.

Something was terribly wrong.

He tilted his head to catch her gaze. Glassy-eyed, she stared past his shoulder. Then she started to shake.

* * * *

As the beautiful giant set her on her feet and straightened disheveled clothing, Grayce's brain shifted into auto pilot. Shutdown process initiated. She hadn't been touched like that in years. By anyone, man or woman. Not since her escape.

The tremble started in her chest, spread to her limbs, threatened to rattle her teeth.

To lose control and slip into her dark place was a luxury she couldn't afford. Not now. Not in front of this man. Desperate for a distraction, anything to wrench her from panic mode, she scanned the parking lot. Her search came to a halt when her eyes rested on the lifeless heap on the ground. Holy fuck, was he dead?

"You're shaking. Do you have a coat?" The undeniable concern in his voice made it harder to pull her shit together.

Throat dry and tight, Grayce couldn't manage to choke a word out. She blinked up at him, reluctant to meet him eye to eye. Before the next blink, he'd wrapped a sweatshirt around her shoulders. That's when the waterworks began. A floodgate opened, releasing a surge of wracking sobs and a heavy flow of tears. Two heartbeats and she found herself tucked gently against warm, hard muscle, face buried in his chest, while he tenderly stroked her hair.

He lowered her to the ground, rested his back against her car and held her snug and tight. Despite obvious differences in size, she fit against him perfectly, like the last piece of a puzzle. His caress soothed, his touch brought solace, not pain. She'd never felt so fucking safe and warm. So she let tears fall and allowed him to go through the comforting motions. When composed enough to form a coherent thought, she realized his lips were pressed firmly against her head.

What the? Defensively, with a sharp shiver, she pulled away.

"Um, thank you, I'm sorry. I just—" God. Just what? What the hell was happening?

"No, don't apologize. You did nothing wrong. But damn, that fucker's going to be sorry he messed with you. That was a mean knee to the balls." A low chuckle vibrated his chest. "You're a tough little cookie, brave too." Awkwardly, he offered his hand. "I'm Z by the way."

Grayce tried to sit up. His arms tensed, held her tighter, then relaxed. A vise gripped her heart and lungs simultaneously. "I'm Grayce. Thank you. I think I'm better now." She wasn't. All the up close and personal made her want to scream.

"Of course you are." Like an air mattress with a slow leak, his taut muscles softened beneath her. He lowered his arms in a slow drag down the length of her body and let them drop to his sides.

Grayce dislodged herself from his lap, handed back his sweatshirt and climbed into her car.

"Can I call somebody for you?" he asked. As he rose to stand, his physique commanded her full attention, sucked the air from her lungs and one by one, brain cells fizzled and popped inside her cranium.

"Like the police?" Grayce asked. Morgue perhaps? A quick glimpse toward the man lying motionless on the ground had her fighting back the urge to scream.

Z shot a glance over his shoulder. "I'll be right back." His jaw tightened. "Please don't go anywhere." He leaned so close, his breath warmed her lips. He clapped her thigh with a hint of warning. "I mean it, don't go anywhere."

"I won't, I promise." Shit. Couldn't move a muscle if she wanted to.

* * * *

Z crouched over the man, checked his pulse, cursed under his breath. Motherfucker was still breathing. Not good. The shithead deserved nothing but dead. If Grayce hadn't been watching, the man would've already been shaking hands with Satan himself. Against every instinct, he pulled his cell from his pocket and dialed 9-1-1. At the same time, a group of boys exited the gym and made their way toward him.

Perfect timing. Cocky, over-pumped teenage pricks would be all over this. "Hey guys."

As if on cue, the gang stopped dead in their tracks with jaws opened as wide as their eyes. Pathetic as hell. They still hadn't noticed the man lying almost dead at their feet. Zander resisted the urge to slap them silly and instead enlightened them by looking down and poking his foot at the fat lump on the ground.

Not a single one of them spoke a word while Z finished the call.

"Listen, I called for help. Nearly tripped over the guy, think the drunken fucker's passed out cold. Can you dudes do me a solid and stay with him until the paramedics arrive?" Zander tucked his phone into his pocket.

After a long bout of blank stares and dead silence, one kid managed, "Yeah, no problem."

Idiots.

"Thanks. My wife is sick. I have to get home." Camera flashes lit up the darkening sky as he jogged back toward Grayce's car. Hell yeah, punks were eating it up. They'd take credit for saving the man. Worked for him.

Now he could concentrate on important shit, like claiming his woman.

* * * *

Grayce watched in awe as Z, with his out-of-this-world body, loped toward her. How could he have thrown that man so fucking far? Fat prick had to weigh damn near three hundred pounds. Did she imagine it? Was it humanly possible to toss a man fifty yards?

Not in her world.

It must be shock. That was the only logical explanation. When he leaned in, hands rested on knees, his chiseled chest flexed and contracted underneath the thin cotton of his muscle shirt. Made it difficult to think straight.

"I called for help. Convinced those kids I'd found him unconscious. They'll stay with him until the police arrive." Boyish, sexy dimples graced his face. "Let me take you home. I don't think driving would be such a good idea right now. Clearly you're still shaken."

"How did he end up way over there?" Grayce asked with a quiver.

There, she said it. He probably had a perfectly good explanation. *Looney bird, that's me.*

Eyes narrowed, brows furrowed, Z emptied his lungs with a huff. "You saw what happened, didn't you?"

Running shaky hands through her hair, she stopped at the crown and squeezed her roots. "I know what I think I saw, but what I think I saw is not physically possible." Over Zander's shoulder, Grayce watched the boys take pictures with their cell phones. Mr. Hairy Knuckles' mug shot had probably been plastered all over the internet by now.

Zander leaned closer. "What do you think you saw?"

Wow, he smelled good. Made it damn hard to focus on their conversation. Instinct urged her to inhale and drag all the yummy masculine scent deep into her lungs. Shit. What was wrong with her?

"I saw you throw him an impossible distance. Like a friggin' teddy bear." White-knuckling the steering wheel, Grayce banged her head against the back of her hands and prayed he wouldn't think her insane. What did it matter anyway? Why was he still talking to her?

"That is what happened."

Grayce squeezed her eyes shut. Sincerity or sarcasm? Past insecurities bobbed to the surface. Come on Grayce, don't be a pussy. In hopes of discovering whether he fucked with her or not, she summoned the courage to meet him square in the eyes.

Bad idea.

The moment their gazes met, Grayce was caught in a whirlpool, sucked deep into his soul. Mesmerized, wholly consumed by heavenly blue eyes filled with conviction. The peculiar connection caused her head to spin, her heart to beat rampant. Any doubt about his honesty evaporated, only to be replaced with the knowledge that if desired, she could steal every thought and emotion from his very being.

"Oh fuck. That's impossible. There is no fucking way you threw that—that thing across the parking lot." Because she'd be lost forever if their eyes locked again, she studied his lips. Perfectly carved, full and enticing, they begged to be nibbled. God she hungered to taste them, feel them brush against her skin. Seriously, what was wrong with her? Had she been hit on the head? Who fantasized about kissing after narrowly escaping a brutal attack?

Grayce averted her attentions to his nose, hoping it would offer no temptation. No such luck. It was incredibly sexy—strong and masculine, creating a perfect balance between his eyes and mouth.

God, she needed to focus.

She tried to hide her embarrassment behind the shield of her hands. Sirens blared in the distance granting a distraction from the torrid path her brain seemed to be following.

"Let me take you home," Z pleaded. Nervously scanning the parking lot, he stood, ran his hands through already messy hair, then squatted back down to eye level.

"What about the police? I have to talk to them." Grayce moved to get out of the car and Z braced the door.

"No. No, you don't have to talk to them. Those boys will take care of it." Becoming visibly more stressed, he chewed on his lower lip. "You saw what I did to him. That's not something we can explain to cops." The sirens grew louder. "We have to go. Now."

"But..." Before she could protest further, a gust of wind stole her breath. Hair whipped at her face with a stinging lash and forced her eyes closed. When able to see and breathe again she was tucked and buckled in the seat of his truck, which made no sense considering it was parked a block and a half away.

* * * *

Tyr watched from his perch as his man failed miserably at procuring Grayce. Simple task. What a shame. He'd been confident Houghton was the best choice for the job. It exhausted him arranging the deranged convict's escape from prison. Houghton was the first human he'd transported. A feat which left him physically and emotionally drained.

Thank goodness for his playthings at home. Of course, considering he'd found his favorite toy, his little dove, the others were useless. Disposable. Two days of rest replenished him fully. Having Grayce near again, his energy recharged two times faster than by the fear he'd been forced to feed upon.

As he witnessed the scene play out below, an excited tingle danced down his spine and caused his cock to twitch. The blond giant possessed incredible strength. When he threw Houghton like a rag doll, Tyr giggled in wonderment. What a beautiful creature. What would it be like to play with the giant and Grayce at the same time? Oh what fun. So many possibilities. What tools would he need to keep this man in check? The playroom would need to be fortified. Could he make it strong enough to hold such a massive, powerful male?

Time for a new plan.

Tyr fought back another cursed smile and crossed his arms. Blocks away, red lights lit up the evening sky. Well, they were in for a nice surprise, weren't they? This pathetic town would soon make national headlines.

* * * *

Z lead-footed his F-450 away from the gym, oncoming sirens and all other bullshit that ruined what should have been a happy union. "I'm sorry. Didn't mean to scare you. The police and I..." He sighed and shook his head. "We don't get along."

No response. Tension billowed throughout the spacious truck cabin for several long moments before Grayce nearly jumped through the roof. "Oh shit! Shit, shit, shit. I have to get to work." Profanities continued softly while she dug through her purse.

Krissy Daniels

Z jerked the steering wheel and slammed the brakes, throwing them forward against their seat belts. "Are you serious? You're worried about work?" The steering wheel cracked under the force of his grip. He relaxed his hands, only to feel the tension shift to his jaw. Fuck. After what just happened, she wanted to go to work? Had to be shock. That, or insanity.

"Listen. We don't know each other, and I won't give you my life story here. I need this job. I can't miss a shift. I'm fine. Working will distract me from whatever the hell happened back there."

A set of piercing angry eyes flashed in his general direction after she'd pulled the cell from her handbag. *Shut the fuck up and drive* was communicated without a word needing to be spoken.

It took three deep breaths for Zander to regain control of heated emotions. Arguing would not be the best course of action. She needed to know. Everything. More than anything, he needed to tell her, right then and there. Blurt it out. Lay it on the table. Timing however, was not his friend.

"Which way?" He grabbed the steering wheel with more force than necessary.

"Jane's Bar on Fifth and Pine." Grayce pointed west. The tension in her face disappeared. No need to upset her. Soon enough they'd be inseparable. Didn't have to happen tonight.

"I know the place. Come to think of it, I could use a drink." Good excuse to keep an eye on her.

"Um, did you really throw that fucking asshole across the parking lot or have I lost my mind?" She fiddled nervously with her cell.

Zander's arms ached with the need to pull her close, tuck her snug against him where she belonged.

"I did. I'm sorry you saw that. I followed..." He cleared his throat. "I mean, when I was heading to my truck, I heard you yell and lost my temper. Didn't think. I just reacted." The Lone Ranger theme song strummed through his brain as he tapped his thumbs against the steering wheel.

"But, how? I mean, you're huge and everything, but how did you toss him that far without breaking a sweat?" She shifted in her seat, glanced his way, then looked straight ahead.

"I'm strong." A nervous chuckle escaped his lips. "I'm very strong." Strong would be an understatement. Superhuman strength and speed. Never been sick. Never seen his own blood. Bona fide freak of nature.

"So, is Z your real name, or does the Z stand for something?"

"It's short for Zander."

"Zander. Nice. Last name?"

"Vascos. Zander Vascos." God, it felt good introducing himself properly. "And Grayce, I don't believe I got your last name."

She quickly turned away. "No. No you didn't." She wasn't going to offer it either, judging by the uncomfortable silence that followed. Not in the sharing mood? Didn't matter. They'd share a last name eventually.

"Well, Zander. Thank you for rescuing me...I think."

Grayce spent the rest of the drive with her head pressed against the passenger side window. Didn't say a word or look in his direction. Gave him plenty of time to consider his next move. Obviously, tonight wouldn't be an ideal time to drop any bombshells regarding their future. They were together. It would do for now.

The truck rolled to a stop and Zander let it run. Grayce sat in silence, palms folded in her lap. He reached across the seat and placed a hand over hers. With the joining of their skin, the bonding energy, unique only to them, surged through their flesh and bones. Grayce jumped and jerked her hands away.

"I'll drive you back to your car after your shift." Secretly hoping she'd invite him home with her, he studied her face for a sign, disappointed to find resolute blankness.

"That won't be necessary. You've done so much already. I can get a ride home." Grayce searched her handbag, fiddled with her phone, jiggled her keys. She wouldn't look his way.

"Grayce. I need you to look at me, please." Her sigh cut like a knife to his chest. Fear twisted his heart as he considered the possibility he'd been wrong, that Grayce wasn't the one. If she were, wouldn't she be responding to their closeness, to his touch?

Tucking hair behind her ear, she half turned in his direction. "What?"

"No one can know about what happened tonight."

Slumping, she buried her face in her hands and laughed. "You don't have to worry. I won't say a word. Who'd believe me anyway? I still don't believe it myself." With a shrug, she opened the door and vaulted from the truck.

"Thank you," Zander whispered.

Her reserved smile, the blush in her cheeks and the sadness haunting her hazel eyes temporarily paralyzed him.

"I have to get in there. You coming? First drink is on me." Tilting her head, she smiled shyly. "No. Not the first drink. As many as you want. On me. It's the least I can do."

Chapter 3

As they entered Jane's Bar, an eerie silence spread through the room. Zander placed his hand on the small of her back and guided her in. Adrenaline burst through veins already burning with an electric heat. The same sensation jolted her senses when he'd touched her in the car, and again in his truck. Did he feel it too? No way was she going to ask. Enough of her crazy side had been revealed for one day.

Unaccustomed to being the center of attention, a heated blush crept its way up her neck and landed hot and throbbing across her face. However, with his six-foot-four-inch frame wrapped neatly with layers upon layers of muscle, all eyes were on Zander. Grayce felt invisible, which was good. Inconspicuous was dead center in her comfort zone.

"Find a seat," she mumbled. "I'll be back in a minute and get your drink." She strode to the back room, shoved her handbag in a locker, changed her clothes and made her way to the mirror.

Mortified by the sight, she bit back a squeal. Mousy brown hair hung frizzed and messy over her shoulders. Flushed cheeks flashed like neon signs across her face.

"Shit." Twisting loose braids on each side of her head, she scrutinized her reflection and decided the crimson glow was pleasant. It brought out the flecks of green in her eyes. Attempting to perk her boobs, she adjusted her bra. Okay. Everything in place. Good to go.

The standard issue black t-shirt bearing the bar's logo was purposely too tight, the v-neck way too low, but Jane insisted she'd get much better tips if she conformed. Income far outweighed pride at this point in her life. Tucked safely under a floorboard at home was six months worth of tips. Escape funds. Drop everything and run for your life cash. Hide from the monster money.

Heart beating a painful rap against her chest, she entered the crowded bar. Immediately, her gaze was drawn to where Zander sat in the darkest corner of the room. How funny, she thought, a man of his stature trying to hide. She drew herself up as she ambled forward. She needed to suck it up and be brave for a few more hours. If he was going to hurt her, he would've done it already. After a few drinks, he'd leave and be out of her life for good.

"Holy Fuck," she whispered to herself.

Settled in the corner with his back against the wall, his industrial-sized arms were folded over a hulk-like chest. Tan skin stretched tight and firm over every inch of him. Dark blond hair sat tousled atop his head, carefree and wicked sexy. And his eyes—his intense blue eyes glowed in the dark. His gaze travelled along her body from head to toe as she drew near. She'd never felt so exposed. Not even in the playroom.

"Okay my superhero, what can I buy you to drink?" The words were barely audible because her throat had closed tighter than a corked bottle. She studied her feet and the scuffed hardwoods as she attempted to clear the shag carpet from her larynx.

"Superhero?" His chuckle soothed her jagged nerves. When he smiled, his eyes shone brighter than the sun making its first break through black clouds after a passing storm. "A superhero wouldn't have given that fucker a chance to get anywhere near you to begin with." The smile morphed to a frown. "I'll take a beer please, whatever you've got. The darker, the better."

* * * *

Jane's Bar wasn't at capacity, though busy enough to keep Grayce from talking to him. He didn't care. He'd found her. Well, he was ninety-nine percent sure she was the one. If not, he'd have to commit suicide because the attraction was not one of earthly origin, but that of the heavens. Now, to find the right time to break the news.

Zander was more than content to spend his evening in the corner. Screw that, he was downright ecstatic. For the first time in his life, the stars had aligned and all was right with his world. Shit, he'd make the very chair he sat on a permanent home if it meant he could get twenty-four hour, nonstop Grayce time.

The woman was jaw-dropping gorgeous with her petite, curvy stature, exotic hazel-green eyes and lips that begged to be devoured. Damn.

Unable to peel his eyes away, it didn't take long to notice the changes in her demeanor anytime a man approached. Her body tensed, tone of voice faltered, facial expressions darkened, even her posture altered with the slightest touch. Where did this fear take root? Who did this to her?

It was his fault. If he'd found her sooner, tried harder, maybe she would've been spared whatever anguish haunted her spirit.

Grayce cleared glasses behind the bar, and occasionally shot a glance his way. Wielding a wet towel and a bottle opener, a voluptuous redhead worked alongside her and gawked like a lovesick teenager. A couple of young women made their way to his table, flirty, underdressed and confident that at least one, if not both, would be invited home with him. Not taking his eyes off his woman, he shot them down and turned them away. If he wasn't mistaken, Grayce fought back a smirk at the shattered expressions on their faces. Made his heart swell. She cared. Just didn't know it yet.

As the night rolled on, Zander's agitation became unbearable. The urge to castrate every man who entered was irrepressible. A feat he could easily accomplish in the blink of an eye. Shit. They wouldn't leave her alone. Every male who walked through the door made a pass at her, whether they came with a woman or not. Fuck, she was like a douche bag magnet.

He growled under his breath but didn't act on his protective instinct. Watching her defend herself proved more entertaining as the evening progressed. Her foul mouth and steely glare were enough to turn any would-be-suitor into a cowering little boy. Her razor sharp tongue had wounded many souls.

If one more drunk asshole made a move on Grayce, Zander was in danger of claiming *numero uno* on the FBI's Most Wanted List for murder, as well as a dozen other crimes he could imagine committing all in the name of defending his lady. If he had his way, he'd throw her over his shoulder and march straight out of there. Never let her come back.

The decision to leave pained him, but Zander decided it safer for everyone within a two block radius of the bar if he did. He scribbled a note on a napkin and snuck through the back door when she wasn't paying attention. Yeah, it was better that way. If he'd waited to say goodbye, there wasn't a doubt in his mind he'd be taking her with him whether she consented or not.

* * * *

"Grayce, I don't know what the deal is, but if you don't take that sexy beast home and fuck the holy living shit out of him, I will." Jane winked and tugged Grayce's braid. "Where'd you find him, anyway?"

"Well, um, he kinda found me." She pondered the day's events. Her brain reeled from her near abduction, but mostly from her overwhelming attraction to the blond warrior sitting in her bar. Oh, what she wouldn't give for a rewind button. If she'd stayed in bed, well, shit, would another woman have been attacked instead of her?

For a fleeting moment, Grayce felt an ache in her gut when she realized Zander's chair was empty. The ache turned to anger as she pushed through the drunken crowd to clear his table. What the hell? Emotions like these were not her style. A note was scribbled on a napkin with a generous tip folded underneath.

I would love to sit here and watch you work all night. It's hypnotic. You are, without a doubt, the most beautiful woman I've ever laid eyes on. However, a superhero's work is never done, and alas, I've been called away. Here's my number, call me when your shift is over. I'll drive you back to your car. Z

"Seriously? Hypnotic? Beautiful?" she asked, grumbling to no one. "Must be drunk." She crammed the note and money into the pocket of her too-tight jeans.

"Grayce." A sharp stinging smack to her backside caused her to knock a half empty glass of beer to the floor. A flood of fury crashed down on her and everything turned red. The table, walls, people. Red.

"What the fuck?" She turned to find a regular, Crazy Joe, as she liked to call him, dragging his tongue across a cracked lip and eyeing her up and down. Obviously inebriated enough to have forgotten she'd nearly broke his wrist last time he touched her, he swayed on unsteady legs and gave her a wink.

"Darlin', you are so gorgeous. Let me take you home tonight." His slurred words were fuel to the fiery anger burning in her gut.

Grayce straightened herself and jetted her chin up. "You fucking touch me again, I'll kill you."

The man smiled and placed his hands on his hips. "Cock tease. Bitch. You know you want—"

Before he could finish, Grayce's fist met his jaw with such force that blood sprayed across the table and landed decoratively on the wall. Stunned, but too drunk to register pain, the man stumbled a step or two, then landed with a loud thud at her feet. Impressed with the strength she'd pulled out of nowhere, Grayce inspected her fist for damage. Nothing. Not a cut, bruise or even a red mark. As she surveyed the room, it was no shock to discover all eyes were on her. But she was surprised to find she was still seeing red—literally.

After her shift, which ended moments after the ambulance carted away the drunk asshole, she grabbed a ride home with Georgia, who conveniently lived a few short blocks from Grayce's apartment.

"Your car in the shop again?" Georgia asked with her trademark sneer. The two had never been particularly fond of each other. Grayce didn't make friends. Why bother? Being on the run wasn't great grounds for nurturing relationships.

"Yes." Grayce rolled her eyes and lied. "She's in the shop again." She lacked the energy or patience to explain the truth. No way was she going to impose on Zander. So, it was take a taxi or accept Georgia's offer for a ride home.

"I met someone. Totally hot. Rich too." Georgia waited for Grayce's response. When it didn't come, she continued. "Get this. He let me drive his Porsche. God, it was amazing."

"Uh-huh." Did Georgia honestly believe she gave a fuck? Grayce nodded and pretended to listen as Georgia rambled. Man, that was the longest ride of her life.

Her apartment was small and cozy. She loved coming home. Her stuff, her mess, her food. No one around to bark commands, tell her what to wear or what to eat. Bed made? No. Dirty dishes in the sink? Yes. They'd get washed when she was damned well good and ready. Hell would freeze over before anyone told her how to live again. Period.

She locked the door, and not bothering to get undressed, headed straight to bed. Too fucking exhausted. The blankets were so warm and inviting she didn't even get her second shoe kicked off before sleep consumed her.

A very restless night ensued. Horrid dreams filled with visions of Tyr. His brooding face, fits of rage. His toys. Broken furniture, dishes. "You're mine." He stroked her cheek with long fingers.

"Oh God. No!" Grayce woke tangled in sweat-soaked sheets. Tyr dreams were few and far between, but when he did haunt her slumber, it put her in the foulest of moods. After a Tyr dream, it was best to stay home and clear of human contact.

* * * *

Grayce spent the morning hours and early afternoon curled up on her secondhand couch. Phone didn't ring all day. Thank God. Wouldn't have answered it anyway. By two in the afternoon her stomach growled loud enough to vibrate the sofa. It took some mental cheerleading but she finally forced herself to the kitchen for food. Hmm... Cereal or leftover nachos? She opted for nachos, cold, and settled back into her warm spot on the cushions. By three her ass was asleep and she was considering a shower when her cell buzzed. She wanted to ignore it. A nagging curiosity made her answer.

"Yeah, what?" She snapped in her grouchiest don't-fuck-with-me tone.

"Good afternoon, Grayce. I hope it's okay I'm calling you." Shit. Zander.

"Um, yes. It's okay. How are you?" Embarrassed by the tremble of her voice, she stumbled to find words. What does one say to an uber-sexy superhero, anyway?

His voice, deep, throaty and silky smooth, could probably melt the polar ice caps. "I'm sorry I left last night. It was my responsibility to get you home safe." He paused to clear his throat. "Can I see you today?"

Whoa, wait a minute cowboy, what? See me? Giddiness crept up her spine and took root in her brain. Grayce didn't do giddy. "Me? Why?"

A deep chuckle oozed its way through the phone into her ear, warming her down to her toes. "I would like to see you."

No. "Um, okay?"

He let out a loud sigh of relief. "See you in a sec."

In a sec? No, not happening. Before she was able to formulate an escape plan, the doorbell rang. A quick peek in the mirror made her wish she'd showered, or at least brushed her hair. Not a pretty sight. Well, if he didn't like the view, tough shit. At least her teeth were brushed.

Of course, Zander looked glorious standing in her doorway. If he'd arrived sporting a halo and backed by a choir of angels, she wouldn't have blinked twice. Damn, he was radiant.

To enter, he had to duck and turn sideways because he was so— massive.

"Hi." A whisper was all she could manage.

"I need to know something." The man exuded sex and power. Confidence, also. Something Grayce had always longed for.

"What?" Awestricken, Grayce unconsciously took a step back from the mountain of masculinity invading her personal space. Dressed in military style cargo pants and a clingy black t-shirt, he could've jumped out of a kick-ass, shoot 'em up video game, larger than humanly possible and able to survive even a nuclear attack. Fierce. Deadly. Determined.

With the tap of his heel, the door slammed behind him. His gaze penetrated with such intensity, she froze, captured and completely at his mercy. A heat spread over her cheeks. God, the way he stared, studied, invaded. She hoped like hell he couldn't read her mind.

With no warning, she was trapped, arms pinned to her sides, engulfed in his embrace. Surrounded by warm, hard male, Grayce couldn't move, breathe or think. Without asking permission, he lowered his head and kissed her. No easing into it, just a full blown, toe curling, tongue swirling kiss.

Much to her dismay, she let him continue.

There was no pulling away, no revulsion, or escaping to her dark place. Instead, every ounce of her turned to soft mushy goo in his arms. And there it was again—the adrenaline jolt, liquid electricity that jetted through her veins, churned in her abdomen and warmed her from the inside out.

Blood pumped from her most guarded organ, rushed to her neglected private parts and beat heavy in her ears. A trail of heat followed in the wake of his hands as they slid down her waist and cupped her ass. In one swift move, she was lifted, spun, then pinned to the door with her legs wrapped around his waist. It all happened so fast. He kissed with fervent need. She'd never been kissed like that. Never believed it possible. He took her with carnal hunger, like he was dying of thirst and she was his first drink.

Unaccustomed to being ravished and uncertain of the proper etiquette in the situation, Grayce could do nothing but grab his shoulders and hold on for the ride. As his hips rolled against her with a subtle rock, a hard erection pressed into the sensitive tissue between her legs, triggering unbidden ripples of pleasure. Oh shit, he wanted sex.

Reality smacked her like a two-by-four between the eyes, or the legs rather, and the electricity fizzled. No. She so wasn't going there. This wasn't one of her fucked up fantasies. She placed her hands on his chest and tried to push herself from his grip with no effect whatsoever.

"Stop." Grayce mumbled through the sweet tortured assault on her mouth. "No. No, I can't do this, stop." With a disapproving groan, he released her lips. Eyes closed, he pressed his forehead to hers.

"I knew it," he groaned between clenched teeth. Grayce was still pinned to the door. Every nerve ending in her body on fire with his erection shamelessly and unapologetically pressed against her now moist and throbbing special place.

"What? Knew what?" Grayce gulped and gasped, trying desperately to catch her breath. What the hell? Her cursed body betrayed her again.

"It's you. You're the one. I knew it." He eased her down the length of his arousal to the floor. "I'm sorry, that wasn't a very gentlemanly thing to do." With palms against the door, he braced her between his arms and lowered his head to capture her gaze.

"I'm lost here. Please, do explain. What did you know?" she asked in a whisper, thankful for being propped against the door so her jiggly legs didn't collapse. He pushed away from the door, engulfed her trembling hands in his own and led her to the couch.

* * * *

"Sit down. Please." After she obliged, he knelt on one knee at her feet. Even kneeling, he towered over her. Intimidating as hell, but damn she felt safe. One hundred percent safe and protected.

"Do you believe in fate? Or destiny?"

Grayce shook her head, not quite sure what to say, or where this conversation was headed. Still reeling from the kiss, she struggled to believe this powerful man who had held her with such tenderness, was here in her apartment. Holy fuck. A man was in her apartment. What was she thinking?

"I do. I believe in destiny." His penetrating gaze pierced her fragile soul. "I'll cut right to the chase." Tension laced his voice. "I don't believe you're a girl who likes to beat around the bush."

Damned straight about that one, she thought, and nodded again.

With a deep inhale, he continued. "I'm different from most people. I'm sure you've noticed." She attempted to speak and he raised a finger to her lips. "I believe humans, but especially people like us, have soul mates, one person we are meant to be with for eternity."

People like us? Grayce let free an exasperated giggle. It was too strange hearing words like "soul mates" coming from the man who knelt before her, so big and strong. His eyebrows furrowed. Oh shit. He was serious.

"You are my soul mate, Grayce. I've been searching for so damned long now." Shoulders slumped, he ran a hand through his scruffy locks. "I can't even begin to tell you how frustrating it's been."

Grayce's hands trembled and her head spun. She was pissed. Pissed because of the undeniable attraction to this man and pissed for putting herself in this situation. And why did she want to believe him so badly? God, how could she be so stupid?

Really? Soul mates? Yeah right. Shit like that never happened in real life. Perfect men didn't appear out of the blue and kiss a woman like his very existence depended on it. There sure as hell wasn't a world full of hearts, roses and chocolate truffles where lovers went to live in bliss. Soul mates? Sounded like a pathetic fucking romance movie. Was the word imbecile tattooed across her forehead?

She fell for that load of crap once. Been paying for it ever since.

The memory of Tyr's seduction all those years ago snapped her back to the reality that was her life. "Is this a fucking joke?" She spit. "Did Tyr send you? Did that mother fucking psychopath send you? How the hell did he find me?" Panic bubbled its ascent from gut to brain, stifling her ability to breathe. "Did he think I'd fall for this load of shit?" She punched him hard in the chest. "Ow, dammit." May as well have been a steel beam.

"Grayce." Grabbing her shoulders, he tried to calm her. Electricity passed between them again, angry and violent this time. "Listen to me. This isn't a joke. I...I..." He shook his head, disbelief etched in his eyes.

"Oh God, please don't take me back to him. I'll do anything. Please." Full blown panic mode set in. "I have money. It's not a lot, but you have to understand. I can't go back."

"Listen, nobody sent me. I found you. We found each other. Let me explain, please." His pathetic attempt at offering comfort only fueled her fire. He reached around to hold her but she squirmed from under his grip, slid to her knees and crawled across the floor. After she'd cleared the dining area, she pushed to her feet, rounded the corner to the kitchen and grabbed her chef's knife from the counter.

"Get the hell out of my house." Did she sound insane? Without a doubt. Could she stop it? No. Emotion had taken over the driver's seat and steered her straight toward Crazyville. "Get out. I'll kill you. I'll kill myself before I let him get near me." Clumsily, she pointed the knife at him. "I will not go back to that life." Head throbbing, she wanted to cry, but she couldn't. Anger held the tears at bay. "No. No! Tell that sick, psychotic piece of shit I'm not running anymore. He can come after me with everything he's got, but I'm not running anymore."

Everything turned red again. A warm glow surrounded her, urged her to continue. "I won't let him touch me ever again." Conviction carried that statement through the small apartment. Bravery replaced fear, and damned if it didn't feel amazing.

Zander's demeanor changed in an instant. One second he was pleading and bewildered, the next, he radiated stone cold fury. A burst of heat pulsed through the room. In a flash, they were nose to nose. The blade of the knife bent like putty in his fist and flew across the room. Cupping her cheeks, he growled.

"Did he hurt you?" He drew jagged breaths. Attempts at freeing herself from his grip were futile. He wouldn't budge. "Answer my question, Grayce. Did he hurt you?" His hands seared her flesh. Or was it her cheeks burning his hands? Hard to tell.

"Let go of me. Get the hell out of my house." She struggled to loosen his grip, to pull heated fingers from her skin, but it was like trying to bend a railway tie. Useless waste of energy.

He released her, and in a split second was gone. A rush of hot air blew her hair up and across her face. Her cheeks burned. Every inch of her skin was hot. She stammered to the couch, threw herself into the cushions and gave in to a full blown snot and tears meltdown.

* * * *

Grayce woke with a jump to a racing heartbeat, spurred by more dreams of the monster. Damn, this had to stop. Peeling her face off the pile of tissues she'd fallen asleep on, she rubbed swollen eyes before she was able to focus on the clock above the television. Thank God, it was only six.

Letting the shower run extra hot, a luxury she rarely indulged in, Grayce curled in a ball under the soothing water. Brushing a finger lightly across her lips, she closed her eyes and replayed the kiss over and over in her head. No revulsion, no compulsion to punch him, no retreating to her dark place. She stayed present. Wasn't afraid. Wanted more. How was that possible? If anything, she should be more afraid of him for the mere fact he was impossibly large and fierce.

Steam billowed around her as she stepped out. She wiped condensation from the mirror and gasped at the sight. Her face glowed where Zander had grasped her cheeks, like she'd spent a day in the sun. She ran her fingers gently across the sensitive skin. They weren't sore, but they tingled, and when she closed her eyes to picture his hold on her face, she was disappointed by the warming in her lower belly. Oh my fuck.

Must be getting sick. It was the only logical explanation, because in no known universe would her body react this way to any man. Least of all this beast who could crush Tyr with one strike of his powerful fist. Grind his bones into the pavement.

Shit. Tyr. Why the nightmares? What's changed? And what's with the freak-outs and losing control? Yeah, she was sick, no question about it.

She cranked the volume on the stereo hoping it would offer distraction from the fear bubbling beneath the surface of her psyche.

The funny thing about hiding from a monster —at some point, she'd have to strap on boxing gloves and fight for her life or tighten her laces and run like hell. It'd taken her years to realize that running was pointless. Nobody ever really got away, especially from the monsters with money and power. So why run at all? Either way, she'd end up six feet under or wishing she was.

Grayce had settled in Chastain, Idaho because it was large enough that she could blend in unnoticed, but remote enough that she could disappear into the Bitterroot Mountains in any direction if necessary. It was a quaint town, populated by nature lovers, retired military, celebrities and the few generations of mining families that stuck around after the Gold Greek Mines shut down in the early 1970s. Most of the large homes sat on acres of land, were second or third houses to the rich and famous and sat vacant for months on end. She'd squatted in a few of them until she found a job and decided to stay.

The town had grown on her and she hated the thought of leaving. So, she had to keep it together, not let Tyr, or memories of him, ruin her life any further. She was staying put, that's all there was to it.

Maybe she'd sign up for additional self defense classes. If Tyr did find her, she wanted to fight like hell. She'd probably go down, but fuck it, she'd go down kicking and screaming, hopefully with chunks of his flesh in her hands and teeth.

Heading for the door, she remembered her car had been left at the gym. "Oh shit!" Her scream to nobody echoed through the small room. Could this day get any worse? She grabbed her phone to call a taxi. A bomb burst inside her ribcage when she noticed a text. From him.

Your car is outside. Z

She ran to the window and there it sat, parked outside, just like he said. Holy cow, did he wash it too? It shined. Even the tires were clean. When? How? She ran through the events of the last twenty-four hours in her head. Of course, he must have brought it when he came earlier. Did he steal her keys? How'd he get home afterward? Too much to process. With a huff, she snatched her handbag and headed to work.

Chapter 4

The bar was busy, filled with rowdy kids, who'd barely reached the legal age to drink, and regulars, who claimed their favorite seats from noon until closing time. The chaos offered comfort. Helped keep her mind off Zander. Maybe she'd scared him off and would never have to see his magnificent face again. Time had allowed ample opportunity for her head to clear and thoughts to be organized. No possible way was Zander working for Tyr. Fuck. She must have looked quite the fool. She'd have to find a new gym, maybe a new job.

"I'll close up tonight. You go have fun," Grayce told Jane. She rolled her eyes as her boss perked her boobs and checked her lipstick in the mirrored wall behind the bar. Once again, Jane had hooked up with a stranger from out of town and couldn't wait to continue her evening with him, for a good romp in the hay, no doubt. Something she did quite often. "Be careful. Men are assholes you know."

Grayce had tried to despise Jane, mostly because of her wanton ways, but was never able to live up to the task. Jane had always been so gracious; hired her without proper identification, paid her under the table, allowed her to pick up extra shifts. Jane knew Grayce had a past without having to ask, and although it went unspoken, the two carried a deep respect for each other. Grayce often wondered if Jane harbored dark secrets of her own, but she would never pry.

"I'm always careful, Grayce baby." Jane winked and sauntered through the door toward a black Porsche waiting outside. A horrifying chill crept through Grayce's bones. She wanted to stop her. Scream for her to come back.

Locking the door, she peered cautiously into the darkness. Looking left and right, then down the alley directly across the way, she sighed and hoped like hell she wasn't going to read in tomorrow's paper that her boss's dead body had been found in a ditch somewhere. As she headed to the back room to finish up, an intoxicating tingle danced across her skin. Oh fuck no. Please no. Not him, not now.

"Grayce." Her stomach lurched. She looked over her shoulder, half hoping it'd been her imagination. No such luck. There he sat, dark and brooding, leaning forward with his elbows on his knees. His lips quivered at the corners, suppressing a smile.

"How did you get in here?" Grayce snapped as she contemplated making a run for the door.

"Grayce." The word slid off his tongue like chocolate silk. Made her almost feel needed. "We have some unfinished business."

It should've frightened her senseless. Odd. Despite what happened earlier and the shameful embarrassment at her outburst, it felt right having him there. Besides, the determined glare in his eyes was a telltale sign he wouldn't be leaving anytime soon.

"Thirsty?" she asked.

"Very." A muscle clenched deep between her legs as his tongue glided across his upper lip. Oh crap, nothing but trouble was coming her way. Pouring his beer, she decided to have one as well.

Strategically positioned on the opposite side of the table, she placed his drink down and tried unsuccessfully to calm her trembling hands. After an intense and uncomfortable stare-down, Grayce decided to start. "Listen, I'm sorry about my meltdown earlier. It's just—"

"Who's this man that hurt you?" Zander interrupted. He hadn't touched his beer. Hadn't taken his eyes off her, not even for a second.

Buying time while she decided what to say, Grayce took a long drink from her glass. "I knew he didn't send you. I—I—panicked. It—it—was just—just too much." Great, now she was a stutterer. She shot a glance to the back door, gauging her chances for escape. Where were her car keys? Could she find them fast enough to make a clean get away? "I was overwhelmed by—"

"Who is this man that hurt you?" he asked again. She noticed a tick in his cheek before his jaw tightened enough to accentuate the muscles in his neck. Fearsome. Still, she wasn't afraid, not of him. What she did fear were the overwhelming feelings his presence evoked. Those terrified her.

"That's none of your God-damned business." Grayce slammed her glass down and crossed her arms. Head cocked to the side, she challenged him with a glare.

"Well, my dear. You're wrong about that." He huffed and for the first time tore his gaze away from Grayce. "It's absolutely my business." His dark tone offered no apologies. He traced the rim of his glass with a thick finger before he lifted it to his lips and drained its contents in one shot.

"Who in the hell do you think you are?" Boiling anger churned in her gut.

Zander jumped over the table and grabbed Grayce by the arm. "Do you feel that?"

Oh yes, she felt it. The electricity. The life force. Almost painful. Her body absorbed it as if it were a drug. She needed it.

"Tell me you feel it. I know you do."

After several failed attempts at swallowing, she managed to choke out a "yes." It took all of her energy, all of her wits to remain strong, be brave, not lose it again. "Please." A whisper was all she could manage. "I don't like being manhandled." *Don't cry. Don't cry. Don't cry.* "Please let go of my arm."

He released her. Regret extinguished the fire in his eyes. "I'm sorry. I didn't mean to, um…" Scratching his head, he took a step back. "I'm sorry. I need you to understand. I don't know how else to show you."

"Understand what exactly?" Hugging herself, she rubbed the warm spots his fingers left behind. "Listen. Just say it. The last couple of days have been insane. I'm going insane."

Lowering his face to meet hers, an exasperated sigh escaped his lips. "You're not going insane. We are soul mates. We were meant, no not meant, we were made for each other." He looked around the room, gnawing on his lower lip. "I'm strong, right? You've seen it."

Grayce nodded. Strong would be an understatement.

"But when you're near, I'm stronger. I'm more alive. That's how I knew I'd found you."

Not the soul mates crap again. Does this work on all the women? "Soul mates, huh? You're still going with that?" Sarcasm coated her voice and she gasped when a burst of heat pulsed through her body. Did that come from her or Zander? Hot flash. Yeah, had to be it. Could've been the beer she gulped. His eyes crinkled at the corners as he glowered at her.

Zander inhaled and held it in. She couldn't help but revel in his breathtaking features. Strong square jaw, glowing eyes, flawless skin. On exhale, the wrinkles in his forehead diminished. "Tell me something, Grayce. Over the past few weeks, have you felt different? Emotionally, physically or anything?" Straightening his back, he crossed his arms over his chest. Clearly eager for a response, his smirk made her wonder if he already knew the answer.

She knew, but pretended to think about it. Needing some space from the giant super-sexy man stealing her oxygen, she headed to the bar, grabbed a bottle of cleanser and squirted a hefty dose over the stainless steel counter.

"Yes."

She didn't look, but his mood shifted, changing the current between them. "I've been more pissed off than usual. I've had more energy. Also, I'm not as..." She looked him in the eye now. "Afraid." She refrained from telling him about her fantasies starring yours truly, how horny she'd been, or how the thought of being touched by anyone had repulsed her until he barreled into her life like a crash test dummy.

"I don't like hearing you were afraid. It makes my blood boil." She believed him. Unsettling as it was, she believed him. May have been the sweet spirit dancing in his eyes, or the fact he felt familiar somehow, but there was no possible way he wasn't speaking the truth. She felt it in her DNA.

"Would you believe me if I promised you'll never have to be afraid of anything, ever?"

"No." A life without fear was unimaginable. Fear of being found. Fear of returning to that hell. Fear of the monster.

"What did he do to you?" Zander took a slow careful step closer.

"Zander, I don't know you at all. Why would I tell you this? Why would I tell you anything? Why do you care?" She'd never told anyone her dirty little secret. Sure as shit didn't want to share it with this beautiful beefcake. He'd seen enough of her crazy. Nobody needed to hear her story. She tapped off another mug and took a huge swig to buy some time. Or perhaps to absorb some liquid courage.

"Tell me, please." He stared right into her soul again, unrelenting.

Maybe she should tell him. Maybe then, he'd leave her alone. It might feel good to tell somebody after all these years. Dump her shit on someone else's shoulders. He had huge fucking shoulders, right? He could take it. Raising the glass to her lips, she finished her drink for dramatic effect, and wiped her mouth with the back of her hand. She'd truly lost her mind.

Fuck. Fuck. Shit fuck.

"I was young. He was handsome and rich. Said all the right things. I thought it was love at first sight." Pausing to take a deep breath, she nervously twisted a braid. "It's funny how easy it was for him to seduce a young girl, especially one with no self worth. Someone with Daddy issues. Shit, mommy issues if I'm going to be honest. He was wonderful, until he'd hooked me. After that, well...you can use your imagination."

There he had it. The very watered down version. Should satisfy his curiosity.

"Grayce. I want to hear you say it." He shifted slightly not breaking eye contact, slanted his head to the side, willed her to continue.

No. Not going there. "He was abusive in every way imaginable. Took complete control over every single aspect of my life. He made me do things that...well, quite frankly, I'm not going to fucking talk about. He was a sick, perverted piece of shit. I knew I'd end up dead if I stayed. I tried to leave twice. Landed me in the hospital twice. With his wealth and power, the police were no help. My mother didn't help me. I'm sure they were paid generously for their silence. When I escaped, I left everything behind. My mom, my friends, everything. Not a penny to my name. I've been running ever since." Okay. So she went there. Now he knew. Perfect excuse to run away from the crazy lady.

"Thank you for telling me." Zander stepped closer making it very clear by hooking his thumbs in the back of his jeans he had no intention of touching her. "Tell me when you started to feel different. You know, braver, more pissed off, like you said earlier." A half devilish smile spread from dimpled cheek to dimpled cheek, like the thought of her being pissed off amused him.

The answer came at once, but again she pretended to think. Should she tell him the truth? Would he laugh?

"The first day you came to the gym." Whew, that felt good to say. Not a clue why, but her head felt lighter. She waited for him to laugh, then sighed in relief when he didn't.

"Greatest day of my life. I fell so fucking hard. It took every bit of self control I owned not to steal you away from there. I walked past you and—*bam*!" He smacked his hands together with a loud crack and Grayce nearly jumped out of her thrift store jeans. "Indescribable energy coursed through me, like fire. Every cell in my body ignited with new life. Almost knocked me on my ass. I'd never seen anyone so beautiful. No doubt about it, you were the one. I just knew you were mine." Expectant wonderment sparkled like disco balls in his baby blues.

Blinking up at him, she digested his words. Wait, did he say beautiful? Holy crap. Hold on. Mine? I knew you were mine? Shock dissipated under a thunderous roar of heated blood pounding in her ears.

"Dammit, Z. Don't say things like that to me." She stomped around the bar bringing herself face to face with him. Or rather face to chest. Her face to his out-of-this-world enormous chest. "Motherfucker. Don't say things like that to me." Tears fought their way to the surface. "I'm not going there with another man. Ever. Fuck this soul mates shit. I'm not yours. I don't belong to anyone."

Tension coiled her muscles with the overwhelming need to punch him. Or maybe touch him. Such a myriad of emotions surged through her. Anger, confusion, lust—fierce. Yeah, that was it. Fierce. Where the hell was this coming from? She glared up to meet his obnoxious, frisky expression.

He returned her glower with equal fervor. "Lady, you have such a foul mouth." Zander bent and brushed her ear with his lips. Muscles that had no right reacting clenched with nauseating need. "You have no idea how much it turns me on."

In one smooth motion, he cupped her waist and brought her to his level. Desperate hunger blazed in his eyes and he tilted his head with the threat of a kiss. Body tense, she braced for impact. Instead, he plopped her ass playfully atop the bar.

"Grayce." He placed his hands at each side of her hips and pressed his forehead to hers. "I'm sorry. I'm so sorry you went through that. Sorry I didn't find you sooner." With a sigh he brushed her heated cheek with his nose. "I'll never touch you without your permission. I'll never hurt you."

Grayce closed her eyes, stealing a moment to think. His breath warmed her face like a summer breeze. She wanted to inhale deeply and never stop. Absorb him into her being. She recoiled, unsure what to make of these foreign emotions. There was no doubt an undeniable chemical and physical attraction. But how could she ever trust again? Especially a man. Would she ever be able to let her guard down?

Memories from her past knocked on the cellar door buried deep in the dark corners of her mind. Memories locked away a long time ago. Memories she'd no intention of revisiting. So, up went her wall.

"Zander, I have to finish up here. I'm tired. I need to go home." Lacking the resolve to look him in the eye, she placed her hands against his chest and pushed. He didn't budge.

With a loud sigh he slumped and backed away. "Of course," he mumbled. "I'll see you tomorrow."

Raw emotion triggered her ugly retort. "See me tomorrow? Pretty fucking presumptuous."

Zander bowed. "I'm sorry. What I meant to say was, can I please see you tomorrow, Grayce?" His eyes and posture reflected complete humility. Her heart dropped at least two inches in her chest. Ouch.

"I'll be at the gym tomorrow. My usual time. I suppose I'll see you there, right?" Grayce feigned indifference. Deep down, she feared that long a wait might be the death of her.

"Yeah, I suppose." He grinned. A crooked playful grin that showed a dimple she hadn't noticed before. "Finish up. I'll walk you to your car." Like she weighed no more than a feather, he lowered her to the floor. "We don't know who may be lurking in the shadows."

* * * *

The moist early morning air clung to his skin and cooled the slow burning embers of need that had tormented him throughout the night. Unbeknownst to Grayce, he'd followed her to the apartment and planted his sorry ass outside the window. His intention was to see her safely home, but after she'd closed the door and turned the lock, he couldn't bring himself to go. For so many years he'd searched. Now they were together. How could he possibly leave?

Nikolas told him it would be like this. Once he found her, it would be extremely difficult to be separated. Bastard failed to mention the mental and physical torture. Every cell in his body had morphed to a singular ball of white hot plasma. Only being near, seeing and smelling her, could quench the searing pain. Grayce was every thought in his mind, every breath in his lungs and every tiny vibration in his ears. The world could crumble at his feet and his sole focus would be protecting his mate.

Finding a soft spot near the window, Zander stretched in the wet grass, the cool moisture no match for the heated lust pumping through his veins. If their bond was this intense already, what would it be like after they made love? Fuck. He couldn't let his imagination go down that path, not yet. Zander grabbed his head and attempted to scratch the thought away.

Hours ticked by. When the sun peeked through the tree line in the distance, he contemplated bringing her breakfast. Nikolas' words rang through his ears. "She needs time. Don't rush this. You've found each other and now you have eternity to spend together." Patience had always been one of Zander's strong character traits. Time? Yeah. He could do that. The girl had issues. Wounds that festered. Only time would heal those.

His stomach growled. He didn't want to leave but breakfast and thoughts of a warm soak beckoned to him. Nikolas and Chelsea would worry if he didn't check-in. He could tough it out for a few hours, right? Before leaving he snuck one peek through her window. Big mistake. The outline of her body and curve of her hip where she lay motionless under a thin sheet gave birth to a raging hard on. He cursed under his breath and headed home for a cold shower.

* * * *

Grayce scowled when she entered Armstrong's Gym. It was packed. She hated having to wait for her favorite elliptical. The one tucked away in the corner where she could crank the volume on her mp3 player, get lost in the music, and hopefully not get noticed.

She opted for skipping the afternoon self-defense class. She'd lost her temper during last week's session, and the instructor had made an example of her in front of the class. Fucking bastard. She'd kill him if it were legal, just for being such a cocky prick. She'd tolerated his touch and tutelage only because it furthered her ability to protect herself should the monster come hunting her down.

"Good afternoon, Grayce." The perky little employee behind the counter beamed at her. "You look great today."

"Thanks, Carrie." Grayce tried her best to beam back, already pulling her hood over her head.

Carrie leaned over the counter to whisper to Grayce. "Did you hear about the man who almost died in the parking lot?"

What? Fuck.

"No." Trying hard not to sound shocked, she took a step closer. "What man? What happened?" Grayce leaned toward Carrie and pulled the hood back off.

"Some teenagers found him outside and called the police. They saved his life. If he'd been left lying there too much longer, he'd be dead." Her cute little button nose scrunched in disgust. "Internal injuries or something like that." She waved a hand nonchalantly in the air. "It was on the news. Police were questioning the employees. Also got a list of members who were checked-in around that time."

Holy. Fucking. Shit storm. Shit fuck. "Does anybody know what happened?" Mouth full of kitty litter, Grayce choked the words out.

"No. From what I understand, he's been unconscious this whole time. Scary, huh? But it gets better..."

Better? No. Make it stop. Grayce didn't want to hear any more. "Better? How?"

"He's a convicted felon. Kidnapping, extortion, drugs. He escaped from prison a few days ago."

Carrie's eyes grew wider and she grabbed Grayce's arm. "No one knows how he got out. Freak up and disappeared from his cell one day. Like a ghost." She released her grip and slapped her hands on the counter. "That's what they're saying anyway."

A painful lurch in her gut forced her to double over. Her legs lost the ability to bear weight as the blood drained from her face. Her world turned black and before she collapsed, steel warmth braced her waist, keeping her upright.

Zander's voice pierced the dark, a lifeline weaved from brilliant light and sound, halting her descent toward la-la land. "Stay with me, baby. I'm here." His words danced in her head. He wrapped his other arm around her shoulder feigning a hug, but she knew it was to support her limp body and hide the fact from bubbly little Carrie that she was barely conscious.

"I've got you," he whispered. "Breathe for me."

Eyes screwed tight to slow the spinning in her head, she pulled one deep drag of oxygen into her lungs, then another. The inhale, exhale exercise repeated while she pulled herself from the brink of a major blackout. The energy they shared became a life force as Zander's chest rose and fell in unison with hers.

"You good now?" His gravelly voice resonated deep. "Is it safe to put you down?" He held on so tight his heartbeat pounded in her ear.

She buried her nose in his chest, the scent of fresh air and sun baked skin mixed with a hearty dose of rock hard male made her a whole new kind of dizzy. Were she a typical female, she would've begged him to hold her that way forever. But she was Grayce, hater of all things men, all things mushy. No, she wouldn't beg. Although, she did hang on a little longer than necessary. "Yeah, I think I can stand now. Shit. Thank you."

He set her down and wrapped an arm around her shoulder.

"Wow," Carrie exclaimed from behind the counter, "you two make a great couple. I love it when gym members hook up." Grayce's attentions snapped to the cheerful girl behind the counter. It was comical, almost, the way Carrie stared at Zander. Wide eyed, pink cheeked. It became less amusing the longer she ogled, downright irritating when she shot him a wink before turning back to her computer.

"Well, it seems you are my superhero." Grayce struggled to stand steady. "That's twice now you've saved me," she joked, a feeble attempt to hide her embarrassment.

With a tender hand, he cupped her face and caressed her with his thumb. "I heard your conversation. Are you all right?"

"Can we get out of here?" she asked, pleading. "I don't think I'm up for a workout." Without a moment's hesitation, he caged her hand in his massive palm and led her out the door.

They drove for several minutes in silence before Grayce released a huge breath. "He was a criminal. Oh my fuck...what if...what would have...he would have..." Unable to finish a sentence, she snapped her jaw shut and stared blankly ahead. Realization hit her like a frying pan to the face. Where would she be right now if Zander hadn't rescued her that night? Would they be pulling her body from a ditch?

"I need to go home. Can you please take me home?" She hugged her gym bag to her chest as events from her past flashed before her eyes. Images best kept locked away, far from prying eyes. Her bed was calling and all she wanted to do was curl up in a ball under the blankets for the next fifty years.

* * * *

As they approached the door to her apartment, a tingle shimmied down the base of her skull and tiny hairs on her neck stood on end. Something wasn't right. Then again, things hadn't felt right for days.

Zander's arm shot out to block her from touching the door. "Grayce, wait," he commanded. Grabbing her keys from her hand, he scooted her behind him. Heat radiated from his body. "Go to the truck. Wait there." His tone was so authoritative and frightening, she didn't hesitate. Only after he watched her lock herself in, did he turn and reach for the doorknob.

With bated breath she watched Zander enter her home. Less than two minutes later, the door flew open and he barreled toward her carrying a duffel bag and wearing a grim expression. The revulsion in his eyes snapped her last cord of sanity, sending her emotions on a downward spiral and her heartbeat into about-to-explode territory. She jumped when he slammed the duffel in the truck bed and yanked his door open. He climbed in, punched the dash and pounded the steering wheel. "We have to go." An order, not a request.

"Wait. Just wait a minute. What's happening?" Grayce fumbled with the door handle as she tried to free herself. Zander grabbed her thigh and held her in place.

"I can't let you go in there." With jaw clenched tight, his eyes reflected pure animal rage.

She glared at him, temper rising. "What the hell do you mean? That's my home. Let me out of here." Grayce shoved his hand from her leg and jumped out of the truck. Before her feet touched the ground, Zander was at her side. Seriously? How did he do that?

With an authoritative grasp on her shoulder, he implored her to stay put. "Please don't do this. Please trust me and come with me, right now." When she met him eye to eye, there was no denying how much he cared. His expression was so sincere, pleading, filled with genuine concern.

"Zander, you're scaring me." She pulled his hand from her shoulder, held it in her own, and clung for dear life. The skin to skin contact gave her courage she wouldn't have otherwise been able to muster.

At first glance, the apartment looked like a paintball battlefield where the soldiers were only allowed to use red paint. If only that had been the case. It was a bloody mess, spattered on the furniture, the walls, even the ceiling.

Photos were strewn throughout the apartment, taped to the walls, tossed across the floor and furniture. Images of her bruised and bloody face, pictures of her bound to Tyr's bed, various shots of her in bondage where she appeared to be unconscious—all reminders of the evil that dwelled in the shadows of her past. The hallway was littered with pictures of Grayce at the bar, the gym and the grocery store. Handwritten in red ink at the bottom of each snapshot was the word *mine*.

Reluctantly, she headed toward the bedroom, hands shaking. Oh shit. Oh shit. Her bedding had been replaced with a blood red comforter like the one Tyr had in his playroom. On top lay handcuffs, a whip she knew all too well and a single crimson rose placed on top of a handwritten note. Lacking courage to pick it up, she stepped away. More photographs were tossed carelessly around the room. Pictures of her asleep in her bed in the apartment. For the second time that day, blood drained from her face and her knees wobbled and buckled under her. Zander caught her before she hit the floor.

* * * *

Jostled by the deep potholes in the dirt road, Grayce awoke, leaning against Zander's warm shoulder in the spacious cab of his truck. Seemed like she needed to say something, but what? Where would she even start? Sure, she could thank him, again, but that was getting old. She could ask where they were going even though it didn't matter, so long as it was far from where they'd come. It would be too exhausting trying to make sense of the horrors they found in her apartment. Not a single word or string of sentences would do justice to the mish-mash of thought and emotion that scene had stirred in her brain. So, she stayed silent, left her head on his firm shoulder, and concentrated on the addictive energy he emanated.

She heard a loud buzz and he grabbed his cell from the dash.

"Hi. We're almost there... Ten minutes. Everything ready? Is Nikolas home?" His body rose and fell as he inhaled deep and exhaled with relief. "Good, good... No, there hasn't been time, but soon. I promise." He tossed his phone across the dash and cursed under his breath.

Grayce didn't pay much attention to where they were going. Honestly, she couldn't have cared less. She didn't want to think, or feel or process any of the last forty-eight hours. Instead, she focused on Zander's breathing and his soothing scent.

Up ahead, a bend in the bumpy dirt road veered left. To the right, nothing but dense woodland, dark and foreboding, stretched as far as the eye could see. Fir trees had grown thick enough to block the sun's intrusion on the forest floor. Instead of turning left at the bend, Zander steered right and drove head on through the thick of trees. As the truck plowed through, the firs misted away like fog.

Oh God, please no more freaky stuff.

Unable to take anymore, she squeezed her eyes closed, hoping to shut out the world. She contemplated visiting her dark place for a while to escape. But if she did that, she'd no longer feel Zander's presence, and right then he was the only thing keeping her sane. How fucked up was that?

Grayce thought back to her first encounter with Zander two weeks ago. He'd burst through the double glass doors of Armstrong's Gym like a predator on the hunt for someone to devour. Aside from his overwhelming size, what had stood out most was his radiant blue eyes. Grayce had been certain he wore cosmetic contacts. Nature didn't create an eye color as magical as his. Dirty blond hair laid a perfect mess on his head. He hadn't struck her as the type to wear product in his hair, but no way could it look that sexy without a little effort. The man was huge, bodybuilder huge but without the bulky clumsiness. He'd prowled through the gym with grace and moved with a suppleness and confidence that commanded respect and a wide berth.

She'd been instantly attracted to him, which was highly unsettling considering the fact she hated men. Hate would be an understatement as neither word nor emotion came close to describing the affect the male species had on her psyche. In her opinion, they should be wiped off the face of the planet—gruesome and painful would do.

When he approached, her cells came to life, vibrating and humming, every last one of them, completely betraying her.

That was the first time she'd considered leaving Chastain. She couldn't afford being attracted to anyone. Attraction had nearly killed her years ago.

She'd considered packing her bags and moving on, but dammit, she had liked it there. Quite frankly, she was tired of running away. She'd even resigned herself to the fact that if Tyr found her, she would fight him to the death rather than leave. Most likely, he'd kill her, but that's how tired she was of running.

* * * *

The truck rolled to a stop, the engine shut down and Zander shifted in his seat. With a sweet tenderness, he rubbed his hand through her hair and planted kisses on her head. His lips were the catalyst to sinfully delicious shivers that frolicked across her skull and spread like a thousand lightning bugs dancing down her spine. "I need you to come back to me now, Grayce."

Zander scooted out of the truck and effortlessly pulled her with him. Cradled in his massive arms, she was carried down a long dirt drive. "I can walk, I'm okay." Not completely confident with her statement, she managed half a smile for him. A sensual groan rose in his chest.

"If you don't mind, I think I'll carry you. You've fainted on me twice today and I'd like to avoid a third occurrence." Nudging her cheek with his nose, he chuckled. "I think I'll carry you wherever we go from now on. This is kind of nice."

"Where are we?" She averted her eyes from his massive chest to the sprawling palatial mansion up ahead. Or maybe it was a castle. Hard to tell. After the day she'd had, it could've been an alien spaceship.

"We're home." His voice resonated with sweet conviction, like he'd been waiting his whole life to say those two words to her alone. Gazing down at her again, he smiled like a smitten school boy. An unfamiliar sensation rippled through her chest. A flutter? A palpitation? Oh, hell no. She didn't do this sappy love shit. No. Men were the enemy.

He opened large hand-carved double doors that revealed a grand entryway. An elegant, intricate design in different shades of hardwood graced the floor. Opposite them a giant window overlooked a plush garden. Up above, the arched glass ceiling allowed light from the bright blue sky to flood the impressive space.

"I'll give you a proper tour later." He turned right and made his way down one of many long corridors. "We'll put your things in my room and then I'd like you to meet a friend of mine." They continued down the hallway to a whole new wing. "This is where we'll be staying for now.

At least until I know you're safe. Then of course, it's your decision." In awe of the enormous home, Grayce was helpless to do anything but gape at her surroundings.

Zander kicked a door open and they entered a ridiculously large but understated bedroom. He beelined for the bed and set her on the edge. His tension was palpable—he wanted to touch her. She felt it, felt his restraint. Instead, he sat with his right thigh pressing heavily against hers. Damn she looked small, so diminutive next to him. Her whole lower body could fit inside his one leg. Every muscle of his thigh strained through the fabric of his workout pants. A strong urge to touch him, feel his powerful body beneath her fingertips, had her clenching her fists at her sides. The disloyal body of hers wanted to be connected to his in every way possible. The voice in her head screamed at her to run for the hills.

"Well, it's been one hell of a day, huh?" Clearly an attempt to break the tension between them, he laughed at himself and relaxed his shoulders. Leaning back on his arms, he sighed. "I can't imagine what's going through your head right now."

What *wasn't* going through her head right now? "He found me. How did he find me? I've been so careful. There were pictures of me..." After swallowing the golf ball-sized lump in her throat, she paused for the few moments it took to get her emotions in check. "While I slept in my bed. He's been in my home. What kind of sick fucked up game is he playing?"

"Grayce." When Zander brushed hair from her shoulder, she flinched and regretted it instantly. He jerked his hand away and dragged it through his own scruffy mop. "He can't touch you here. He won't find you again." Leaning forward with eyes squeezed shut, he declared under his breath, "Fucker won't live long enough to find you."

Grayce gasped and turned to Zander. "He won't stop. You don't know him." With dramatic flair, she threw herself back on the bed and covered her face with both arms to hide the fear. To hide the tears she'd been fighting. Just to hide.

"I know me." Zander growled, his tone heavy with the promise of retribution. "I know what I'll do to keep him from touching you, or even laying eyes on you again." Zander lifted her arms and pulled her back to the sitting position. "He left a note, a warning." The letter appeared from behind his back.

"Shit." She didn't want to read it, but curiosity got the best of her.

My dearest dove,

It saddens me deeply that I wasn't reunited with you as planned on Saturday. It appears my efforts to reclaim you were thwarted. It won't happen again. Mr. Houghton lies nearly dead in the hospital. What a shame, I toiled so to free him from prison.

Who is that beast of a man who so heroically came to your aid? I must know more about him.

You've no comprehension of the misery I've endured during your absence. Rest assured, I will have you, soon. That's my vow to you.

Forever you are mine.

Tyr

A cry escaped her lips as the note became confetti. Zander wrapped himself around her and she was blown away by the raw emotion that pulsated through him. "Tyr sent that man to attack me."

Zander's solid form fit perfectly around her tiny frame, as if he'd been built for it. To hold, comfort and shield her from the horrors of her world. The protective space between his arms had become a haven, and damn if that wasn't scarier than knowing the monster had found her. It felt too good, too right, and that could only be very bad. Feeling all sorts of smothered, Grayce wiggled and pushed herself from his overwhelming embrace.

"Grayce, I want to introduce you to my friend, Nikolas Compton. He's a brilliant doctor. Taught me about our kind and helped me deal with my issues. He's been eager to meet you."

Oh, what the hell? She was about as low as she'd been on the "how fucked up can her life be" scale in a long time, there was nowhere to go but up, right? She rose from the bed and let him lead her down yet another long corridor. She should've been too tired or wigged out to notice, but she appreciated the way he carried himself—all sexy bad ass and don't-fuck-with-me attitude. He palmed a decorative mirror that hung at the end of the hall. The glass lit up and beeped, then a wall panel slid open to reveal an elevator. Grayce shot him a quizzical glance which he reciprocated with a playful smile.

"Security." He held the door open and gestured for her to enter. "You'll be programmed in soon enough. This is your home too."

* * * *

They entered a pristine, well lit room. Everything was white. Facing a leather couch in the center of the space were two matching leather armchairs with a wooden table nestled between. A panel door in the far corner slid open and out came a tall, handsome gentleman dressed in a black dress shirt, tie and fitted black slacks.

With his broad shoulders, slim waist and olive skin, he could've been mistaken for a fitness model. Sharp facial features were enhanced by his shaved head, but what dominated his handsome mug were a set of bright, almond shaped green eyes that, like Zander's, glowed and were far too mesmerizing to be real.

"Z, my man." He gave Zander a quick handshake and a firm pat on the shoulder. Zander pulled him into a hearty embrace.

"Nikolas. This is my...um..." Clearing his throat he shot a sideways glance at Grayce. "This is Grayce." In an outright possessive gesture, he grabbed her elbow and pulled her close.

Grayce offered a trembling hand to shake but Nikolas laughed, threw his arms around her instead and squeezed too damn tight. "Grayce." Holding her at arm's length, he studied her face and shook his head. Disbelief flashed through his stunning green eyes.

"Oh my God, woman, you are gorgeous. You don't know how happy we are to finally have you here." His genuine smile put her at ease. Grayce was impressed at how she managed so far, considering she was trapped somewhere underground in a small space with two men. First instinct? Jump behind the couch and hide, or grab the small table and do her best to beat them away. She suppressed the urge. Yeah, she held it together pretty well, she supposed.

"I, um, thank you," she sputtered.

Releasing her, not nearly as soon as she would've liked, Doctor Compton gestured for them to sit. With way too much grace for a man, he lowered himself into one of the armchairs. Zander claimed his spot on the couch nice and tight against her.

"I hope you don't mind, but Z has told me about what's been going on. He also told me he tried to explain his..." He scratched his head. "Attraction to you." He looked her square in the eye. "And yours to him?" Raising his right brow, he waited for her response.

"Ah, yes, the soul mates bullshit." Grayce huffed, folded her arms and slouched like a spoiled teenager. More of the sappy romance shit? Fucking awesome. Zander tensed next to her and squirmed in his seat. "He thinks we are connected somehow. Says we are meant to be together."

Doctor Compton nodded at her, his expression unreadable. The man was so proper the way he sat in his chair; back straight, hands folded politely on his crossed leg, chin lifted, not arrogant but respectful in manner, giving her his full attention. Strikingly handsome, Grayce thought. But so was Tyr and look where that got her. Fuck. Tyr. She cringed with the thought. Bile rose in her throat.

"My dear, I've known this big lug for many—" A big sigh followed by a roll of his eyes hinted at a playful side that seemed at odds with his professional air. "Many years." He smirked and tossed a quick glance to Zander, who reciprocated with a middle finger. "I can assure you with every fiber of my being the connection you share is very real."

His large confident smile showed off perfect white teeth, five shades brighter than the walls and furniture. "And now you two have found each other, the bond will get stronger."

Oh crap. Not him too. Uncertain if it was the stark room and bright light or that she was in the presence of two males, but agitation swirled like a fog in her brain. Stifled, heated and angry, she shook her head in an attempt to clear it of some of the chaos. "I can't do this right now!" She didn't mean to scream the words, they just came out that way. Shocked at her own outburst, she jumped to her feet.

"Dammit." Zander's deep voice vibrated through her. "You need to hear this." A heavy fist pounded the couch cushion. "This is my life. Our life." Frustration thick in his voice, he pounded again.

Grayce jumped back, wild with fury. Something cracked inside her, opening a chasm deep, deep down in the darkest depths of her soul. An intense heat rose from the abyss and filled her insides.

"You fucking men are all alike." Leaning forward, bringing herself nose to nose with Zander, she read the regret in his eyes.

Too late for regret.

"Don't you ever fucking raise your voice to me. I'm not some pussy ass little bitch you can bully around." Her breath caught in her throat as the internal heat fueled her anger, boosted her nerve. Urged her on. "I've been a pathetic victim for too damn long. I'll be damned if I let you walk into my life and stake your claim. What did you think I would do? Swoon and fall into your arms? Are you fucking serious? Soul mates? What the fuck does that even mean?"

Grayce shot a glance over her shoulder to make sure the other asshole was paying attention. Doctor Compton had a death grip on the armrests.

"I gave my life to a man. Once. I will not do it again. Do you understand?" Zander leaned back as she stabbed at his chest with her index finger. Both heartbreak and remorse were evident on his face. Tears stung her eyes. She let them fall. Wiping them away would be useless.

"Where were you when I was still worth saving?" she asked, knowing it would cut deeper than if she'd stabbed him with a sword. As the heated rage swelled, spreading from belly to limbs, her confidence grew. "He took everything. He ate me alive, and I let him." An unwelcome memory of Tyr's playroom sent violent shivers through the churning heat straight to her bones.

"I hate all of you! Soul mates my ass. I'm holding on tight to the little piece of my soul that's left." Salty tears blurred her vision, but not so much that she couldn't read the confusion in Zander's eyes. "My soul. Not yours."

His own baby blues puddled as she fisted his shirt. "You fucking men should be thrown into the deepest pits of hell for what you did to me." The anger was so intense, she saw nothing but red. Mind, body and soul, she was nothing but fire and fury.

Zander's shirt shredded like tissue under her grip. Tears poured down his face while Grayce threw all of her pain, all the rage and every prick of fear at him. God, it felt so good. Zander tried to place his hands on her wrists and she threw them off, taking a piece of his shirt with her.

"Don't. Ever. Touch. Me!" she shouted. Her own voice was frightening, like she'd been possessed and a demon spoke through her. She wanted them to feel every horror that'd been bottled up inside of her, wanted to punish them for what Tyr did to her. And more than anything, she tried to will her anguish into their souls and free her own from the burden she'd carried for too damned long. She tore her shirt over her head. "Look at me. Look at what he did to me," she screamed, throwing her arms out wide.

* * * *

Mouth agape, Zander stared at his woman, his future, his life. His lungs ceased to perform their duty. He fell on trembling knees at her feet. "Holy Christ." It pained him to look, but he couldn't tear his eyes away. Scars riddled her torso. Some were small and round, a few were jagged and raised, most were long and thin. Not a damned one of them should've been there.

"Who would want to be with this?" Her fury manifested itself as a red fog charged with electrical currents. In seconds, they were engulfed in a swirling gust of heated energy that crackled and buzzed in his ears, churned around the room, swirled and billowed between them.

Aching to hold her and offer comfort, he raised his hands. She backed away and tore the thin cotton bra from her body. Round firm breasts, perfect in proportion to her narrow waist and full hips, bore as many, if not more, of the same sickening marks as her stomach.

He glanced at Nikolas. A sheen of moisture coated his head and face, his eyes wild, not with fear like they should've been, but anticipation.

"Z! Are you seeing this? You've got to calm her. Fuck. This is unbelievable." Nikolas jumped from his chair, ran to the corner of the room and disappeared through the door panel.

"How can I ever be whole? I hate you. I hate you!" Grayce screamed. A loud, guttural, soul-cleansing release.

The deepest sadness filled Zander. A terrible ache permeated his bones. How could he let this happen? Why didn't he find her years ago? Try harder? She could've been spared this anguish, this endless torment to her spirit. As she purged herself in front of him, he tried to absorb it, take it away from her. The physical pain was bad, but the emotional blow was downright devastating. He couldn't fathom the amount of strength required to carry that much baggage around for so long.

"Grayce, baby." His voice trembled. "I'm sorry. I'm so sorry for scaring you. You have to stop. Look, look what you're doing." He gestured to the burning couch. Hair whipped around his face. The red energy consumed the entire room. He rose from the floor and locked gazes with her.

"Look at me. You can't hurt me. I won't hurt you." With caution, he stepped forward. She didn't back away. Good. Her eyes reflected unspeakable pain. "I won't hurt you," he murmured softly. "I will never hurt you. I can't." Slow and gentle, Zander grasped her hands.

Her chest heaved with heavy jagged breaths. "I'm hot. Oh shit. It's so hot in here." A layer of moisture coated her body. It bubbled and danced across her heated skin.

"Keep looking at me," he whispered warily. "Breathe. That's it. Breathe, baby." Her breasts rose and fell as she slowly calmed. He inched his arms around her, never breaking eye contact. Grayce stared up at him, utterly lost.

"What have I done? Help me." Pleading eyes begged him. "What's happening?" His tears still fell but he wiped hers away with his fingers. The temperature of the room dropped almost immediately.

"That's a potent temper you have," he breathed against her ear. His lips brushed her cheek. "We'll have to work on getting that under control." Drawing a deep breath, he dropped his arms. "Nikolas," he shouted over the panel. "You got an extra shirt back there?"

Grayce looked down at her naked body, then snapped back to Zander. She swayed, her eyes rolled into her skull and he caught her, just before she hit the floor.

"Not again."

* * * *

Grayce woke in a sweat, heart racing, legs tangled in the sheets. Zander burst through the door practically freeing the hinges from the jam. "What is it? What happened?" Two strides and he'd settled her in his lap, twisted bedding and all.

Her first urge was to curl into a ball and protect herself, but he cupped her chin with a strong hand and lifted her face. There they were again, those eyes. It really wasn't fair, the power his gaze held. She wondered what would've happened if she'd made eye contact with him weeks ago when he first made his magnificent appearance at the gym.

"It was only a bad dream." She tried to sound stoic, knowing he wouldn't buy it. "Nothing to worry about."

"You were screaming. I could hear you down the hall." His nimble fingers worked their way through her tangled hair. Head pressed to his chest, his heart beat like the sweetest lullaby in her ear. She tried, but couldn't hold back an exhausted yawn.

"You need to sleep." His body shifted gently and he laid her across the bed. A pang of fear stabbed her chest. No. No sleeping. No dreaming.

"Please don't leave." Surprised by her own words, a blush warmed her cheeks. "Please, stay here with me. Don't go."

Zander's face lit up. "I would like nothing more than to stay with you." His eyes sparkled. "Let me get the chair." He pointed to the overstuffed cream lounger occupying the far corner of the room.

No. Too far away. She scooted over and gestured for him to sit on the bed. "Please, I don't want to be alone," she whispered.

Looking extremely pleased, he straightened the sheet and comforter and pulled them up to her chin. The mattress slumped when he lay down next to her on top of the blankets. Acting the noble gentleman, he stayed close to the edge. A feat not easily accomplished with a physique that spanned half the space. Desperate to be nearer, Grayce wiggled herself under the covers until she could feel his warmth. His breath caught and there was the slightest pause before he enveloped her in a hug and pulled her closer.

Talk about epic progress. She couldn't believe she was sharing a bed with this man. And felt safe. Certainly, she'd wake from this dream disgusted with herself. At least it was Zander, not Tyr invading her sleep time.

"Thank you."

She yearned to say much more, but the words lulling around the tip of her tongue scuttled to the back of her throat to be swallowed.

* * * *

Grayce woke feeling warm and refreshed. For the first time, she surveyed her surroundings. The wall opposite the bed consisted of one big window that overlooked a plush green valley. The sun's rays, weakened slightly by the sheer curtain, blanketed half the room. The four poster bed was made of pale wood. The bedding, plush, fluffy and perfumed with lavender, was hands down the most luxurious place she'd ever laid her head. An oval hand carved mirror hung above a matching set of dressers, also pale wood. The walls were void of any artwork and there were no personal items of any sort on display. Must have been a guest room.

Zander's arm lay heavy across her hips and his face nuzzled her neck. She needed to stretch but she enjoyed the warmth of his breath on her skin and didn't want to disturb him. How was it possible she could come so far in a few days? She's hated and feared men for so long. Now, she wanted this beautiful creature wrapped around her like a warm blanket. Was it the violent purging of her anger yesterday?

Yesterday. Oh crap. It came crashing back to her like a giant wave of angry memories. What had she done? How had she—

As if sensing her tension, Zander tightened his hold. "Are you okay?" His deep voice, thick with sleep and incredibly sexy, took her breath away.

"I could have killed you." Due to the massive arm hanging over her, it took much effort to turn and face him. She cupped his face with her hands and waited for his eyes to open. "Please just give it to me straight. Did I make that fire? Did I do that?" He nodded yes. "Was I able to do that because of you?"

"No." He pulled her closer and kissed her forehead. "Because of us. It's a part of you. It's always been there." His hand found its way to her heart. "You, are..." he paused, started to say something and paused again. "I tried to tell you before. We're stronger together than we are apart. You have an incredible gift. It's unusual for powers to manifest as quick as yours did. If you're this strong now, I can't fathom what you'll be able to do after—" He stopped and squeezed his eyes shut. "Never mind. You shocked the hell out of Nikolas. I'll bet he's been in his lab all night trying to figure you out." A playful, crooked grin spread across his face.

Powerful? Grayce remembered something and smiled up at him.

"What?" he asked, brushing his finger across her bottom lip.

"I liked the way it felt...yesterday. I did feel powerful." She loved having the ability to hurt him, or any man for that matter.

"I've never lost control of my temper like that before. I mean, I've been angry for so long, but never out of control." Worried she might say too much, she paused to collect her thoughts. It did feel good to talk to someone. She'd never had a confidant. For some reason, she wanted to tell this man everything. "I don't think I could've stopped myself. I would've killed us all. I wanted to burn and burn and keep burning until the pain went away."

Zander chuckled.

"What's so fucking funny?"

"I have what some might call an anger control issue myself. But yours, baby. It makes me look like a saint." An angelic smile swept across his face. "And that foul mouth of yours. Shit. Makes me want to..." He shook the thought away. "You're a little firecracker, you know that?"

A question burned on Grayce's lips. It took a few moments to build the courage to ask, afraid the answer might be exactly what she suspected. "How are you able to soothe and calm me just by making eye contact?" She picked at a loose thread on his shirt.

"Soul mates." She loathed those two words. This time however, she was a little more inclined to believe him. He kissed her forehead and pushed himself off the bed. "I need a shower, how about you?"

She lifted the blankets and looked down at herself. Crap. Someone had covered her with a large black t-shirt. Zander, no doubt. "Um, I've got no clothes."

Zander pointed to the dresser on the right. "I filled your duffel bag yesterday, you know, before we um..." he scratched his head. "I put your clothes in there. We'll get you more soon."

"I'm never going back to my apartment, am I?" It figured. Forever on the run. Her life story.

"No Grayce. This is your home now." He disappeared through a door she hadn't noticed before and failed to close it behind him. The whoosh of running water piqued her interest and she lifted her head for a gander. Oh, for the fucking love of everything. Zander. Naked.

A drift of searing heat made its way through her lungs and spread through limbs, heart and head. In her wildest dreams she couldn't have imagined a more perfect, beautiful man. The way his skin stretched taut and smooth over every muscle and vein on his sun kissed body reminded her of golden caramel. His chiseled muscle from head to toe didn't look real. One hundred percent pure, raw, male power stood only feet away and the need to claim him overwhelmed her.

She spied as he stepped into the glass encased shower. When she leaned over the bed to get a better view, a thumping, aching heat pounded in between her legs. The sensation was so intense her thighs clenched together. Shit. What was happening? She'd never felt anything like this. A flush burned her cheeks and her head felt detached. A relentless rhythm pounded down there. Was this lust? Was this what it felt like to want somebody? Unable to peel her eyes away, she shifted to get a better look until he disappeared behind the steam.

Oh fuck, what now? Her body screamed for something. A release. It needed a release—or him. Why? A few days ago, she would've killed anyone who suggested she'd ever need a man, want a man. Her core grew hotter and a light sheen of moisture formed on her skin. Every muscle ached with hunger.

* * * *

Accustomed to being alone, Zander neglected to shut the door before he stripped his clothing and stepped into the flow of steamy water. He lathered up and hoped like hell to wash away the lustful urges he'd been battling for days.

Laying in bed with Grayce had almost been his undoing. The beast in him had wanted to rip off her clothes and take her, because it was his right as her mate. The man in him had lain heartbroken, searching for a way to put the puzzle pieces of her life together.

Zander had been tempted many times before by desirable women. He always turned them away. It was a no brainer. Cheating wasn't his nature, and although he'd yet to meet Grayce, knowing she existed was more than enough to keep him faithful. Temptation was no match to the desire to be the man she deserved. He had spent many tortured nights alone in bed, starving for his woman's touch, her embrace, her naked skin pressed against his.

Being a male and human, there were of course physical needs. He dealt with those just like any other warm blooded male. An active imagination, his right hand, and quality time with himself added up to a daily ritual that he sure as shit wasn't going to miss.

Sharing a bed with Grayce and knowing he wouldn't touch her soft, warm skin, or taste her full pink lips had been pure torture. Hands down, the most difficult night of his life.

As he tried and failed to wash away the torrid thoughts, a wave of fear and panic washed over him. And something else.

Something was wrong with Grayce.

Not bothering to dry off, he abandoned the shower and ran to the bedroom. His heart dropped to his gut, bounced around a bit, then settled somewhere near his groin. Grayce sat on her knees in the center of the bed and frantically rubbed at her arms. A deep red glow illuminated her skin.

"Grayce?"

With imploring eyes she begged. "Please help me."

"Oh shit." A hungry growl escaped his lips. He captured her gaze, hoping to give the comfort he could so easily offer. She only stared back, eyes pleading with carnal need.

The desire he'd washed off in the shower? Yeah, it was back, with a vengeance.

"Please help me," she sobbed. "Please." She glanced down at her body then back to him, lost, helpless and terrified.

At her side in an instant, he threw the bedding across the room. "Tell me what you need. I'm here, baby."

The room temperature rose. "Touch me," she begged.

"I know you're scared, love," he whispered. "I'll be gentle. I promise." Zander leaned forward and planted a reassuring kiss on her head. "I'll never hurt you. You know that, right? I'll never do anything to hurt you." He flinched when she placed blazing hands on his heaving chest. Fuck. She was on fire.

"Grayce, can I kiss you?"

Through labored breaths she groaned. "You're asking my permission? Now is not the time to be a gentleman."

Now was exactly the time to be a gentleman. This needed to be right. She needed to know she had complete control. "May I touch you?"

"Please." Grayce's tormented plea battered his spirit. Hell, it damn near gutted him. This wasn't the way he'd imagined their first time playing out. With her past, he had been certain it'd be a long time coming. There were spiritual, heavenly forces at work, urging them to come together. It was more than physical. The need to be inside her, to claim her in the most primal way, surged through his body and soul like a tsunami. Even if he'd wanted to, he was powerless to stop the inevitable joining of their bodies.

Blood filled his sex with ferocious heat. At first, he claimed her lips with tender nudges. The kiss turned into a fevered assault the moment she reciprocated. With unrelenting urgency, he deepened his exploration, cupped the back of her head and urged her to lay back. She trembled under his touch, whimpered when he trailed his free hand down the front of her shirt, groaned when he brushed a finger across the top of her panties.

Reaching under her shirt, he rubbed his fingers across her abdomen, making his way over heated skin to her breasts. She was so much softer than he'd imagined. Her breasts were full and as they heaved with her gasps, he marveled at how perfectly they molded in his hands.

"Is this what you need?" He brushed the pad of his thumb over a taught nipple, her moan an assurance he was headed in the right direction. With little effort, he tore her shirt right down the middle, exposing her naked, scarred and glowing body. Pink, pebbled peaks greeted him with promises of fleshly delight. He had to taste them. When he brushed his tongue against one hard nub, she nearly bucked off the bed, so he continued, exploring every inch of her breasts with his mouth. The unrelenting flow of blood had his cock crying for mercy. When she arched her back and held his head to her chest, he damned near lost his composure.

Satisfied he had properly tended to her breasts, Zander wandered lower, savoring her flavor with each kiss, each nip of desire-basted skin. He paused and lightly traced his fingers across the largest battle wound she wore. It started underneath her left breast, stretched in a jagged arch across her stomach and landed a finger's width from her right hip. Goosebumps popped across her skin as he studied her with eyes and touch. He stopped to watch a single tear trickle down her cheek.

"I wasn't there to protect you." With a final kiss to her hip, he positioned himself lower. "You have my word. I'll be there every fucking day for the rest of your life." His breaths came deep and ragged as he slid her panties down around inviting hips, past lean trembling thighs, and swept them from her feet. Nestled between her legs, his erection strained hard and heavy toward the only place it was ever meant to be. Home. He couldn't help but drink in her naked body. So voluptuous for such a small frame. So perfect. All his.

"I can't believe how beautiful you are."

Grayce blinked away another tear and reached up to him. Zander leaned over, hands fisted on the bed. The red glow spread, enveloped them both in its warmth. Grayce's hazel eyes burned with hunger.

"Please, I need you now." Fingers curled around his neck. She drew him down for a hard kiss, expressing just how carnal her need. God, he needed her too. His body was coiled so tight he thought he might snap. Blood pounded through his ears in a thunderous roar. The tip of his erection found her plush folds. As he eased into her heated flesh, she flexed her hips to meet him. With ardent grace, she wrapped her legs around his thighs in attempt to force his entry.

"Slow down, love," he panted. "I don't want to hurt you." It was impossible to hurt her physically, but since this was his first time with her or any woman, Zander didn't want to explode before satiating her completely.

"Zander!" Desperate pleas shredded his sanity. "It hurts already. Can't you feel me burning alive?" With a shift of his hips, he delved further. Silky. Tight. So fucking warm. Full breasts bounced and teased as she arched and clawed at his back.

"Oh hell." Wits completely unraveled by her need, he thrust deep and hard. She took every inch and bit back a scream. "Fuck, Grayce. You're on fire." He took pause, allowing their bodies to acclimate to one another, stealing time to get emotions under control. He wanted to revel in the moment, commit it to memory—her glow, her smell, the way her sex enveloped his, the way their bodies fit together, a seamless knitting of flesh. Face buried in his chest, she whispered something inaudible and tightened her embrace. Teeth gritted, he withdrew and slammed into her again.

"More," she cried. "Please, more." Nature guided his movement. In. Out. In. Out. She met him thrust for thrust. Each time he impaled her, he claimed victory over the war with the dark and lonely days of his past. Each sheathing, a claim to his throne. He continued again and again, each time burying himself deeper. God, he couldn't believe how lucky he was. He'd never felt so empowered. It was worth the countless years spent frustrated and angry. Zander fisted the sheets on either side of her head and buried his face in the mattress next to hers.

"My sweet, sweet Grayce." Needing to be deeper, he wrapped an arm around her waist, pulled her hips tighter to his, then lifted his head to find her eyes. She gazed through heavy lids then tossed her head back into the mattress. Back arched, her sex convulsed with violent spasms around his erection, pulling and pulsing, taunting him to the point of painful ecstasy. "Grayce. Oh fuck...I..." He struggled for breath, and with one final desperate thrust, exploded inside of her with savage tremors.

His release was excruciating, exhilarating and exhausting all at once. As he pumped in and out of slick, heated flesh, he feared it would never end, he'd continue exploding and filling her to the brim. Grayce clung to him with desperate unrelenting convulsions. Her orgasm was every bit as overwhelming as his. And damned if that didn't make him the happiest man on the planet.

Chapter 5

Blinking sleepy eyes open, Grayce was, for a fleeting moment, in a state of complete bliss, an emotion both foreign and elusive. The moon flashed a bright smile through the open window, illuminating the dark room with milky rays of light. Zander clung like a protective shield. How she wasn't crushed under his massive weight was a question only briefly entertained.

The grumbling that vibrated her midsection reminded her it'd been hours since her last meal. Attempts at wiggling free of her Z blanket only caused him to hold tighter.

"Mmm," he purred, "you're hungry." How did he know? Should mind reading be added to the growing list of weird?

"Hungry is the understatement of the year," she grumbled, still unable to move. If her bladder weren't about to burst, she'd consider staying like that all day. She tapped his arm locked in a tight vice around her chest. "Let me up."

"No. Do I have to?" he asked with a pout. Pouting from a man would, under most circumstances, be a major turn off, especially a man of Zander's stature. However, the resonance of his voice, combined with the sensation of his warm powerful body against hers, had the opposite effect. "I'm not ready to let go yet."

"Please. I need to use the bathroom." She wiggled about, trying to worm her way under his arm. "You'll be sorry in about ten seconds if you don't let me go," she warned in a vain attempt to sound agitated.

He rolled off and stretched underneath the comforter. Clasping his hands behind his head he watched with an amused grin as she wrestled free of the bedding. "You are so fucking sexy."

Grayce had no idea where her clothes were, but oddly, she didn't feel modest. Was it the mind blowing sex? Maybe it was because with him, she felt absolutely safe. Perhaps she was dreaming. If that were the case, she'd have to remember to send a thank you note to Mr. Sandman.

She decided to take a quick shower while in there. When she returned from the bathroom, buffed and shined, Zander stood by the bed dressed in perfectly worn out jeans that did nothing to hide the muscled sculpture of his thighs and a white, fitted cotton tee. It hugged him so tight, it could've been body paint.

"Come here." With a firm pat of the mattress, he gestured for her to sit next to clothing folded neatly on the bed. Tilting her head she raised an angry eyebrow. "Please." He smiled.

Grayce obliged. He unfolded a yellow cotton sundress he must've grabbed from her apartment. Her favorite lazy day outfit. "Lift your arms." Deep dimples made a playful appearance. "Please."

With surprising skill, he lowered the garment down her midsection. Ecstatic waves of pleasure pulsed through her as his fingers traced seductively down her sides.

"You disintegrated your bra. We'll have to get you another one. Or not." He reached around, grabbed her panties, knelt down and lifted first her left foot and then her right. His thumbs caressed her skin as he slid the garment up her calves.

"Stand up." He groaned. Her insides clenched with his carnal show of want. Grayce stood while he slid her panties up her thighs and over her rear. After straightening them, his hands drifted sensually to her stomach. His finger left a trail of blazing skin as he traced the length of her scar. Wrapping his arms around her waist, he hugged, pressing his nose against her abdomen. An intimate act that bordered sensory overload. With jaw clenched, she fought the impulse to recoil, forced leaded arms around his head and hugged him back. Her stomach grumbled, protesting its neglected state.

"Well, my little firecracker, we better get you some food." Zander released his hold, scooped Grayce into his arms and whisked her down a long wide hallway. The vestibule brought to mind images Grayce had conjured as a child on the rare occasion her mother read a story about the prince who rescued a princess from an evil queen. Deep burgundy walls were adorned with large cast iron mirrors and sconces that lined either side. Dark wood floors held a mirrored shine and not a speck of dust or lint could be detected. Grayce smacked his arm. "Put me down. I can walk." With his large strides, they were already halfway down the corridor.

"But this is more fun."

Anger welled like a raging flood. Bad enough he dressed her like a child, now he had the nerve to carry her too? "Dammit. Put me down." She shouldn't have raised her voice, but her temper was so volatile, there was little time to register the mood change, let alone filter her verbal response. The rate at which she shifted from content to turbulent left a disconcerting knot in her gut.

He dropped her feet and they swung mere inches from the floor. Cradled in his other arm, she punched at his chest. "Show off. Fucking put me down, now," she commanded through clenched teeth. Her skin heated with rapid force. Zander felt it too. His expression changed from playful to regretful in a blink. When he dropped her, the floor seared her bare feet like hot coals.

Grayce looked up into captivating blue eyes. "Thank you," she said, sugarcoating her words. To assure him rejection hadn't been her intent, she hooked his elbow and gave him a bump with her hip. Zander sighed deeply and slowed his pace so she could keep up with his strides. "Is this a heated floor?" she asked.

He snorted. "No baby, that's you. If we don't tame this temper of yours, we'll have to fireproof the entire estate."

* * * *

The walk to the dining room was an exercise in patience as well as self restraint. Patience on Zander's part, self restraint on Grayce's. Holy fuck. Each chamber they passed was larger than the last, each hall lined with countless doors. Grayce wanted to sprint into each room and spin like a school girl then bellow into the vast space to test for an echo.

Never had she seen, let alone imagined, a home so enormous and full of wide open space. Zander watched with a pleased grin as she explored, opened doors and peered through windows. If hunger pains hadn't been raking her insides she would've insisted he gave her a full tour.

Grayce was ravenous by the time they reached the dining room. Platters of food covered most of the ornate wood table that stretched the entire length of the room. The aroma made her stomach twist and growl. Zander pulled out a chair and kissed the top of her head as she sat. Electric currents danced across her scalp.

"This isn't all for us, is it?" Grayce practically drooled on herself. Damn she was hungry.

"I don't know what you like, so I asked Chelsea to make a little of everything." Nonchalant and clueless to the bomb he just dropped, Zander started to fill his plate. No big deal. Another woman in the house. Just Chelsea.

"Chelsea?" A strange feeling poked and prodded the back of Grayce's mind. Jealousy? No, couldn't be. For some odd reason, she wasn't so hungry anymore.

"She's Doctor Compton's soul ma—er, wife." He smiled down and handed her a plate. "The woman loves to cook. What do you wanna start with?"

Wife. Muscles relaxed. Fingers unclenched. "A little bit of everything please."

They ate in silence. Zander was big, gargantuan even, but Grayce was still shocked by how much food the man put down. She'd filled her plate twice and felt like a boulder had taken up residence in her stomach. Zander worked on helping number four and showed no signs of slowing his pace. Unable to take another bite, she decided to break the silence.

"Why is this table so big? How many people live here?" she asked.

Zander held up a finger while he finished chewing. With aristocratic elegance, he wiped his mouth and hands with a linen napkin, then, after a crisp fold, laid it next to his fork. "Nikolas and Chelsea live here with me—I mean, us. They have their own wing but we share the kitchen." His hand slid from the arm of his chair to her thigh. Heat charged her skin on contact.

"You said us." Grayce voiced dryly to him.

"Yes I did." The perplexed expression in his eyes irritated her, like he expected her to accept his word with no questions or concerns.

"This isn't my home. I don't live here." She shook her head at him. Grayce never had a real home. Her apartment was the first place she'd called her own. She'd never been fool enough to believe it wasn't temporary. Before that, it was one crappy hotel room after another. Always on the move, always looking over her shoulder. One step ahead of the monster. "You said the same thing earlier, about this being my home now."

"Grayce." He scooted his chair, turned it toward her and rested his elbows on his knees. "I know you don't understand, not yet. But this..." He waved his hand, presenting the kitchen to her. "I built this for you. I knew you'd be coming soon."

"How did you know?" Oh, this ought to be good. Her skin tingled with annoyance.

Zander reached between Grayce's legs, grabbed her chair and scooted her close, bringing them nose to nose. "I searched the planet multiple times trying to find you. Gradually, the pull became stronger. I knew you were close, but had a hard time pinning you down. It was so fucking frustrating. At first I thought something was wrong with me. Nikolas explained that perhaps I couldn't zero in on you because you were on the move. We joked about you being in the circus or some traveling show. I passed through this area many times. Our connection was always strongest here. I felt you getting closer, so I built this home."

"So you're saying this was built for me?" She looked around. "All of this?" She glanced back to his serene face. A pool of liquid warmth formed between her thighs. Shit. Betrayed again. By her own blood and bones.

"Yes. I know it must sound crazy. You have to know I'm one hundred percent sincere. I couldn't lie to you even if I wanted to."

Ha! Couldn't lie. What man didn't lie, or do everything in his power to deceive the women in his life? No man she'd ever known.

"I'd been out of town for several weeks on business. When I returned, a shift had taken place, not just in me, but around me. I sensed you. I followed the energy and it led me to the gym. Every cell in my body vibrated when I stepped inside. I zeroed-in on you, tried to make eye contact, but you avoided me at all costs, like you were afraid. So, I didn't push. Nikolas warned me to take it slow. God, it was fucking torture." He searched her eyes, she had no reaction to offer. "Anyway, you know what happens next."

"If we're connected like you say, why didn't I feel you? Why didn't I feel a bond or a pull?" Her bones ached with an unexpected sorrow, like she'd missed out on an important rite of passage.

"You did. You do. You're so guarded you couldn't or wouldn't recognize it. That's one hell of a wall you've built around yourself." Sadness spread over his hard masculine features. An unusual urge to comfort him unfurled through her veins.

"So now what?" She surrendered her hands to the air. "Are you expecting me to call a minister? Buy a puffy white dress? 'Cause let me assure you, I'll do naked cartwheels through Disneyland before shit like that goes down."

"I'd like to see that," he chuckled. "We can take it slow. Or not at all, if that's what you choose. But you need to know something." He paused and rubbed his face roughly, drawing Grayce's attentions to his rugged hands. They knew her intimately, gave her pleasure beyond reason, and despite being masculine and powerful, she didn't fear them. It was ironic, really. Tyr's long manicured fingers were far too pretty and delicate for a man, and with them, he'd only shown her pain.

"What?" She barked.

"Now that we've found each other..." He looked hesitant, afraid even to say what needed to be said.

Oh fuck, this was going to be bad.

"I'm with you forever. Mind, body, spirit. I'm yours. You are..." He stopped. He wanted to say *mine*. Zander knew better and didn't want to ignite her fury again. Good boy.

"I can't make you stay here. I'll never force you to do anything. But you need to know that wherever you go, I'll be there. If you never want to see me, you won't. But I'll be there in the shadows. If you want me to be your friend, we'll be friends. If you need a father figure, brother, security guard...I'll be there. If you're ever sick, in danger, trouble of any sort, it'll be me keeping you safe. If—"

"Stop. You're killing me." Grayce silenced him with a finger over his soft lips. "I get it. Fuck. I get it." Her hand lingered. The skin to skin contact was like a shot of happy-happy-joy-joy without the nasty side effects. He nipped the pad of her palm and chuckled.

"Why the foul language, Grayce?" His eyes saddened as he grabbed her hand and placed it on his knee. "Don't get me wrong, it turns me on." He added quickly.

Grayce shrugged in mach indifference. Yeah, her foul mouth was a tool used to keep people at arm's length. Didn't take a PhD to figure that out. No one wants to get to know the crazy girl who drops the F-bomb in every sentence. She didn't want to talk about herself. Not now. Not ever. Besides, if she did open up and spill her guts, the fire and fury might come back. It'd be a shame to burn such a lovely house.

"Never mind. It doesn't matter." Zander shook his head. "Would you like a tour of your maybe home?" Grayce nodded, hoping to walk off the obscene amount of food she'd scarfed. That, and give her some time to think about her possible place of residence, and Zander, too. Shit, she couldn't believe she was even considering this insanity.

The forty-five minute jaunt ended in a large home gym decked out with top of the line workout equipment. It didn't go unnoticed that a set of elliptical machines matching the one Grayce favored at the gym were placed side by side in the corner of the room. The man paid attention.

"Wow." Grayce gasped when they entered. "Why would you ever buy a gym membership when you have this at home?"

His laugh bounced off the wall to wall windows. "I've never had to work out a day in my life." He smiled. "I went to Armstrong's to be near you." The steel framed bench creaked in protest as he sat. "You went every day. I thought you might like to have your own gym here. I built this for you. Finished a couple days ago."

Unable to help herself, Grayce threw her head back in laughter. "You're kidding me, right?"

Her feet left the floor and her ass landed on his thighs faster than she could blink. "I'm not kidding. What's so funny?"

"I hate going to the gym. I'd joined a couple weeks before you came in, to take self defense classes, which I loathed by the way. I kept going back..." She couldn't believe she was admitting this. "Because I wanted to see you."

Zander squeezed tight and laughed with her. Grayce hadn't laughed like that since she was a child...a million lifetimes ago.

* * * *

"Grayce. Grayce. Baby wake up." Her eyes snapped open, releasing her from the nightmare. Hands trembled in panic as she loosened the death grip on her own throat. Zander nestled her to his chest and stroked her hair. "Hey. I'm here. You're safe." Soft kisses tickled her scalp.

No. Not the damned nightmares again. Why was this happening? She searched his gaze for the solace only he could offer. "He's in my head again. God I hate this shit." Grayce scrubbed the forming tears away, along with the goo that'd collected in the corners of her eyes from a hard sleep. After planting a few kisses on her cheek, Zander grunted and rolled out of bed.

"Come, Chelsea's making breakfast. She's dying to meet you." He planted one last soft kiss right on the tip of her nose. A prickly heat shivered down her spine and spread like wildfire across sensitive skin. Never in her wildest dreams did she imagine being so receptive to a man's touch. Waking in bed with one, safe and warm? Well, miracles really did happen, didn't they?

They dressed and headed to the kitchen. The aroma of bacon overwhelmed her senses and her stomach roared. Zander heard it too and laughed. At the sink stood a tall, raven-haired curvaceous woman. Couldn't have been older than thirty-five. As if she felt them enter, she squealed and dropped the pan she'd been drying onto the counter.

"Grayce, I would like you to meet Chelsea." Voice thick with pride, Zander beamed. She'd never seen him smile so wide.

"Oh my." Chelsea cupped her mouth. Deep green eyes gleamed with pure joy. "May I hug you?" she asked, choking back tears. Not waiting for an answer, she lunged at Grayce, throwing delicate arms around her neck. She squeezed so tight, it left Grayce grasping for breath. "You're

here. You're finally here." A sob escaped her lips followed by the most
unladylike sniffle. She held Grayce at arm's length, gave her a once over,
then hugged her again. "You're more beautiful than I could've possibly
envisioned." Like a mother hen, she scooted Grayce to the table. "Sit, sit.
Breakfast is almost ready."

The strangest sensation swept through Grayce. A warm-and-fuzzy,
cinnamon roll-and-coffee, gossip-over-a-glass-of-wine kind of feeling.
How could someone she'd never met feel this comfortable and familiar?

Chelsea zipped over to Zander and embraced him in a bear hug. "I'm
so happy for you Zander." He embraced her back, swung her in a circle
and kissed her cheek as he set her down. "Nikolas is waiting in the lab.
I'll let you know when breakfast is ready."

"Yes ma'am." Zander grinned, shot Grayce a wink and headed for
the doorway in the far corner of the room.

"Okay. Got rid of him easily enough," Chelsea snickered at Grayce.
She shifted her dress and positioned a chair to bring them face to face.
"How are you doing?" Dainty fingers enveloped her hand and squeezed.

Grayce avoided eye contact for fear of having a meltdown. "I...
um...I don't know. This is...overwhelming." She looked down at their
clasped hands. "Unbelievable is more like it."

"I know what you're going through. I truly do. It's going to sink
in eventually, I promise." Chelsea tucked a long slender finger under
Grayce's chin and lifted her face to catch her gaze. "I'm here for you.
One hundred percent. I've got your back, whatever you need." Her eyes
glowed a brilliant jade green. What was the deal with everybody's eyes?
Chelsea's smile was so warm, inviting and maternal that Grayce couldn't
help but feel at peace, at home. "I think we should spend the day together,
just the two of us." Her eyes widened and glittered with anticipation.
"Would you like that?"

Yes, for some bizarre reason, she did want to spend the day with this
stranger who radiated warmth and love. This woman who wouldn't judge,
who didn't have a nasty bone in her body. How did she know that? What
the fuck did it matter? Weirder things had happened. Say like, in the past
three or four days.

"That would be nice." Besides, she needed a break from Zander, a
reprieve from the foreign emotions that attacked from every direction.
Work had offered a minimal distraction, but not enough to...

"Oh shit!" Work. She'd missed her shift. "I have to get to work. I
didn't call them yesterday. Fuck. I'm going to lose my job for sure."

Chelsea giggled and rose from her chair. "Zander was right. You do have a colorful vocabulary." She grabbed plates, then glasses from the cupboard. "From what I understand, it's not safe for you to go back."

Crap, she was right. Tyr had been watching her. She'd be a fool to go back. He'd be waiting.

"The boys are coming," Chelsea proclaimed. How did she know? A few seconds later, heavy footsteps preceded hearty laughter. Doctor Compton entered first. "Good morning, Grayce." A warm smile and wise eyes greeted her.

"Morning, Doctor Compton." She breathed a sigh of relief when he didn't come in for a hug.

Chelsea snickered. Nikolas snorted.

"Oh God, child. We're family, call me Nikolas." He headed for his wife, kissed her hard, then grabbed the dishes from her hand.

Family? Sure, in theory the idea was kinda awesome, but in reality? Yeah, right.

Zander scooted his chair close enough to Grayce's to keep their thighs in contact. It would've been annoying as hell if she didn't crave his touch so damned bad.

No one talked much at the breakfast table. Seemed as if a secret lingered between her three hosts. They made eye contact and small talk, with nothing of much importance being said. No one delved into her personal life. Thank God. They took turns checking on her. Kept her plate full, asked if she wanted more coffee. Small stuff. So many questions burrowed through her brain. So much she wanted to know but was afraid to ask.

Chelsea winked across the table at Grayce. "I'm sure you have a ton of questions." Shit. Was she a mind reader too? Grayce nodded and poked at her scrambled eggs. It felt like she'd been sucked into an alternate universe. She was surrounded by people who obviously loved each other and carried a deep respect for one another. When they spoke, the words were kind and thoughtful. They made eye contact and shared gentle, trusted physical touch. No one yelled or barked commands. No one was drunk or under the influence of illegal substances.

"If you'd like," Chelsea continued. "We can go for a walk after breakfast. I'll tell you anything you want to know. The men can join in, or we can go alone, it's your call."

Grayce glanced at Zander and melted a little in her seat as he flashed his sinfully sexy eyes her way. She didn't know how to act around all this normal, happy family, breakfast at the table, have a nice day shit.

Irritation rumbled through her bones like an oncoming storm. Conflicting emotions muddled her brain. For so long, she'd survived on pain, anger and fear. How could she let that go?

It couldn't be that easy, could it? It couldn't be that easy to just trust somebody? All these years she'd shielded herself from physical and emotional contact. Protected her heart and mind from the inevitable pain that accompanied intimate bonding, on any level, with another human. Now, her own body had double-crossed her. This damned attraction to Zander was fucking unbearable. She not only needed, but wanted him near. Why? Maybe she should run while she still had the chance. Never look back.

And what was with all the creepy shit? She practically ignited into flames when she got mad or saw Zander naked? What the hell? There hadn't been time to tackle that subject. Maybe she didn't want to. Then there's the whole topic of Zander's super strength. What was he? What the fuck was she, for that matter?

Questions, questions, questions. Unable to bear any more bombardment, Grayce slammed clenched fists on the table hard enough to make plates jump. "I have to get away from here. How the hell do I get out of here?"

Zander jumped to his feet so fast his chair flew across the room and splintered against the wall.

"I can't take all this nice." Grayce held up hands that glowed a crimson red. Sweat beaded across her skin. Her core churned with molten energy.

"Here she goes again," Nikolas proclaimed, wearing a shit-eating grin as he placed himself between his wife and Grayce.

In a blurred sequence of actions, Grayce was lifted, sucked through a vacuum, then set on a giant rock. The boulder protruded from the shore out across a crystal blue lake.

"All right baby, this good? You pissed?" He cocked his head and gave her shoulders a squeeze. "Let it out. Let it all out right here." Zander took a step back, placing himself between Grayce and the water and only a few feet from the edge of the slippery rock. "You wanna hit something? Here I am. You wanna burn something?" He slapped his fist against his chest and winked. "Bring it on."

What the fuck was he doing? Grayce trembled with hands fisted at her sides. Her mind reeled from the fact they traveled from the kitchen to wherever they were in mere seconds.

"Come on baby. Give me all you've got." Zander squatted and bounced, shifting his weight from side to side. What? Was he trying to piss her off more?

"That sick fucker fucked you up real good, didn't he?" He taunted.

Oh. He didn't just go there. Why would he do that?

"What? You don't like the foul language? You can dish it out but you can't take it?" Standing up straight again, he folded his arms across his chest. "Maybe you don't want me bringing *him* up?"

Her stomach clenched. White heat burned deep in the pit of her soul. It swirled and spread, searching for a way out.

"That's it Grayce, come on. You getting pissed?" Back in a semi-squat, arms held wide, he jutted his chest toward her, as if bracing for impact. "I can see how angry you are baby. I can feel it." He smirked and nodded. "Now show it to me."

Oh fuck no. Was this a challenge?

"You fucking bastard." Her body grew hotter by the second. She didn't want to do this.

"He's out there right now, looking for you." It was obvious by the catch in his voice that it pained him to speak those words, yet he continued. "He's coming for you. What are you gonna do about it? He wants you baby. You're his, remember?"

Oh God, why would he say that? The world turned red. Heat and energy swirled around her in a dizzying frenzy. Leaves, twigs and dirt blew around her feet, caught in a tornado of outrage. Energy snapped and popped in her ears as it buzzed through the air.

"You want to go back to that cock sucker? You want him back? You like the way he made you feel?" Zander's lips were drawn tight and an icy steel gaze hammered into her, threatening her sanity.

The last string of reason that held her psyche in balance snapped. All at once, Grayce was nothing but fire and fury. She wanted to kill him and keep going until every fucking male was wiped off the face of the planet.

The surrounding trees bowed and bent with the force of her vehemence. The energy consumed her as it traveled through her blood and cells, danced across heated skin, freed her from the binds of limited physical human ability.

She had ultimate power.

Zander continued to goad her, except she no longer heard his voice, only the current pulsing through her veins. The hypnotic rhythm encouraged her. Hands raised toward Zander, Grayce guided the heat, the fire and hatred right at his beautiful warrior body. "You motherfucker!" Her scream was surreal. She doubted it came from her lungs.

Zander stumbled backward, but maintained his composure. He shook his arms, cracked his neck and nodded, as if giving her permission to go again.

Yeah right, like she needed permission.

Oh fuck, the release felt good. With a confident step forward, she struck again.

Eyes flashing with disbelief, Zander leaned into the assault and slid farther along the boulder until he teetered on the edge.

She didn't allow him time to recoup his balance. When she hit again, he was lifted off his feet and disappeared beneath a plume of water. A wave temporarily flooded the rock and soaked her clothing.

Seconds later, he surfaced. "Good job, baby." He dared to wear a prideful grin. "That was awesome."

Why was he smiling? Didn't he know he was about to die?

Grayce stepped to the boulder's edge. "Oh...baby." She shook her head slowly. "I'm not finished yet." She didn't recognize her own voice. Deep and fearsome. Horror flashed through his baby blues before he ducked back under the water.

Grayce simmered in one big burning ball of energy. With a deep breath, she sucked in all the rage, all the hatred and anger and fear. She drew it deep into her being and with all that she had, with every god forsaken bit of her soul, she forced it at him. A thunderous roar tore through the wilderness as the entire contents of the lake were pushed in one giant swell, up and over the trees.

No longer able to bear weight, her legs collapsed beneath her. On hands and knees, she watched the massive wave devour everything in its path with a deafening rumble. Trees broke under the weight of the water, the force sweeping away the forest floor.

She was spent. Her lungs refused to take air and she struggled to remain conscious as she leaned forward onto trembling arms.

Was he dead? Did she kill him? Oh shit, what did she do? A thick steam rose from the lake bed making it impossible to see the bottom. Grayce looked to the left, then the right. The forest was decimated for at least a hundred yard radius. Nothing left except ash. *"Oh fuck, I killed him,"* was her last thought before blackness consumed her.

* * * *

Feeble fingers gripped the bark of a hefty fir. Exhausted and hungry, the small boy crouched behind the tree taking extra care not to make a sound. He peeked around to find a giant man and a tiny woman standing on a huge rock above the water. He watched in silence as they argued. He was good at being quiet and very good at hiding.

He rubbed his eyes when a red glow formed around the woman, afraid it was his imagination. As it grew brighter and wider around her, his own insides warmed. The sharp hunger pains in his belly melted away. Blood pounded through his veins with the need to be near her. He felt strong and brave, and for a moment, like nobody could ever hurt him again.

No way. She's like me.

He should've been scared. Should've run, but he couldn't stop watching. The red glow swirled like a tornado around her and then flew at the man like a ball of fire. The man's body sucked it up. Sucked it right up. He was so huge it didn't even hurt him.

Then the air got super hot and he couldn't breathe. Still, he watched. It seemed like she pulled all of the fire into herself and then just exploded. He didn't see much after that. Everything turned black and the force of the blast threw him into the trees. His fingers were torn and bloodied from his tight grip on the rough bark. Oh man, it was hot. As ash blew around him, he ducked deeper into the ground. When the air cleared enough for him to see, he snuck around the tree in time to watch the woman fall. The giant man with huge muscles picked her up, walked toward the thick trees, and disappeared in a flash. Whoa.

They're both like me. I'm not a freak.

The small boy, weak and frail, hobbled back to his tent, stuffed as much as he could in his backpack and fought off a smile. Smiling hurt and made his lips bleed, but he couldn't stop. Maybe he didn't have to be by himself anymore. By sheer determination alone, he managed to lift the heavy bag onto his shoulder, and head in the same direction as the fighting couple.

Chapter 6

Pain hammered her skull as Grayce struggled to lift weary lids. It was too damned sunny. She attempted to lift an arm to block the painful intrusion on her optical nerves, and found she was unable to move. A sweet, melodic voice came from her left and subdued the panic that rose within her like a bat out of hell.

"Grayce, you're awake. Oh thank goodness." Chelsea stood bedside and straightened the thin sheet. The lingering scent of fresh baked cookies ignited a rumble in Grayce's stomach. "Nikolas. Honey, she's awake." Delicate fingers worked at Grayce's wrists. "Here, let me get these off." Chelsea released the cuffs that bound Grayce's arms to the bed. "You were thrashing. We didn't want you to rip out your IVs." Grayce massaged her wrists while she shielded her eyes from the damned light.

"Is that too bright?" Chelsea pattered to the wall and hit the dimmer switch. "Sorry about that." Back at Grayce's side, she offered much needed comfort with the simple gesture of holding her hand.

"Well, well, well. Look who's decided to join us." Nikolas leaned over Grayce's chest and gave her a scrutinizing once over. "How are you doing, girl?" With a sympathetic pat to her thigh, he checked her vitals.

"Did I kill him?" Grayce winced. "I'm so sorry, I didn't mean to..." Tears became a nuisance under eyelids that felt like sandpaper.

Chelsea provided a reassuring squeeze. "No, Grayce. Oh heavens no. He's fine."

"You scared the ever living shit out of him though." Nikolas interrupted. His pearly whites were a stark contrast to his olive complexion. He was laughing. How could he make light of this?

Chelsea leaned over Grayce and punched him in the shoulder. "Knock it off Nikolas."

"Why am I here? What happened?" The room was decorated in soft muted tones. Medical equipment surrounded the bed. Opposite where she lay, a large flat screen television hung on the wall. A peaceful nature scene adorned the wall to the left. To her right a picture window overlooked a small grassy area shaded by an overgrown maple tree that looked to be over a hundred years old. The room resembled a luxury suite at a hotel rather than a hospital.

"Grayce." Nikolas scratched his head. "How can I put this simply?" He looked to Chelsea for guidance and continued after they exchanged warm smiles. "You burned yourself out, so to speak. When Z brought you here, you were dehydrated, exhausted and well...done. Wiped out, mentally and physically. You've been sleeping at least...um let's see..." He glanced at his watch. "Forty-seven hours now. I'll get these IVs out of your arm."

"Why is my skin burning? Shit, it itches like hell," Grayce complained and rubbed frantically at her arms.

"Hmm. That's interesting." Nikolas poked and prodded for a few minutes then turned to his wife. "Darling, how long has Zander been gone?"

"Close to an hour now, lover." The way Chelsea regarded her husband made Grayce's heart ache. Such love and adoration. And it came so naturally.

"Grayce. You're having withdrawals."

"No, I'm not. I've never taken drugs. Not even to experiment." Drugs were her mother's gig. No way did Grayce want to follow in mommy's footsteps.

Nikolas laughed. "I want you to rest. When you're feeling up to it, we'll sit down and talk. There's plenty to tell you." The doctor blew his wife a kiss. "I'll be outside if you need me." A quick wink to Grayce and the door closed behind him.

"Where's Zander?" Grayce asked with a shameful tremble to her voice. Chelsea plopped herself on the edge of the bed and blew an unruly hair from her forehead.

"He'll be back. He's been by your side the whole time. Something important came up. It killed him to go."

"I tried to reduce him to ashes. Why would he want to come back?" Turning a heated cheek into the pillow, she replayed the events in her head. How could she lose control like that? Or was it take control? It was amazing and terrifying at the same time.

"You've got some serious shit bouncing around that brain of yours." Chelsea clasped a hand over her mouth, as if horrified for saying *shit*.

"I know." Grayce almost wanted to smile at the expression on Chelsea's face. Almost.

"Someday, you'll have to open up about it. It's not healthy to hold such dark secrets. I hope if it's not Zander, you'll trust me enough to share. I'm a good listener."

Grayce managed a half-hearted shrug. "I've never trusted anyone. Don't think I know how." That was a little white lie. She had trusted somebody once. He stole her soul.

"I'm going to get lunch ready. I'll be back soon." Chelsea tossed a remote on the bed. "Here, help yourself. There's at least three thousand channels to choose from. Should keep you busy until I'm back." Grayce was left alone, hungry for cookies and facing a huge decision. What channel should she watch?

* * * *

Homemade chicken soup and warm wheat rolls had satisfied her appetite, but did little to soothe the violent itch ravishing her flesh. Neither did the stunning view through the picture window. Channel surfing had offered some distraction before lunch. Maybe she'd try again.

Where was Zander? Would he speak to her again? If he were smart, he'd be halfway to the moon by now. Probably much safer there.

Soul mates? Yeah, right. Soul mates wouldn't try to kill each other. Proved his theory wrong. She turned on the television to distract her mind from traveling to the dark place it wanted to go.

"Oh fucking hell." Jane's face was on the big screen in glorious high definition. Grayce fumbled with the remote.

"The body of Jane Christine Montgomery, owner of Jane's Bar in downtown Chastain was found today in this apartment complex." The pretty reporter gestured to Grayce's building. "Police are not yet releasing the tenant's name, but have confirmed disturbing evidence was found inside."

Grayce sat up and feverishly tried to find the volume button. "Sources are telling us Ms. Montgomery has been missing for over twenty-four hours. An anonymous phone call led detectives to this address."

She flipped through channels hoping to find more information. A bleach blond woman wearing too much eye makeup talked to the camera with an almost believable pretending-to-care face. "Authorities have confirmed the victim appears to have been tortured." The camera panned behind the reporter and scanned the parking lot.

Grayce's heart dropped to the pit of her stomach. Oh, God. Please, no. As the camera angle widened, she got a spine-chilling gander at a tall, dark and demented nightmare. Beyond the crowd of police officers and curious onlookers, leaning casually against the exact black sports car she watched Jane drive away in, stood Tyr. Smug as shit, looking straight into the camera and smiling. Oh fuck, oh fuck, oh fuck. He killed her. Holy shit. Grayce threw off her blankets and came two feet short of the bathroom before her lunch made an unwelcome reappearance.

After cleaning herself and the floor, nervous energy nixed any desire to return to bed. A pale blue sundress hung neatly over the back of the chair. No doubt left by Zander. He seemed to have a thing for short, barely-there attire. She dressed and headed outside to the patch of grass she'd admired earlier.

The sun, despite its biting heat, eased some of the unrelenting itch. It also reminded her of Zander and the sun kissed glow he carried. She sat and stretched her legs. It was safe there. Even with the knowledge that Tyr was close, she felt sheltered, hidden from the world. For a moment she allowed herself the luxury of accepting this place as her home.

As she lay on her back in the spongy grass and inhaled the summer air, Grayce hoped that someday Zander would be able to forgive her. She'd never desired absolution, nor had an inclination to offer any. With him, everything was different. The rage needed to be tamed. What if someone else had angered her? Somebody who didn't have Zander's strength or power or whatever the hell it was?

Under Tyr's control, she hadn't been allowed to show anger. Couldn't show any emotion without being punished. If she'd known her power back then, the fuck-head would be stewing in a lake of fire, somewhere between Hitler and Charles Manson. The mental image brought a wicked smile to her face.

Why kill Jane? Did he think she'd go to him if he threatened people around her?

"Firecracker." The familiar tingle jetted down her spine and ignited the energy explosion through her veins. *Oh thank God, he's here.* In an instant she was flushed, swollen between her legs, and tempted to pounce like a cat on the hunt.

"Zander." Shit. Where did she start? How did one apologize for attempting to annihilate the other? He crouched, flaunted his dimples, and she knew in an instant, forgiveness was hers without having to ask. "I thought I killed you. I thought..." He placed his index finger over her lips to silence the unnecessary explanation.

"You can't hurt me Grayce. I've told you that before." He traced her bottom lip with his forefinger. "I'm sorry for the things I said. I needed to know how far you'd take it." He stood and brought her with him. "Walk with me?"

They strode hand in hand through the small meadow just beyond the ancient maple tree. "I didn't think you'd come back." The forest floor passed in a blur as she stared at her feet, unable to bear the weight of his gaze.

Exasperated, he sighed. "There's nothing you could do to keep me away. I'm afraid you're stuck with me firecracker." Zander grabbed Grayce's hips and effortlessly swept her over a bubbling brook that trickled through a patch of tall grass.

"I'm completely blown away by you." He whispered as he set her down.

"Blown away? You're joking." Grayce fought hard not to smile. "That's not funny."

"I'm sorry. Hey, I want to show you something. Come this way." Zander grabbed her hand again and led the way to a small footpath that took them up a hill through a dense patch of pines. On the other side, it opened to a grassy area that overlooked a deep wide valley thick with wildflowers and blackberry bushes.

"This is my favorite spot."

"It's beautiful." Grayce turned her attention to Zander. Hungry, heated blue eyes stared down at her. A gaze so intense, so filled with promise, her sex clenched.

"You're beautiful." He brushed her cheek with the back of his hand and let it rest at the nape of her neck.

Her dark side wanted to push him away, while the rest of her wanted to eat him alive.

He teased with a feather light kiss. Squeezing his eyes closed, he pleaded through gritted teeth, "Let me love you, Grayce. I can wash the dark stains away." Slowly he opened his eyes and searched hers for a response.

With a force she'd never felt, her heart pummeled against the restraints of her chest. The familiar burn of insatiable need rose through her center. How was it possible, this intense desire? Why would this perfect man want her, when she was so damaged? Fuck her, but at that moment, she didn't care. The formidable ache in her soul, in her heart, overrode the self hatred.

Rising to the tips of her toes, she placed her hands around his neck and pulled him toward her, never breaking eye contact. Powerless to say no, or refuse him anything when lost in those eyes, she licked his soft, full lower lip, then grabbed it with her teeth and nibbled. The moment she released him, a groan rose from his chest and he devoured her mouth.

With lips locked, Zander lifted Grayce by the waist and wrapped her legs around his middle. His scent, mixed with the flavor of his kiss, sparked a hunger that disintegrated any and all inhibition. He walked with her coiled around him until he found a soft patch of grass. As he released her mouth to let her down, Grayce protested with a whimper. It hurt to be separated for the few seconds it took him to remove his shirt and lay it in the grass.

"Holy fuck." Grayce mouthed to herself. He was so impossibly perfect and sexy kneeling there, shirtless. Not a flaw anywhere, only muscle that bulged and writhed, performed a mating dance under his taut skin. Grayce's own muscles tightened as heat swirled and churned in her belly.

"Grayce." He whispered as he slid his hands up her thighs and under her dress. With adept fingers he explored and rubbed her abdomen, then made his way to her backside. "I need to tell you something."

"Shh. I don't want to talk. Please, not now." A warm glow spread across the surface of her skin.

"My firecracker. You're hot for me already." Pulling her close, he guided her panties down her hips and thighs, her calves and ankles.

He pulled the hem of her dress over her waist and held it in place with one hand at the arch of her back. With the other, he traced her scar, pulling her near to kiss the spot where it met her hipbone. Shockwaves rocked her body as his lips brushed against her skin. Weak in the knees and head spinning, she rested her weight on his shoulders to stay upright. Nimble fingers leisurely made their way across to her navel, his lips in hot pursuit.

Trailing kisses downward and stopping at the apex of her thighs, he cupped her ass on both sides, squeezed and pulled her closer. A yearning groan escaped his lips as he buried his nose in her moist folds that ached with need, then inhaled deeply. "Good God, baby. You smell like heaven."

Grayce gasped as he guided her legs apart and his tongue invaded her like wildfire, doing things she never could've imagined, let alone considered pleasurable. With her head tossed back, she buried her fingers in his hair and pulled him harder into her. Strong arms held her steady as he massaged her trembling rear. Her hips swayed and pushed against him as he continued his slow sweet exploration.

Greedy for more, needing him deeper inside her, she lifted her leg and rested it over his shoulder. His tongue and lips explored, pleasured and pushed her body beyond any emotion, thought or reason as they circled, kissed and loved her down there. Her hips ground against his mouth as her body hummed and her blood turned to warm oil oozing through her veins.

Molten once again, the fire swelled, a good burn, not angry, and definitely not out of control. Her climax built rapidly. She wasn't ready, didn't want the pleasure and escape to end. But shit, how she needed the release. With a death grip on his head, she gyrated, harder and harder against him until... "Oh fuck. Oh Zander. Fuck." Grayce came undone and collapsed into the strength of his arms. Zander supported her full weight through the last jagged breath, last quiver and last whispered profanity.

After one final lick of her sensitive nub, he lowered her to his lap. His erection rubbed against her moist sex through his sweatpants. "Kiss me, baby." He begged.

Grayce lifted her chin to oblige and was shocked by the flavor and scent of her arousal on his lips. "Now that wasn't a gentlemanly thing to do, was it?" She moaned and licked the taste from her lips.

"I did ask first." Zander leaned forward on powerful haunches and lay her on the shirt he'd spread in the grass. As he stood to remove his unwelcome clothing, Grayce gasped at the sight of his erection jetting between his prodigious thighs. It bounced thick, proud and heavy. How, in the name of all that was holy, did that thing fit inside her?

"Grayce, I can't hurt you, remember?" He knelt next to her. "We were made for each other. Every inch of our bodies."

She wasn't sure what he meant. In that moment, she didn't give a shit. She only wanted him on her, in her. Wanted him to fill her until there was no room for loneliness, fear or self loathing.

"Let me love you, Grayce." Laying next to her, he peeled one spaghetti strap off her shoulder, then the other. One at a time, he circled his thumb over her nipples then pulled the bodice of her dress down to free her breasts. He leaned in to kiss her chin, her neck, then her shoulder. With each brush of his lips across sensitized skin, shivers danced through her soul. Cupping one breast in his hand, he nudged it to his lips, then paused to meet her gaze.

Grayce fisted the grass at her sides. She couldn't help but swivel against the erection that lay heavy and heated across her leg. Warm summer air swirled around them and filled her lungs with the scent of pine, wildflowers and sex.

"Your body makes me crazy." His tongue flicked over her nipple and her body spasmed. He pulled it into his mouth, teased, taunted, pulled and sucked. Grayce squirmed under him, tried to control the fire that seared her insides. Fuck. How could she feel pain and such intense pleasure at the same time?

"Zander, please," she whimpered.

"What, my little firecracker?" With liquid heat, his tongue danced across her chest toward the other breast. "Tell me what you need." The neglected nipple was sucked and nibbled while he rubbed his hand down her stomach to her heated, moist sex. Tenderly, he brushed his thumb back and forth across her swollen clit. "Is this what you need?" He rubbed in a slow circle with torturous pressure.

"Oh fuck, Zander." Her body temperature spiked. The red energy swirled with rampant need and enveloped Zander in her fiery shield. "No!" Grayce shouted as panic attempted to punch through her wall of ecstasy.

"Look at me Grayce." He grasped her chin and turned her head to meet his lusty gaze. "You have to trust me."

She was captured, lost in the sea of blue, drawn into him alone.

"We can do this," he whispered as he eased her legs apart.

Her insides clenched at the husky promise.

"We can do this," he repeated. The energy surrounded them, warm and comforting like a favorite blanket.

Zander positioned himself between her legs and eased the tip of his erection into her swollen folds. She stared into his eyes and bit back a scream when he fully sheathed her and a current of purple light flashed across his retinas. With each thrust, the color intensified until the blue had changed to an electric purple that flared and popped like a lightning storm.

Mesmerized, she cupped his face and rubbed the pads of her thumbs across his cheeks.

As he invaded her, stretched her with agonizing pleasure, Grayce met him thrust for thrust, bucked wildly to meet his hips and pull him deeper inside. He pounded with relentless force, leaving no doubt he was staking his claim. She took it all. Wanted more.

"Fuck, Grayce," Zander unleashed a guttural heartfelt cry. As he reached his climax, his eyes glowed a steady purple and for a brief moment, his very thoughts and emotions became hers.

Love. Pure fierce love. He would die for her. As they shared the intense and deeply personal moment, her body found its own release. She screamed his name as the orgasm shook her with painful, soul cleansing tremors, lifting their bodies off the ground. A brilliant burst of energy blasted around them, dissipated into the trees and over the valley below.

Zander collapsed at her side, pulled her to his heaving chest and cursed under his breath. Sated and weary, she closed her eyes and dreamed of a vast house and a giant man.

* * * *

"Zander, what are we?" Grayce examined her fingers. They were so small and delicate intertwined with Zander's beefy digits. The size difference was laughable. How was it possible her petite frame held so much power?

"You sure you're you ready to hear this? You have to promise you won't freak, okay?"

"Why, is it that bad?" Her mind reeled with the possibilities. Aliens? Chemical spill? Scientific experiment gone wrong? Radioactive exposure, perhaps? She propped herself on her elbows to give him full attention.

"You've heard of fallen angels, right? Angels cast from heaven because they believed they could place themselves on a throne higher than God? Chose darkness over the light?"

"Zander, please don't tell me you're a fucking angel." Angels? Definitely not on her list of possible explanations. She'd been to church once or twice as a child. Mommy dearest dragged her there after a mad binge or two, prayed and wept, hoping to free herself of the sins she'd committed. Grayce had seen statues and art depicting the divine creatures, but never gave them much thought. Matter of fact, they creeped her out.

"No. Grayce, I'm not...I mean, we're not angels. Hear me out. The dark ones were cast from heaven. In a final act to spite God, they spread their seeds on the earth. Planted their evil in the wombs of humans."

"So they made more angels?"

"No." Zander shook his head. Rays of sun caught in his blond locks and mimicked a halo. Grayce couldn't stop herself. She had to touch, needed to run her fingers through his silky strands. Zander's breath hitched before he continued.

"Angels can't create angels. Only God can create angels. The fallen took human form and mated with humans. They bred warriors so that over the millennia their darkness would spread through humanity and turn against God. However, they hadn't considered free will. Many of our ancestors chose light over the darkness, good over evil. It's a constant battle. We fight the darkness on a daily basis."

Grayce knew the darkness all too well. It had beckoned for as long as she could remember. Hell, with the life she'd been cursed with, it was nothing short of a miracle that she wasn't queen of the fucking underworld by now. It was often her hiding place, especially when Tyr had his fun. It had protected her on countless occasions.

Zander inhaled, deep and slow, then continued. "We were assigned mates to insure a strong, pure lineage. Problem with that was again, free will. Human nature had us so caught up in ourselves, our own desires, that we pursued earthly pleasures—lust, greed, pride. You get the picture. We didn't wait to be with our true mates but followed our own paths and started marrying, mating with whomever we wanted. So, for most of us, our powers lay dormant. We live our lives never knowing what we are, never realizing our true potential. So we're human, we do know that much. We're just more than human. Beauty of it is..."

He cleared his throat and looked down at her. Fire spread through her veins as he ran a finger up and down her back. "After we connect with our soul mate, our powers or gifts, or whatever you want to call them, are amplified. Sometimes, they even change completely."

"How did you know what you were?"

"What we are," he corrected.

"We," Grayce snapped back and rolled her eyes.

He shifted onto his back with a sigh. "It's rare for males to realize their powers unless they've bonded with their true mate. Some develop with puberty. Mine have been evident since I was a small child." Zander's face drooped, overtaken by sadness. "I had a hard time...well, um, not breaking everything I touched. Toys, doors, glasses. You name it, I broke it. I hurt my parents more than once—not on purpose. They tried to hide their fear, but I saw it in their eyes. They tried to teach me to be gentle, but it's difficult for a small child to master control over his body." He threw an arm over his face attempting to hide his emotion.

"When I hit puberty, the dreams and the voices started. They tried to tell me what I was. I thought I had lost my mind. I ignored them. Eventually, they went away."

"Your parents, were they like us? Where are they now?" Grayce sat up straight and caressed his chest, partly because she wanted to offer comfort, but mostly because she craved the contact.

"They were killed in a car accident when I was seventeen. I've been on my own since. Far as I know, neither one of them had any special talents. They weren't true mates." A half smile peeked out from under his arm. "So, I've been on my own since then. Until I met Nikolas."

"Tell me." Grayce pulled Zander's arm away from his face. "How did you meet?"

Zander sat up and stretched, naked and beautiful, arms spread wide. Grayce inhaled sharply at the view.

"I call it an accident. Nikolas will tell you otherwise. He calls it destiny. Long story short, I was full of pent up anger, started a bar room brawl and didn't restrain myself. Fucked a guy up real bad. Left him for dead in the alleyway. I left him there for quite some time. Guilt got the best of me so I went back. Took him to the emergency room. Nikolas was on his way out when I carried the guy to the entrance. My intention was to leave him there on the sidewalk and disappear. Nikolas saw it the moment we made eye contact. He knew we were alike and persuaded me to come inside while he patched up the asshole I'd brought in. I don't know why I agreed, but I did. There was something innately familiar about him. Not long after that, he told me what I was. We've been working together ever since."

"But how did he know?"

"Nikolas listened to the voices in his head. Paid attention to the dreams. He's researched our kind for most of his life. We have a network of people working for us with resources that reach around the globe."

"I feel like I fell asleep and woke in some crazy comic book story." More like fucked up fairy tale. Oh, what a bedtime story that would be. Psycho princess rescued by ginormous prince. Yeah, right.

"I know. It's a hard pill to swallow and takes more than a few days to digest. If I'd found you sooner, it would've been easier. You have no idea how much it kills me that I wasn't there for you."

"How long did you search?"

"My whole life, I think. I always felt you, just didn't know what it was. It frustrated the hell out of me. I'm convinced that's where my rage stemmed from. It wasn't until I met Nikolas that I learned it was your pull. That's when I started to focus my energy. I had a mission, a purpose, and it was you."

* * * *

After a casual lasagna dinner, Grayce helped Chelsea clean up. Zander and Nikolas excused themselves to the lab.

"Please go." Chelsea scooted them off and shot Grayce a wink. "We need some girl time." Chelsea grabbed her hand and pulled her into the common room. In the center sat two oversized cream colored sofas that overflowed with pillows of various colors. Bright happy colors. Reds, greens and vibrant blues. A flat screen television occupied the center wall. Inset speakers were strategically placed around the room for optimum sound.

Over the course of a few hours, Chelsea talked, Grayce listened. She learned the circumstances that brought Chelsea and Nikolas together as well as how Chelsea's powers developed.

"I don't like to use them, though," she confessed. "I always felt like an outcast until Nikolas found me."

Chelsea shared her life story but Grayce struggled to focus. She'd only been away from Zander for a short time and already found herself crippled with need for his presence and starving for his scent and touch.

"Would you please show me to the lab?" Embarrassed by her desperate craving, she hung her head.

Chelsea's motherly smile was a soothing balm. She grabbed Grayce's hand. "That's an incredibly strong bond you two have. Most of us can go at least twenty-four hours before we start to feel the effects of being separated. You've only lasted a couple."

With a weary sigh, Grayce squeezed Chelsea back. "This is all so strange."

"I know dear. You're handling it like a champ." She giggled and captured Grayce in a warm embrace. "Before we head downstairs, I have something to show you."

"What's that?" Grayce had the feeling she'd never be able to say no to Chelsea. Despite the screaming need for Zander, she grabbed the proffered hand and followed behind.

The Compton's had their own wing on the east side of the home. Grayce was grateful when Chelsea didn't stop to give a tour. They headed straight through one of the guest bedrooms into a walk-in closet.

Chelsea turned on an overhead light. "I know you left your things behind in your apartment, so I took the liberty of buying some new clothes for you."

Grayce's jaw dropped. The closet burst with brand new clothing. Shoes were stacked against the far wall. Handbags and belts were organized by color in the corner.

"But how?" Covering her mouth with her hands, Grayce shook her head. She was surrounded by her favorite styles and fabrics.

"I can read people. I know things about them without having to ask. That's one of my special skills." She winked. "I hope it's okay that I did this." She placed a hand on Grayce's shoulder. "If there's anything you don't like, we'll donate it."

Grayce nodded, already sure she'd love every piece. As she glanced around the closet, which was larger than her former bedroom, she was overwhelmed with a sense of belonging. With a thud, she dropped to her knees and cried.

"What's wrong?" A soft, warm arm embraced her shoulder.

What's wrong? Well, where to begin?

"Grayce. Don't worry. If it's too much, we'll get rid of it. I promise I won't take offense. We'll go shopping, and you can pick whatever you want."

Did she want to explain? Did she want to go there right now? Painfully aware of heartbreak in her new friend's voice, Grayce decided to share a bit of her past.

"No, no. That's not it. Everything is perfect. I just—" She choked back a sob. "I wasn't allowed to wear anything I liked. You know...before. I was dressed in designer gowns and designer lingerie. I hated it." She pulled at her hair. "I couldn't even brush my own hair. He brushed it. He styled it. I was his fucking life-size doll. If I fidgeted or fussed, I'd be punished." As she wiped tears with the back of her hand, Grayce felt a sense of relief. She'd never said these things out loud before. Sharing wasn't so bad. Felt kind of good.

"I'm so sorry." A tissue was produced out of thin air. "Thank you for telling me." Chelsea waited while Grayce blew her nose. "Come. Let's go see what our boys are up to."

* * * *

"Ladies!" Nikolas beamed when the women entered. Grayce took a moment to adjust to the bright light. They were surrounded by white, stainless steel and glass. The only color in the room came from the four people standing within.

Zander wrapped an arm around Grayce the moment she crossed the threshold. The edginess that had grated her nerves melted away like a sugar cube in a steamy cup of coffee. He bent to press a kiss to her cheek. "I'm happy to see you."

Shit, she was happy too, although agitated by the dependency for this man.

Nikolas pulled a remote from his pocket and pointed it toward one of the stark white walls. A panel opened to expose a large flat screen. "This is so exciting." Staring raptly at Grayce, he asked, "Do you have any idea how powerful you are?" He didn't wait for an answer. "Watch this."

A video played on the screen. It was from her last visit to the lab. The day her power erupted. Watching herself come undone was excruciating. She looked pure evil, crazy, insane. Oh fuck.

Grayce had to look away.

"This is where it gets real interesting." Nikolas paused the playback. Grayce stood naked from the waist up. All of her scars, every hideous reminder of her own personal hell on earth, were on display for everyone to see. The image on the screen expanded as he pointed his remote. "Look, look at this."

Grayce ignored Nikolas. She couldn't tear her gaze from the image of Zander's face. He was devastated. Pain seethed from his beautiful blue eyes. It chilled her to the bone.

"Grayce, can you see this?" Nikolas asked, exuberant.

"What? What? No. I don't see anything." Because she wasn't looking. Her heart shattered to a million pieces at the sight of Zander's mournful expression.

"You're focusing the particles. You're focusing them at Z. The energy is surrounding you, and yes, it was hot, but the particles struck him. Only him."

She moved closer to get a better look at whatever the hell he was trying to make her see. He pointed to a tiny spot on the screen and zoomed in on the image. There it was. Looked like a shooting star. Although the red energy had consumed most of the room, hundreds, maybe more, of minuscule shooting stars were aimed right at Zander.

Oh shit. "What does this mean?"

"It means, you can control this. The energy field around you isn't the dangerous part. It's what you can do inside that field." Remote pointed at the screen again, he rewound the image and played it back. "Look Grayce, I'm caught in the red field. See that? At first it felt like a hot wind storm. There were a few zaps and zings like electricity, but it didn't hurt me." The picture paused again. "See here? You're screaming and then a large burst radiates out of you. That's when I decided to high tail it out of there. But you didn't hurt me. You directed the dangerous fireballs right at Z."

"My little firecracker." Zander chuckled.

"Why didn't Zander burn?" she asked.

Nikolas turned to Chelsea, who nodded and took a couple steps back. "Better to show you than try to explain." Pulling a pair of scissors from a nearby drawer, Nikolas threw them right at Chelsea's heart. As if a protective shield surrounded her, the scissors bounced in the opposite direction and fell to the floor. He threw a scalpel with the same result. "We can't hurt our mates. It's physically impossible. It's one of the many perks."

"What about the lake?" she asked, and threw her hands in the air. "I relocated a whole fucking lake in one shot. Never mind the fact that I turned a significant patch of forest to ash in an instant."

"I don't have all the answers yet." Nikolas folded his arms and stared, eyes glazed with wonderment.

"For you to be this powerful before even consummating your...um, I mean connecting with Z, I can't understand how some of this wasn't present before." Nikolas placed his hands on Grayce's shoulders.

Wait a minute. What did he just say?

She shoved her face closer to his. "Consummating?" Her insides heated.

Zander wrapped his arm around Grayce and pulled her from Nikolas' grip. "Grayce, we haven't had time to talk about all of this. Please don't get mad."

"I assume you mean sex. Am I correct?" She looked at Nikolas. If she made eye contact with Zander, she'd be done for.

From behind, Chelsea cleared her throat. "Boys, if I may." With a quick shove, she pushed Zander away and stood in the line of fire.

"Hi." Head tilted, she pursed her lips in a playful manner.

Not funny, Grayce thought. Why was she making light of this?

Chelsea placed a comforting hand on Grayce's shoulder. "Everything's happened so fast for you, I know that."

"No shit, Sherlock."

"So you haven't had time to learn everything. And with your anger issues...we've been trying to give you some time before throwing it all at you."

"Just get the fuck on with it please," Grayce growled under her breath.

"People like us. Or I should say, women like us, we are bonded with our soul mates." She said *soul mates* with a careful hesitance.

Grayce was a blink away from losing it again.

"We are forever linked with them from the second we connect. Sometimes it's a touch. For most, it only takes eye contact. Everybody is different."

That much Grayce had figured out already.

"Our gifts emerge, or if they're already present, grow stronger or reach their full potential after the first time we..." She scrunched her face. "You know, have sex."

"Or consummate the bond," Zander piped in, face full of playful grin. Why did everyone think this was funny?

"You make it sound like a marriage," Grayce snapped.

"Grayce, for all intents and purposes, it is a marriage." Chelsea grabbed her hand and held it to her chest. "Once we've bonded, we cannot be separated—physically, mentally or emotionally. We just can't do it. You felt it today. He was only away for a few hours and you were having a hard time. We're like a drug to each other. So yes, we call it consummating. We're sealing the deal so to speak."

Grayce seethed. "So, I'm stuck with him forever? I don't get a choice in the matter?" Any woman would kill to be with this man. She should consider herself lucky, but fuck, this was a bombshell she hadn't expected.

"So, the other night, when we..." She cocked her head and raised her eyebrows. "You knew we would be bound together, forever?" Still wearing the boyish grin, he nodded. "And you didn't stop to think that maybe I should know what I was getting myself into?"

His smile turned to a pout. "Come on Grayce. Do you honestly think it would've mattered? Did you forget already what happened with your body?" He shrugged his shoulders. "I couldn't have stopped if I'd wanted to."

God he looked sexy. She wanted to jump into his arms and suck on those pouty lips. Grayce gave herself a mental slap across the face. *Pissed, remember? Stick to the subject.*

Would there ever be a time when she'd be in control of her own life?

"So, why was I having Zander withdrawals after a couple hours, when most can last at least a day, like Chelsea said earlier?" She pounded her hands to her hips.

Riddle me this, Batman.

"I have a theory about that." Nikolas closed the wall panel and stepped to the table in the corner of the room. A computer rose from the center. "And you should know, you lasted a couple hours. Z only lasted a few minutes." A heavy crack echoed through the room as Nikolas slapped Zander on the back. "Poor bastard was going out of his mind down here."

Nikolas typed on the keyboard and pulled up a clip from the news. "It's him."

Tyr's face filled the screen.

"For the holy fucking love of everything." Grayce clapped her hands over her mouth. "Please, not him."

"He's the reason." Zander inhaled sharply. His jaw clenched tight and a pulse of heat emanated from his body.

"What in fuck's sake does Tyr have to do with this?" Would she ever be free of this monster? He needed to die.

"It's quite simple really." Nikolas tapped a key on the keyboard and the image enlarged. "You're in danger. As long as you're in danger, the two of you need to stay close to each other. Remember, you're stronger together than you are apart. Your bodies know that, your brains just need to play catch up."

"What do you mean, danger?" Grayce was afraid to ask. "If we have these powers, how can we be in danger?"

Nikolas enlarged the picture and zoomed in on his face. "Look at his eyes."

Holy shit. They were black as coal, but his irises were outlined in red. Blood red. His favorite color.

"He's one of us." Grayce shook her head. How could this be?

"I'm going to kill the motherfucker." Zander disappeared in a frenzied gust of heat and wind.

"I'll never get used to that," Chelsea grunted and patted her hair back into place.

* * * *

Ready to burst with rage from the information that'd just been vomited all over her, Grayce excused herself to her new room. She assumed it was her room, anyway. It was the one she'd been sleeping in with Zander. Her heart swelled. Yeah, she could share a bed with someone. Enjoyed it even. Although, if what she'd learned was true, it couldn't have been anyone else. Her body knew better than her brain. How fucked up was that?

Zander had been gone for hours. No idea how long exactly, but it drove her crazy to watch the clock tick. Her agitated stated made it impossible to sit still. She decided to visit the home gym. If she could find it again.

The workout room felt empty and stark but Grayce needed to burn off the negative energy that boiled to a steamy crescendo with Zander's absence. She couldn't let her cork pop inside the house, so she put on her headphones and cranked the volume. Eminem's "Lose Yourself" seemed a fitting way to start her workout. It was precisely what she needed to do, get lost in the pound and hum of the music and push through the horrendous burning itch that devoured her sanity.

She opted for the treadmill. Running seemed the right thing to do. Running, although not in the literal sense, was what she did best. The faster she pumped her thighs, the better she felt. So, she pushed on and soon became lost in thought as she pondered the events in her life that brought her to this mansion. This room.

Grayce was eighteen when the monster had sucked her into his black hole of a soul. She hadn't been hard to catch. She had been so damned easy to manipulate and deceive. A product of an alcoholic mother who somehow managed to hold down two jobs and shuffled through men faster than Grayce changed panties, she never stood a chance. She'd always felt alone, unworthy, and she had, for the most part, raised herself.

When she met Tyr with his striking handsome features and obvious wealth, which he brazenly flaunted, it had taken all of two seconds to fall head over heels. The man had spoken exactly what she needed to hear. Master manipulator and seducer, he'd filled her head and heart with promises of fairytale romance, unyielding love and rescue from her desolate life.

What a stupid fool she'd been.

She hadn't protested when he moved her into his penthouse, nor had she bothered to tell her mother in person, figuring a note would suffice. Who would turn down the chance to move from a rodent infested motel to a castle in the sky?

Her virginity was the first thing he'd stolen from her; her freedom was the second.

Mere days passed before the obsessive behavior started. He controlled her meals, clothing, even trips outside the home. Buffed, shined and polished to perfection before put on display in his social circle, Grayce hadn't time to notice the subtle shift from fairytale princess to prisoner.

Their first evening, and incidentally last time out as a couple, she'd been surrounded by rich, prominent men. Wanting to please her prince, Grayce had smiled, laughed and made polite small talk with the gentlemen. Tyr had appeared to be proud of his shiny new trinket. However, his bright mood shifted to darkness the moment they'd returned home. Out of the spotlight, out of the public eye.

"Did you like those men? Did you like the way they made you feel?" He'd chastised her in a jealous rage. That was the first time he'd forced himself on her, then introduced her to his playroom. The following night, he had thrown his first exclusive Grayce party. Only the most distinguished members of his social circle had been invited. The men that wanted Grayce, that paid her the most attention the previous evening, were the ones that paid a small fortune for a tiny amount of time with her in the privacy of his playroom.

To these men, for reasons she couldn't begin to understand, she was more potent than any drug. Tyr knew that if he controlled her, he controlled the most powerful men in the state. There was nothing he couldn't gain by dangling his little dove in front of them.

Fuck, enough reminiscing. Grayce looked at the clock. Two hours had passed. What the hell? Thirty, maybe forty minutes of cardio usually kicked her ass, but two hours? Impossible. Stranger still, she wasn't shocked to find the red glow hovering over her skin.

She stepped off the treadmill and was hit with the familiar buzz through her bloodstream. He was back. She turned to find Zander leaning against the door jam, arms folded with a hungry grin stretched across his face. Holy fuck, he was a sight for sore eyes.

"How long have you been standing there?" Grayce asked, a little too loud over the thump of her headphones. Her legs wobbled underneath her. Not because of the two hour run, but because he was so overwhelming to look at.

He laughed. "Too damned long." He ran his hand through his tousled hair. "Firecracker, you look so sexy right now."

Grayce removed her ear buds and took a slow step toward him. With a malevolent smile, Grayce took aim, threw her energy and hit him dead center. The beast didn't budge. A low, sensual growl rose from his chest as the red heat fizzled and disappeared into his skin.

"What was that for?" He glared through lowered lids.

"You left and it hurt like hell," she growled back. "Don't ever fucking do that to me again." Grayce closed the distance between them, leapt into his arms and claimed his mouth. Damn he tasted good.

"Grayce, do you realize what you just did?" Zander mumbled under the assault on his lips.

"Hmm?" She hummed.

"You just controlled your energy."

She chuckled, and came up for air. "Not really, I burned it off on the treadmill, lucky for you."

Supported fully by the strength of his arms, she kissed him slow and savored the flavor of his lips as he carried her back to bed.

Chapter 7

"Where did you go?" Sprawled naked and limp across Zander's chest, Grayce straddled him with arms hung lifeless over his sides. Mind, body and soul, he was completely satiated after having brought her to the height of ecstasy three times in one hour. There hadn't been time for talking, only sex. The bedroom was destroyed, but if that's what it took to replete the emptiness and hunger they suffered from being separated, so be it.

Zander sighed and wrapped his arms around her waist. He could lie like that forever, never have to eat, drink or breathe again as long as he had Grayce, safe and happy by his side.

Now he had to tell her he failed. He left to find the monster and destroy him. He wanted so badly to tell her it was over, Tyr was finished, and he would never hurt her or anyone again.

"I searched everywhere. I searched the whole God damned town. That bastard is a ghost. I wanted to keep looking, but Chelsea called me back. She was right to do that. Being away from you drove me insane." The thought of being separated from Grayce again sent a shudder through his body. She responded to his quiver by hugging him tighter.

"We need to search together, Zander." Tender kisses trailed across his chest, no doubt planted to ease the blow of the insane suggestion thrown at him.

"Like hell." He stiffened. "The only thing worse than being away from you, would be to put you in danger."

"He'll keep hurting people. Won't stop. He wants me, and he'll tear apart everyone on this God forsaken planet until he finds me." A single tear rolled over his chest and down his ribcage. "We have no choice."

Oh, he had a choice. He could kill the psychopath, rip him to shreds and leave nothing of him but a bloodstain on the ground. Even that would be too kind. Nothing short of grisly torture followed by a personal escort straight to the depths of hell would be suitable.

"No. End of discussion," he snarled.

Grayce fell to the bed as Zander turned on his side. He assumed their usual sleeping position and pulled her into his protective embrace.

"End of discussion?" With gritted teeth and a grunt, Grayce tried to push herself free. "Fuck you. I'll discuss this further if I damned well want to. Who in the hell do you think you are?" She kicked and punched to no avail. "This is my fight, not yours."

A growl rose from his chest and tickled his throat. The ferocity of the warning surprised him. Driven by a primitive, dominant need to protect, Zander caged Grace. He straddled her thighs, pinned her arms to her sides and returned her fiery glare with his own. "This is my fight. You are my fight. You are my life. Get that through your thick skull. I won't let you near him. Do you understand? Even if I have to tie you to this fucking..." He regretted the words before they left his lips to hang in the air like a poisonous gas.

Rage and hurt dulled the shine in her eyes as she sunk lifeless into the mattress beneath him.

Shit. Stupid fucking short fuse.

"I'm so sorry. I shouldn't have—" An explosive force blasted through the room and he landed upside down in the corner, underneath an overturned chaise lounge chair. As Grayce rose from the bed, crimson waves of heat danced and swayed across her skin.

God she was beautiful.

"Tie me to what? This bed? Is that what you want? Me tied? At your mercy?" With hands fisted at her sides, her murderous glare warned off any sudden moves.

"God no." Zander righted the chair, rose to his feet and backed himself to the wall. "That's not what I meant. I would never want that."

"I've been a kept woman." She prowled closer.

Merely an arm's reach away, her heat buzzed in his ears. He didn't move.

A tempest brewed in her eyes. "I've been at the mercy of a sadistic fuck. It won't happen again. I'm here by my choice. Get that through your thick skull. I'll leave by my choice, not yours. If I want to go after him..." He cringed as she stabbed his chest with her finger. Not because it hurt, but because he'd hurt her. "My choice. Don't ever fucking forget that."

He resisted the temptation to scoop her into his arms. His erection rose to full attention as heated blood surged through his veins. The need to dominate, to protect and prove his worth as her man, diminished, replaced by the primal hunger to feel her heated flesh, silky and slick caressing the full girth of his sex. Hands down, she was the most tempting creature he'd ever laid eyes on with her petite, curvy frame and soul piercing hazel eyes. Every moment of their time together was a struggle, a constant battle to control his mating instincts.

But hell, when she was in her fiery form, he was downright insatiable. The need was painful. If it weren't for the torment in her eyes, he'd have her pinned to the wall and be buried balls deep in her sweet flesh. It shamed him to feel that way, knowing how she'd been objectified. He'd never consider himself in the same league as the men who abused her, but he understood the attraction. When it came to describing Grayce, irresistible would be an understatement. Her pull was stronger than any drug. Her aura was a bright beacon, a siren's call, the strongest magnetic force. Her spirit filled him with an all-consuming need to be near, and fuck if it wasn't tearing him apart.

A hand around his hardened flesh nearly brought him to his knees.

"You're a damned lucky bastard, you know that?" Stormy eyes peered at him through lowered lashes. Holy shit.

"Why's that?" he asked with a hoarse whisper.

Grayce gave him a good squeeze. "If I wasn't desperate to have you inside me, you'd be burning along with this room." She lowered herself to her knees.

Zander looked down at his broken lover. Her beauty almost overshadowed her vulnerability. But it was there. Vulnerable. Scared. Out of place.

No. This was all wrong.

With a shaky grip, Grayce stroked him.

He grabbed her wrist and held her steady. "Stop."

"Isn't this what you want?" She stared at his sex. Her eyes void of any emotion. Why was she doing this?

"A frail woman at your beck and call?" She continued to stroke him, her lips dangerously close to the head of his erection. "A woman who'll bow to your every whim, obey every command?"

The floor bounced as Zander's knees hit the floor. "Never." He cupped her face and forced her to look up. "I never want you on your knees. I never want you lowering yourself, degrading yourself for me. Holy Christ. Have I given you any reason to think I want that from you?"

A salacious smile spread across her face. "That's what every man wants, right? A toy, a plaything. A beauty to put on display. Someone who won't talk back. Someone who'll laugh at every joke. Suck his cock. Stroke his ego—"

"Stop." Zander scooped Grayce off the floor, pinned her against the wall and held her at eye level. "Listen to me. I am not like those men. I am not like him." He searched her eyes for something, anything to tell him he was getting through.

"We are not all bad. I'm sorry for what you went through. I'm sorry for the shit in your life. I would take it away if I could. But I can't. What I can do is protect you from any more shit. That's why I don't want you going after him. God damn, Grayce. I don't want to control you. I want to shield you. It's my fucking job. Let me do my fucking job."

"Why?" Her eyes glistened with unshed tears as she melted against him.

"Because I would die if anything happened to you. I would die. Simple as that." He choked back his own emotion, couldn't find any more words. The thought of losing her was too much to bear, let alone try to articulate.

"Don't ever threaten to tie me," she whispered.

Not a problem. Lesson learned.

A new light flickered in her eyes. "Kiss me."

Also, not a problem. No need to ask twice.

"I promise, it won't happen again." He smiled and found her mouth soft and welcoming. She wrapped her legs around his waist and shifted to allow him entrance into her molten, silky folds. It was heaven.

He took his time filling her, and basked in the tightness and heat, the stretch of her flesh, the small spasms that gripped him when fully sheathed. Grayce cried out, her voice an anthem. He clamped an arm around her hips. With the other, he cupped her head, held her tight against his chest as she rode out her orgasm. With a final thrust, he found his own release and buried his face in her hair.

He'd known happiness as a child. A sense of family with his parents, then with Nikolas and Chelsea, but there had been something missing. He'd never been whole. With Grayce wrapped around him, he couldn't imagine anything greater. She needed him. She accepted him physically and emotionally. They were one. Mind, spirit, body. He overflowed with complete happiness, pride—wholeness.

Life was good. Not just good. Fucking amazing.

* * * *

Early morning rays played peek-a-boo through the trees. Grayce and Chelsea, adorned in hiking shoes and heavy sweatshirts, trekked through the woods for an overdue session of good-ol' girl time. Chelsea had begged Grayce to join her on her sunrise walk, explaining that Nikolas would be too exhausted to rise and shine for their daily ritual. He'd been working nonstop since Grayce's arrival and she expected him to sleep through most of the morning.

Grayce had accepted the offer the prior evening and was already happy that she'd agreed. The brisk air alone was a better kick-in-the-ass, rev-your-engine, energy boost than even a whole pot of Chelsea's thick black brew of caffeinated bliss. Or maybe it just felt that way, since she'd already indulged in three cups before putting on her shoes.

Chelsea rubbed the back of her neck. "Something doesn't feel right."

"What do you mean?" Grayce stopped for a breather. "Are you getting sick?"

"No, it's not that. Since yesterday, I've had this nagging tingle, like someone is in trouble. But that's all I can feel. I can't figure out who." She shook her head and continued walking.

Grayce stayed a few paces behind. As she approached the tree line, an unpleasant aroma invaded her senses and brought the sting of tears to her eyes. Onion, urine and must.

"Shit. Do you smell that?" Grayce slapped a hand over her nose.

Chelsea nodded. As they continued, the stench grew stronger. Chelsea stopped dead and with eyes glazed, scanned the area around them.

Dread crept up Grayce's back, followed by goose bumps. The foul odor was so strong she covered her mouth and nose with the sleeve of her sweatshirt.

"No. It can't be," Chelsea cried, and sprinted toward a thick of bushes. Grayce followed, hot on her heels. She only traveled a couple yards before tripping over a makeshift tent nestled between a rotten stump and a moss adorned boulder. The funk hung so heavy she battled to keep her coffee and scone from making a reappearance.

"What the fuck is that?" Grayce mumbled.

Two small bare feet, cut blistered and bloody, poked out from under a mud and mold stained blanket.

Chelsea fell to her knees. "I called Zander."

In a gust of air, Zander stood by Grayce's side. "What happened? Everyone all right?" He paused, looked down, then disappeared along with the child. Shit, would she ever get used to his super speed?

Grayce offered a hand to help Chelsea back to her feet. "Come on, let's go."

By the time they'd made it back to the house, Grayce was out of breath, not from fatigue, but worry. Chelsea led her down a set of stairs and several hallways, then through a swinging door into a hospital room.

Grayce found Zander's eyes immediately. Her heart danced when he flashed his "I'm so fucking happy to see you" smile. On a sharp inhale, he turned his attention to the small boy lying on the table. The child looked like bones dipped in ash and dirt. The stench was enough to knock anyone to their knees, but Nikolas, seemingly oblivious to the fact, wasted no time checking vitals and cutting clothing from his body.

Chelsea stood in the corner, face wet, eyes red and swollen, staring at the skeleton of a boy sprawled lifeless before her. She visibly trembled and it broke Grayce's heart to see her upset. Chelsea, who did nothing but smile, laugh and fill every room she occupied with blinding sunshine, now stood ghostly and frail.

Her friend needed her. Needed comfort that she didn't know how to give. Well, no time like the present to pop her compassion cherry. And there wasn't a soul more deserving of it than Chelsea.

Not knowing what else to do, she grabbed Chelsea's hand. "Come on, let's get some coffee. The boys can take care of this." Chelsea nodded and followed. Grayce was relieved for the opportunity to get away from the unbearable odor hanging heavy in the room. After they passed through the door, machines started to beep.

"Oh shit," Nikolas shouted. "He's coding."

"No! He's so little." Grayce turned on her heel and pulled Chelsea back into the room. When she reached the bedside, the machine's alarms stopped, and his heartbeat showed steady on the monitor.

Nikolas shot Zander a quizzical glance. "Grayce darling, do me a favor would you?"

She nodded through teary lashes.

"Walk into the hall again and stop right outside. Stay there until I call you." She did as told. The alarms beeped as soon as the door closed behind her. A few long and torturous moments later, Zander called her in. When back at the boy's side, the noise subsided and his heartbeat steadied.

"What the fuck?" Grayce whispered and clasped her mouth with a shaky palm.

"Ditto that." Zander wrapped his arms around Grayce from behind and gave her an assuring squeeze.

"He's one of us." Nikolas' eyes lit up like fireworks. Chelsea gasped in the background.

"Chelsea, how did you find him?" Nikolas drew her to his side.

"I felt him yesterday. I shook it off because I knew you were all safe. Thought I was overtired, or something." Her voice trembled. "He was in the woods, Nikolas. No food, no water. God, he's so little."

Hugging his wife, Nikolas changed topic. "Grayce, he's feeding off your power. You're keeping him alive right now. This is unbelievable."

"What do you mean, feeding off my power?" Pulling away from Zander, Grayce leaned against the bed and touched the boy's hand. "This is insane."

Nikolas released his wife and adjusted knobs on one of the machines. "Grayce, you are one potent lady. What I wouldn't give to trace your bloodline."

Good luck with that one. No clue who her father was and dear old mom, well, she'd most likely dug herself an early grave. Even if she were alive, Grayce had no desire for a reunion.

Not a chance.

* * * *

Tyr watched from across the room as his toy struggled to pry her eyes open. Confident she could still see him through her swollen lids, he took his time undressing. Made sure she could read his intentions. The pathetic creature whimpered, but it'd become hard to distinguish between her sobs and those of the body sharing the bed. It pleased him when she thrashed. The thing still had some fight left. It was a surprise that she lasted longer than the others, having been the easiest one to seduce. She'd break soon though, and he intended to drain her dry before that happened.

"Although you've been quite entertaining this afternoon..." He scraped a fingernail over her nipple then down the center of her belly.

She bumped against the naked flesh next to her as the bed dipped under his weight.

"I've determined that you are quite useless in the information department." He grazed her chin with his teeth and pressed his heated erection against her thigh. "But you, my dear, are stronger than most."

With his nail, he drew circles around the top of her pubic area then took his time working it down her cleft. Not for her pleasure. To prolong the agonizing anticipation of what was to come.

"So, I've decided that since you are such a spicy little nugget, I'm going to play with you for a while longer." As he thrust two fingers inside her, he covered her mouth with his own to stifle the scream. She tasted salty. His little dove never tasted that way. Then again, he never could bring her to tears. Not like the rest of the pathetic females. No. His little dove was special.

He released her mouth and reached over to shake the limp body lying next to her. Not dead yet, but close.

Wrapping his fingers around the nugget's cheek, he forced her head toward the body sprawled next to her on the bed.

"Carrie. No. Not Carrie," she screamed and pulled against the binds at her wrists and ankles.

"I'm afraid your girlfriend here is no longer of any use to me." With that, he leaned over the trembling bitch and snapped the deadweights neck.

* * * *

Chelsea released a deep slow sigh. "He's getting stronger. I can feel him getting stronger." Grayce and Chelsea flanked the small child. Exhausted from maintaining constant physical contact with him for the past twenty-four hours, Grayce only nodded.

"I wonder who he is," Chelsea whispered, smoothing her fingers through his thick, wild hair.

"Can you read anything about him?" Grayce didn't fully understand Chelsea's gift.

"He's dreaming." Chelsea smiled. "The images are scattered."

"How does it work? Your gift, I mean." After lifting one hand from the boy and replacing it with the other, Grayce rubbed her tired eyes.

"It overwhelmed me when I first gained my power. People's thoughts, emotions, everything hit me like a flash flood. I thought I'd gone insane. I couldn't go out in public, you can imagine why. It took years to learn to filter people, block them out. It took almost that long to realize I could put thoughts in other's heads. Now, it's second nature. I don't peek into people's brains unless I have to. Nikolas, of course, is always open to me. It's a trust thing."

Grayce didn't want to pry. "What about Zander?" Okay. Maybe she did.

Chelsea's eyes lit up and paired nicely with the brightness of her smile. "One thing that's prominent with Zander, like a big flashing neon sign, is his love for you."

"He can't love me. We barely know each other." Grayce shook her head. "I'm having a hard time accepting this."

Chelsea assumed her motherly pose with hands on her hips, head tilted and eyebrows raised. "So, you can accept super speed and strength, mind reading and that you're a human blow torch, but you can't accept that someone could be in love with you? Do you know how ridiculous that is?"

Good point, Grayce thought. Didn't make much sense to her either. She shrugged her shoulders.

"It's who we are," Chelsea continued. "That's the only way I can explain it. I will say, though, there is something extra special about you two. Your connection is stronger than any I've ever sensed." She laughed. "I'm almost jealous."

Intense? That would be an understatement of epic proportions. "How long have you and Nikolas been together?" Grayce shifted, hoping to get some blood flow to her derriere.

After a long pause, Chelsea looked up with worried eyes. Grayce's scalp tightened. "Forty-two years. We've been married forty-two years."

Grayce snorted. "Yeah, right. Seriously, how long?" It was odd that Chelsea would tease her. She'd never joked around, not like that.

"I'm telling you the truth."

"Come on Chelsea, you don't look a day over thirty."

"It's one of the perks, dear." Her sympathetic smile did nothing to ease the tension. "The aging process slows down considerably once we've found our mate."

"Perk? You call that a perk?" For the first time in countless hours, Grayce stepped off the stool and stood, keeping a firm grip on the boy's frail hand. "So let me get this straight." She shook the numbness from her legs. "Number one, I'm stuck with Zander, unless I want to suffer excruciating withdrawals. Number two, aside from this fire burning out of control inside me, I'll be living this nightmare for what, at least one hundred years? Maybe more?"

Grayce slapped her free hand on her thigh and lowered her head. Her body grew hotter by the second. She drew three deep breaths and concentrated on cooling the fire.

"How old are you, Chelsea?"

Chelsea fiddled with the corner of a pillowcase. "Seventy-seven."

"Fuck." Grayce winced and lowered her voice. "Is there anything else I should know? Any more bombs to drop?"

Chelsea rose and moved to the end of the bed. "There is one more thing."

"Just one? Great. Let's hear it." With a slow deep inhale, Grayce closed her eyes and focused on staying calm. She was not going to put them in danger.

"As far as we know, if your mate dies, you die too. Not physically at first, but mentally, spiritually, emotionally. There's no hard evidence, not that we've found anyway, but I had a sister. Her husband was killed..." Chelsea eyes filled with tears. "She lost all will to live, became a vegetable. Couldn't feed herself, couldn't speak, never got out of bed. Then one day, she disappeared. We haven't seen her since. It's been fifteen years. I don't have proof she's dead, but before the tragedy, I was able to read her no matter where she was on the planet. I couldn't read her after she disappeared. I can only assume that means..." She couldn't finish the sentence.

"I'm sorry you lost her." Grayce had never mourned anyone. She'd never been close enough to anyone to care if they kicked the bucket. Sorrow was evident on Chelsea's face. Grayce tried to sympathize. How would she feel if something happened to Chelsea? Or Zander?

Her chest ached at the thought.

* * * *

Stephen stretched and groaned. His yawn was stifled by a cough. When he breathed, it burned like fire down his throat.

He blinked his eyes open. "Where am I?"

For the first time in his whole six years of life, he woke feeling warm. Heavy, soft blankets covered his body. He squeezed his eyes shut again afraid he'd wake from the dream, afraid he'd wake cold and wet. Something soft rubbed his head. Something else tickled his arm. Oh yes, this must me a dream. Or did he die? Were angels taking him to heaven? The air smelled clean, his skin no longer burned or itched. It must be heaven.

"Sweetie."

Oh, angels had such beautiful voices.

"Hi there little guy. Can you open your eyes?"

No, he didn't want to. He didn't want to wake up.

"You're safe here. It's okay to open your eyes."

The voice was so sweet and kind. He forced them open, one at a time and gasped when he saw the woman from the woods smiling down at him.

"I found you," he whispered. "Are you an angel?"

"No, I'm not an angel." The angel blinked at him. "You found me? Were you looking for me? Do I know you?" Her smile was pretty, like his mom's.

He smiled back at her. "I saw you by the lake. You made fire. You were fighting with a giant." Her fingers felt like magic on his skin. His mother used to rub his arm that way, when she wasn't acting crazy from the pills or the medicine she put in her body with needles.

"Oh. Oh no." The angel frowned. "What were you doing in the forest? Were you alone? Where's your family?"

"I don't have any family, not anymore." But he would get her back, as soon as he was strong enough.

"Do you live in the forest?" The angel who'd been rubbing his head, leaned forward. Yum. She smelled like cookies.

"Sometimes." He shrugged.

"What's your name?"

He looked back to the angel who rubbed his arm. Wait, if they're angels, they should already know this stuff.

"Stephen." He hated using that name. His mother made him promise never to tell anyone his real name.

"I'm Grayce. This is Chelsea. It's very nice to meet you Stephen."

A loud grumble vibrated under the blankets. "I'm hungry." Pulling his hand from Grayce's grasp, he clenched his stomach.

"I bet you are. I'll go get some food and the doctor. He'll be so happy to hear that you're awake." Chelsea bounced through the double doors.

Stephen looked around the room and struggled to focus. "The doctor? Am I in a hospital?" He'd never been in a hospital before. His mom never took him to the doctor when he didn't feel good. She said people would take him away. It was fine with him. He only felt sick when she forgot to feed him.

"No, not really." Grayce stood and stretched. "It's like that, but in a house."

Secretly, he was glad. "It's warm here. And it smells so good."

"Yeah, it does, doesn't it?" Stephen reached out to Grayce and grabbed her hand. He felt so much better when she was touching him.

* * * *

Chelsea stumbled as she skidded into the office, face flushed, chest heaving. She grabbed the corner of the desk to avoid a bump-in with Zander.

"Nikolas, Zander." Struggling to catch her breath, she hunched and gripped her knees, then flashed her pearly whites in her husband's direction.

"My love." Nikolas pulled her to his chest and kissed her hard.

Zander folded his arms, rested his hip against the table and waited for the finale. When the Compton's greeted each other, it always started with a kiss and ended with an ass squeeze and a groan. At least once a day, when they thought no one was looking, Chelsea's hand would slide down to Nikolas' crotch and she'd whisper something into his ear. Zander didn't mind their public displays of affection. Hell, they'd been flaunting their sexual attraction for so long now, he hardly even noticed anymore. If they didn't grope each other every time they were in the same room, it would worry the shit out of him.

Chelsea pushed herself free and turned to Zander. "He's awake. He's smiling and talking. His eyes are bright."

"That's wonderful." Nikolas pried his eyes away from his bride to study the document that inched its way out of the printer.

Concern clouded Chelsea's angelic features. "Something is bothering you, love. What is it?" She sauntered to her husband's side.

"You're not going to believe this." Nikolas gestured for Zander to come closer as Chelsea took the document from his hand.

After a short perusal, her face lit up. "Does this mean what I think it means?" Her head bobbed in barely contained excitement.

Zander rolled his eyes. "Anyone want to fill me in?"

Nikolas took a deep breath and let it out slow. "We can't tell her, not yet."

"Tell her what?" Zander demanded.

Chelsea handed over the printout. He read it. Looked at Nikolas. Read it again. "Impossible," he whispered.

"Listen, Zander." Nikolas snatched the paper from him. "Not a word. I want to run more tests."

Zander scratched his head. "Yeah, you're right. That's a bomb we don't need to drop on her right now." Or ever. He roughed his hands through his hair. How would he break this new mind blowing, life altering revelation to her? Was she stable enough to hear it? Would she be happy, or freak and disappear? Would she reject a child? His heart seized for a fleeting moment then beat double-time. Nikolas was right. It was too soon to tell her. First things first.

He kissed Chelsea on the cheek and made a beeline for the door.

Zander strode through the hall anxious to get to Grayce. He was hesitant to update her about the latest reports on the morning news programs, but decided it would be worse if she heard it on her own. Shit, Carrie from the gym found dead in Grayce's car. And Georgia, another employee of Jane's bar, was missing. He hated to admit it, but if they were going to find and stop this maniac, they'd have to work together. The sick bastard was going to keep killing people until he found her. Zander trembled with rage. Grayce was his number one priority, but fuck, they had a responsibility to protect anyone else who might get in the monsters path, didn't they?

Zander had grown up hating the curse. That's what he called his power. A curse. It frightened his parents and left him no choice but to hide from the world. People had a hard time accepting things they couldn't control or explain. That was one lesson he learned early in life.

After he met Nikolas, his feelings changed. He found a purpose. Grayce. Grayce became his focus, his new life mission. He never took time to consider what would happen after he found his mate. But maybe, just maybe, their new role as a couple was to wipe the psycho killer, Tyr, from the world.

"Baby!" The door flew open and made a god awful racket as it crashed against the wall. Zander hadn't intended to scare anyone, but he was just so damned happy to be near his lady. Grayce stood bedside, fluffing the boy's pillow. The young child's eyes burned blazing white and before Zander had a chance to react, Grayce was thrown to the floor and a blue streak of light had him pinned to the wall of the hallway outside. Stunned, he watched a blue bolt of electricity fizzle and fall in tiny sparks to the floor. The boy stood with brave form on the bed holding unsteady arms toward Zander, ready to shoot again.

"Leave her alone. I won't let you hurt her." His threat was backed by a whole lot of attitude and absolutely no muscle.

Stunned and more than a little embarrassed, Zander stood in the sterile hallway. Not what he'd expected. "Fuck." He rubbed his shoulder. The kid packed a powerful punch.

Grayce jumped to her feet and placed herself between Zander and the boy. "No. No. No. You've got it wrong Stephen." She tried to coax the child to sit. Stephen wouldn't budge and with noble resolve, refused to take his eyes off Zander.

"Grayce, step away from him," Zander commanded as his protective fury echoed through the room.

He recognized the look in the boy's eyes, the primal, uncontrollable emotions radiating from deep inside his tiny body. Zander had been there and knew exactly what was going through Stephen's frightened little mind.

"No fucking way," Grayce barked her refusal. "Stephen, he isn't going to hurt me, you can lie back down."

"Firecracker, it isn't a request." The instant Zander took a step forward, another bolt flew past her head and grazed his ear.

Shit. That was close.

"Very well, then." Zander smirked.

He stalked past Grayce, held up an arm to block another strike and pinned the boy's deadly weapons to his sides. "You and me are gonna have a little talk. Somewhere safe."

The boy weighed less than a sack of potatoes. With one arm, Zander tucked him safe and secure against his chest. He gave Grayce a hard peck on the cheek. "Watch your language around the boy, baby." He goosed her ass and gave his best Terminator impression. "I'll be back."

"Zander!" Her scream echoed through the corridor as he made his exit. "I fuc—I had this, you mother fu—ooh!"

He smiled wide. His lips sizzled with her lingering fury as he engaged super speed and headed for safer ground.

Chapter 8

Growing restless, Tyr stretched on the bed next to his toy. While she was no doubt easy on the eyes, she was beginning to lack in the recharge department and didn't come close to giving him the buzz he needed. Not like his little dove, anyway. Of course, there wasn't a woman on earth who could fill the deep chasm her absence had created in his soul—if he had one.

Thinking about his little dove made his erection stand proud. He hadn't used it against his other playthings. No. He reserved that for Grayce. Funny, before meeting the woman who'd given birth to his power, who was responsible for his reign of terror, he'd fucked whomever he chose. Rarely had to do little more than fake interest and flash his net worth to get a woman in bed.

After Grayce? His sex drive didn't fizzle. He merely lost interest in sticking his member anywhere other than between *her* legs. That didn't stop him from having fun with the other females. He simply changed tactics. Didn't take long to figure out that he could feast on their fear, that it fed his dark energy. Wasn't the same, but it would do, until he got his little dove back.

From a young age, the darkness beckoned to him. Fuel to a starving soul, it guided his actions, encouraged his impulses, cloaked his spirit with confidence and a sense of omnipotent self worth. His wealth, social status and power; he owed it all to the darkness. After accepting who he was, everything came easy, especially the women. Simple, pathetic creatures. They weren't even a challenge anymore.

After a lazy stretch, he rolled over and bit his blond toy's nipple, hard enough to draw blood and a scream that didn't disappoint.

"Wake up, toy." With a shove, he forced his fingers between her teeth and pulled her face toward his. "I'm bored, let's play." With a long, slow stroke, he licked the hot tears that cascaded down her cheek. "There will be no more crying today, do you understand?"

From under the blanket, he retrieved his large metal hook. Her eyes widened and she twitched and shook violently against the binds that tore her wrists and ankles. Fear pulsed through him as it rolled off her skin in vicious waves.

Yes, that's what he craved. Fear. It would do for the time being.

"What?" Waving the hook over her face, he couldn't hide his pleasure. "Does this frighten you?" Gray eyes rolled into her skull as she nodded.

"Good."

* * * *

Plopped down faster than he could protest, Stephen took in his surroundings. Oh, man. He was standing on the tip top of a mountain with nowhere to go but down. And to go down, he'd have to scale rock cliffs. He could see nothing but smaller mountains and tree tops for miles. Confused and cold he blinked and looked around again. Fear sent prickles across his scalp.

Oh no. He screwed up. He scared them and they didn't want him. Nobody would ever want him. What a freak.

With all the courage he could muster, Stephen turned to face his punishment and bounced off a rock hard leg. Large hands grabbed his arms before he fell backward.

"Sorry about that little man." The giant squatted. "I couldn't have my lady in the line of fire. I'm sure you can understand that."

Stephen looked into the giant's blue eyes. Gulp. "But I saw you fighting with her by the lake." Blinking, he looked down at his feet. "I thought you were going to hurt her."

The deep chuckle that rose from the giant's throat made Stephen's stomach feel a little less queasy.

"I get it little man. I feel you." He patted the ground, motioning for Stephen to sit by him. Stephen sat and felt no bigger than a mouse.

"You pack quite a punch. Let me feel those muscles." The giant lifted Stephen's arm and squeezed above his elbow. "Hmm...impressive. You work out much?"

Stephen laughed. It came out too fast and sounded girlie.

"What's your name?"

"I'm Stephen." He didn't like the way his voice trembled.

"I'm Zander, but my friends call me Z." He held out his massive hand but Stephen only stared. It was huge.

"Little man, it appears we have something in common." Z's dark blue eyes had Stephen spellbound. "We both want to protect Grayce."

"Yes, I thought you were gonna hurt her."

"I would die before I let that happen." Zander leaned toward him, and instinctively he leaned away. "What you saw by the lake, that was nothing. Grayce doesn't know how to control her power yet. She needed practice. I was helping her."

"Oh." Stephen scooted his butt toward the edge of the mountain and strained his neck to see over the side. "Why did you bring me here? Are you going to kill me?"

"No. I'm not going to kill you. We just need to get a few things straight. You were trying to protect her, I get that, but you could have killed her. That's why I brought you here. Where nobody could get hurt." Zander grabbed Stephen's waist and pulled him away from the edge. "That's quite a skill you've got."

"My lightning. I'm sorry if I burned you." He didn't want to cause pain. He wanted to use his power to save people. To save his mom.

"Have you hurt people with your lightning?" Zander rubbed his shoulder.

Until that point, Stephen hadn't realized that his lightning hadn't damaged Z. "Yes."

"Was it an accident?" Zander wrapped a large arm around Stephen. It felt better than the warm blankets he woke under. Safe and strong.

"Yes. My mom. He was yelling at her. I tried to stop him, and the lightning came out. It hit them both. She told me to run. She told me to run away and never come back." Memories of her frightened face caused him to cringe. He'd seen his mom scared before, but never as bad as that day.

"Listen, I know what you're going through. That's way too much power for a boy your age. How would you like to stay with us for a while?"

"Really?" He was so tired of camping.

"Really. Besides, we need another man around the house. You know, to help out."

"Cool." He turned toward Zander. "Help with what?"

Zander curled his arms. "You see this? You know how I got these big guns?" He flexed and posed, showing off his unreal size. "Chelsea's cooking. That woman makes way too much food. I can't let things go to waste, you know. It would be awesome to have someone help me eat it all."

Too much food? How was that even possible? "Will I get big muscles?" he asked.

"Yeah, little man. You will." Zander smacked his back.

It hurt, but he tried not to show it. A loud gurgle came from somewhere in the lower region of his body. "I'm hungry, can we go back?"

"Sounds good. But you have to promise me something."

"What?" Another loud grumble. Stephen wrapped his arms around himself.

Zander stood, lifted Stephen, and held him at eye level. "There are some very special ladies in the house. As men, it's our job to protect them. So, you can never, ever use your lightning indoors."

Stephen sagged like a rag doll in Zander's big hands as he was lowered back to the ground.

Zander bent at the waist and held a palm out. "Deal?"

"Deal." Stephen grabbed his hand and shook it up and down with zeal.

"It's pretty fuc—I mean, it's pretty cool though, your lightning. Maybe we could practice using it outside. Would you like that?"

"Oh yeah." Stephen's smile stretched so wide he felt a cut open on his cracked lip.

Zander scooped him off the ground and tossed him over a shoulder. "Let's go eat."

A couple of blinks later, they were seated at a kitchen table stacked with turkey sandwiches, grilled cheese, tomato soup, a tray of vegetables and all kinds of crackers and cheese.

Zander chuckled and handed Stephen a plate. "See what I mean?"

Stephen couldn't remember ever seeing so much food on a table. "I think I love this lady!"

* * * *

The boil now a slow simmer, Grayce attempted to join the others for lunch. Her temper had lost most of its steam. They were safe, for now.

Hip against the door jam, she crossed her arms and watched. Zander and Stephen devoured their lunches together. They laughed. Joked. Shoved unnatural amounts of food in their mouths. Zander was a completely different character around the boy. Playful. Young. Wow, she didn't even know how old he was. Didn't know much of anything about this man she was bound to for eternity.

She should've pulled up a chair. But that damned mouth of his hypnotized her. It didn't matter if he chewed, smiled or talked, her gaze settled on those lips and she was helpless to do anything but stare. She craved them now, wet and warm against her skin. She shivered with wanton desire as warmth settled between her thighs. Oh fuck, seriously? Now?

Hatred and fear had been the driving force in her life for so long. What compelled her now? A fucking desire she couldn't explain or resist, and a lust that overshadowed the repulsion toward physical contact she'd harbored for years.

Now, there was a boy and some crazy connection to him. A few weeks ago, she would've left him to die, feeling justified that she'd prevented another male from staining the earth with his putrid soul.

Nikolas entered across the room. He swung Chelsea in a wide circle, kissed her with unbridled passion and didn't give a shit who watched. Their love billowed around them like a pink haze—hearts, cupids and all. It would've been nauseating if it weren't so pure and unfeigned.

She'd never be able to love like that. Wasn't capable. Love didn't live in her heart.

No room.

With Zander, it would always be about need. Her body needed his. It wasn't enough to carry her into a bright happy future, but damn if it wasn't the one thing keeping her going.

Zander glanced over his shoulder, his dimples deepened by the wicked smile he wore. With one bite, his third sandwich disappeared. He whispered something to Stephen and excused himself from the table.

In two strides he was at her side, and much to her chagrin, she was breathless.

"Walk?" Tucking his arm under her elbow, he led her to the back door. Her shoes squeaked across the tile as she dug in to hold her ground.

"No," she whispered, and made a pathetic attempt to free her arm from his grasp. "I'm really fucking mad at you."

"Really fucking mad?" He let her go. Emptiness replaced the heated flow of energy. "Firecracker, you know how it turns me on when you talk like that." He raised an eyebrow and gestured to the erection that threatened to make confetti out of his jeans. Male pride shifted the features on his face. His eyes sparkled like marbles set in a windowsill on a sunny day.

Damn. She was helpless to do anything but wipe the drool from her face and nod.

"Can you be really fucking mad later?" Zander lifted Grayce's chin. She was spellbound, caught in his heated gaze, completely at his mercy.

"You fucker. That's not fair." Heat wafted through the air. Her heat, her desire, her hunger for him. "I had things under control with Stephen. You had no right to—"

With a gust of air and a dizzying whirl of color, Grayce was back in bed, pinned beneath hard, heated muscle. His erection pressed against her groin with enough pressure she felt his blood flow in sync with hers.

"You were saying." Soft lips tickled her ear.

"I don't need rescuing." Gulp. "Get off me. I don't want this right now." She did want him, in every pathetic, girlie way.

Zander removed himself from the bed and stood by the window. His body cast an eerie shadow across the room. "What *do* you want?"

"How old are you?" Grayce sat up and scooted herself against the headboard.

Zander smiled and crossed his arms, mimicking her. "I'm thirty-eight, almost thirty-nine. How old are you?"

"I'm twenty-eight and I'm asking the questions."

"All right. Fire away." He gestured for her to continue, then resumed standing like a statue, his erection still putting up a fight against the bind of his clothing.

She strained to keep her gaze above his waistline. "What do you do for a living?"

"I'm your man. That's my only reason for being," he answered, expression unwavering.

"Be serious, Zander. Do you have a job? You have to make money somehow. This is quite a spread you have here. It didn't come cheap."

"First of all, this is our spread, not mine." Arms still folded, he crossed the vast gap to the bed and sat on the edge. "Nikolas and I have made wise investments. Nikolas is a brilliant businessman. We've been partners for years. My parents were well off, so I received a hefty inheritance after they died. I didn't squander the money."

"So what you're telling me is that you don't have an actual job." She rolled her eyes.

"No, I don't. You'll never have to work either, not if you don't want to."

Tyr had spoken almost those exact words to her right before she'd been caught hook, line and sinker into his net woven of lies and deceit, greed and domination. Only difference was, she hadn't been offered a choice. She was told. "You'll never work." Period. End of discussion.

Zander stretched and lay across the end of the bed. "Why all the questions, Firecracker?"

The anticipatory throb, in that most private of places, beat rampant. There wasn't much time. She'd have to pounce soon or explode.

"I don't know you. I don't know anything about you." With a sigh, she leaned forward and crawled to him. "Isn't that what we are supposed to do? Get to know each other. You say we're stuck together, but what if we don't like each other? How does it work then?"

His deep throaty laugh threatened to disintegrate every brick of every wall, plow through each barricade and melt every layer of her protective coating.

"What's so funny?" Her attempt at scowling proved a challenge when his smile was so effusive, his gaze so solicitous.

"That had been my original plan, you know. Ask you on a proper date or two. Get to know you. Ease you into this new life of yours. Fate had other plans. But here we are and I happen to like you already. Very much." He trailed a finger up her arm, over her shoulder, across her chest and stopped at the dip between her breasts. "You wanna date? I could take you on a date. We could chit-chat. Have a few drinks, shoot the breeze."

Grayce reminded herself to breath. He was too close, his body, his scent, his touch, too overpowering. Fuck talking. She wrapped her arms around his neck and went in for the kill.

Before invading his mouth with her tongue, she whispered, "I hate dating."

* * * *

The floor trembled. Pictures swayed on the walls. Stephen gripped the edge of the table as the chair danced under him.

"This is fun." Stephen giggled.

A black mist oozed from the center of the coffee shop floor and thickened as it rose. Pictures jumped from their hooks. Glasses and mugs dove off the shelves. The shatter of glass rang in his ears.

The size of Chelsea's eyes made his heart stop. Uh-oh. This wasn't supposed to be fun. Danger. Chelsea grabbed his hand and yanked him from the dancing seat. "Grab the back of my coat and don't let go Stephen." People screamed. Tables and chairs were thrown about as they pushed and fought to get through the door. Chelsea banged a chair against the window, once, twice before glass sprayed everywhere. "Stay behind me."

The black mist grew larger. As it swelled, it sucked people in. It surrounded them and they just disappeared. It made its way toward the little girl that'd been smiling at Stephen from across the room. No, he wasn't about to let it get her. Still clinging to Chelsea's coat, he raised his free hand and shot his electricity at the black mist. It jerked, vibrated and shrunk. The girl, now in her mother's arms, smiled and waved as she disappeared into the crowd.

Stephen made a pistol with his hand, pointed his finger to his lips and blew.

Chelsea tugged his arm, pulling him against her side. The black mist turned its attention toward Stephen. As it thickened even more, a mouth shape formed at the center and called his name. It was a loud, terrible screeching sound. "Steeepheennn."

"Chelsea, Chelsea, we need to go." A face jetted from the oily mist and stopped inches from Stephen's nose.

Oh my God. Shayde.

The mist screamed loud and shrill, showing rows upon rows of perfectly sharp and pointy teeth. Black drippy arms grabbed and clawed at him.

"No!" Stephen sat up, throwing his pillow across the room. "Shayde. He's here. We have to go. We have to leave." Taking a moment to catch his breath he realized no one was around to hear him. It took great effort to free himself from the mountain of blankets Chelsea had covered him with. When finally untangled, he marched to the room next to his and pounded on the door.

"Little man, what's up?" Z's hair was a mess and stood straight up on the top. Stephen fought back a snicker. No time for jokes.

Grabbing Zander's shovel-sized hand he pulled him out of his room. "We have to train."

"Whoa, whoa, whoa." Zander squatted and grasped Stephen's head in his hands. "It's six in the morning. What happened? Bad dream?"

* * * *

"Z, listen to me. This is important. We have to train. Now." Stomping his feet and shaking his fist in the air, Stephen looked hell bent and more than determined. Zander glanced over his shoulder to the warm naked body lying under the sheet. His hope for a good morning romp fizzled like a defective firecracker. Shit. He scratched his head and pulled the bedroom door shut. Grabbing the boy's hand, he let himself be led, half naked and barefoot, away from his love and down the long hallway.

He rubbed the stubble on his chin and squatted in front of the boy. "Mind telling me what this is all about, little man?" The troubled expression on the young sleepy face set off alarms in Zander's head.

"There's a bad man. Very bad." Fisted hands shook in the air. "He's the one who hurt my mom. I'm dreaming about him. That means he's coming. He's coming. My lightning can hurt him. So you need to teach me how to use it."

The determination on Stephen's face and sheer force of will in his eyes, told Zander that anything other than a "hell yes" would have been unacceptable.

Zander knew all too well the devastating effect fear and ignorance could have on a child wielding power as strong as Stephen's. At least he'd be able to keep the boy safe. Stephen grunted a "thank you" as Zander threw him over his shoulder and headed out. Shoes be damned, he wasn't going to let this young one down.

The ladies of the house were going to be pissed.

With Stephen in tow, Zander bolted east, deep into the mountains. The sun was already hard at work evaporating the morning dew when he found an ample sized clearing miles from civilization. Far from the threat of prying eyes or discovery.

"That was so cool." Stephen's hair looked as if it'd been sucked through a vacuum nozzle and plastered with quick-dry cement. Zander held back a laugh.

"Okay my man, let's do this." Zander squatted. Stephen's eyes grew to the size of Chelsea's pancakes as they studied the expanse of his bare chest. The boy inflated his own chest and looked down at himself with lips pursed. It was comical, yet heartwarming to watch the small, breakable child size himself up with such confidence.

"First, I want you to show me what you've got." Zander pointed toward a boulder across the clearing at the base of a hill. "Can you shoot that far?"

A snort escaped Stephen's lips. "Um, yeah. I think so."

"Well, let's see it." Zander stood back resting his hands on his hips. The boy widened his stance, stretched his left arm toward the boulder and inhaled. With a shrug of his shoulder, he shot a bolt of blue toward the stone. It struck the outside left and sent shrouds of dust and shards of rock flying. Pride filled his hazel eyes as he turned toward Zander.

"Interesting." He smiled, nodding. "Can you do it with the other hand?"

Stephen, overconfident, shot another bolt from his right hand and missed by a few feet. Without hesitation, he threw his arm back up, paused to aim, then shot again. He hit the target, just shy of a bull's-eye.

"Good job." Zander grabbed Stephen's shoulders and gave him a playful shake. "Can you use both at the same time?"

Without a word, the little boy with the big power, shot two bolts of blue electricity and struck the rock dead center, transforming it to a pile of dirt and pebbles.

"Now that's what I'm talkin' about." Stephen jumped up and down. With hands raised in the air he performed a little dance. "Oh yeah, oh yeah."

Zander let Stephen have his moment. His skin already tingled and itched from being so far away from Grayce. Fuck, he didn't like this withdrawal shit.

Time passed in painful waves of ravenous craving and burning prickles while he allowed Stephen to target practice. Little more than an hour had passed and already the gnawing need to be near Grayce drove him out of his mind and nearly out of his skin. If they were going to keep up this training, it would have to be closer to home.

"Or, you could bring Grayce with you," Zander heard Chelsea's voice in his head. *"Come home boys, breakfast is ready and your woman is going to burn down the house if you don't get back soon."*

Oh shit. He hadn't considered Grayce's withdrawals. There'd be hell to pay when he returned. The thought made his pulse quicken and his cock throb.

* * * *

A faint, thermal glow dusted Grayce's skin. It would've taken a chainsaw to cut through the tension that hung thick as lard in the air. Lips drawn tight, she mumbled under her breath, words not appropriate to speak in front of a child. Zander let her spew. It was kinda cute.

She continued until Nikolas whisked Stephen and Chelsea to the lab. Stephen was the youngest one of their kind to surface with active powers and Nikolas had been eager to start running tests on the boy. Before the door shut behind the doctor, Grayce was straddled in his lap. He cupped her ass and hunted down the tender region in the crook of her neck.

"Fuck Baby. I need to be in you." He worshiped her musky skin from her neck to the deep dip between her breasts that had become his favorite spot. Her moan was the only invitation he needed. Before she protested, he had them back in their bedroom. They'd hammer out their issues the fun way.

Zander lowered Grayce to her feet, then bent to taste her succulent pink lips. Her kisses were his nourishment. And he was a greedy bastard.

He kissed her until she melted against him. He ran his hands down her backside and pulled her to the floor as he knelt. "Fuck, I can't get enough of you."

"Zander," she whispered. "Get naked, then I'm all yours."

"You want me here on the hard floor?" He patted the ground next to him.

"No. I want you here." She pointed to the heavenly place between her legs. "And I want you fast and hard."

Before the last word left her lips, her panties tore at the seams and drifted to the ground. With eager hands, his shirt was removed and his erection was freed from his jeans. Grayce mounted him. He leaned back on his arms to allow deeper penetration and to watch as she had her way with him. This woman of his was pure, unbridled sensuality.

Lean thighs supported her weight as she stroked his cock with her silky heat. She rode him with wild abandon. Hair tossed back, lush lips parted, nails scoring his chest. Her slick, tight insides pulled and massaged him with perfect friction. Nothing in the world was more satisfying than being inside of her. Nothing.

Grayce pounded against him one last time, ground their hips together, kissed his chest, then stood and backed away.

His heart skipped a beat or two, amazed that someone so breathtaking was hungry for his touch. He laid back, crossed his legs and folded his hands behind his head.

He groaned. "We need to get rid of that dress."

Her eyes darkened to a sultry hue. "You take it off," she teased and inched toward the bed.

Her shy smile made his balls tighten. He jumped to his feet, removed his jeans and prowled after her. The dress was removed with a simple rip and tug. The dark peaks of her breasts puckered in anticipation. He stood back to enjoy the view.

"That was my favorite dress," she murmured.

"That's a shame." He shook his head and smiled. "But I like you so much better without it."

He was about to go in for the kill, but came damn close to hitting the floor when Grayce crawled onto the bed and positioned herself on hands and knees. He'd never taken her from behind. Feared it was too dominating a position and would flood her with unwanted memories. But she offered herself to him with complete trust.

He swallowed the lump in his throat, then cautiously positioned himself behind her.

Grayce turned her head to meet his gaze. "Fast and hard, Zander. Please." There was no fear present in her eyes. They burned with hunger.

"Are you trying to kill me?" he asked through gritted teeth.

Before she could answer, he was buried so deep she yelped. Her flesh gripped hard and he pulled out with a steady drag. His erection glistened with her slickness. He could've continued with the slow burn. Could've watched his cock enter and retreat her backside all day. But his firecracker wanted fast and hard. Who was he to deny her wish?

With one hand gripping her hip and the other splayed across the small of her back, he rammed her again and again. Through her whimpers, her moans, he pumped and ground his hips against her perfect round ass. Fast. Hard.

He continued until her sex clenched and spasmed around him. With one last forceful thrust, he exploded inside of her, then collapsed on the bed by her side.

Without a doubt, he was the luckiest man alive.

As he skimmed the sultry surface of the naked body sprawled next to him, Zander had a heated debate with himself. He knew what needed to be done. He hated it, but fuck him, there was no better option at this point.

"We're going to train. We'll start tomorrow."

"Why the sudden urgency?" Turning toward Zander she pulled the sheet up to cover herself. "You're keeping something from me. I can see it in your eyes."

Zander rubbed a finger over the curve of her ass. With a less than convincing smack, she put distance between them. "What's going on?"

He had to tell her.

"He killed Carrie. Another woman from the bar is missing too."

The fire in her eyes dulled to ash. Grayce sat and curled into a ball.

"Oh my fucking hell." Fisting her hair, she rocked back and forth. "We have to stop him."

Zander's heart split into a thousand tiny shards seeing her like that, scared and frail, retreating to her dark place. "There's more." Before continuing, he sat and pulled his precious, broken lover into his lap.

"What? What more?" Grayce shivered then relaxed into his hold.

"He left Carrie in your car in Armstrong's parking lot. They haven't found the other girl, Georgia I think her name is."

No need to talk about the horrific condition Carrie was found in. Grayce shouldn't hear about the wounds, or the torture devices he left with the body. Most likely, Grayce had seen those tools up close and personal. Tyr wanted her to see them. Zander would not let that happen.

The rocking continued. "Why is he doing this?"

Unable to bear it any longer, Zander untangled Grayce's hands from the strands of hair she frantically twisted. He turned her to face him.

"Because he can. Because he's insane. Shit. He's been consumed by the darkness, that's why his eyes are black." Zander had only heard of the evil ones, he'd never come face to face with one. Nikolas and Chelsea had. Loved ones had lost their lives during the horrific encounter.

"He's one of us," Grayce whispered.

"Yes. But he's not like us, not anymore. He's pure evil, the darkness owns him, controls him. Nikolas believes he has the ability to teleport. That's how Houghton escaped from prison."

Mindful of her fragile disposition, Zander pushed. "I know this is hard to talk about, but if you have any information that may help, we need to hear it. We need to know everything we can about him."

"Fuck Zander, what can I say? We lived in California. I never met his family, but I know they were stinking rich. He had an older brother. I've seen pictures, but he never talked about siblings. I didn't ask. If he had powers back then, it was kept from me.

"Grayce, baby. Think back. Do you remember anything peculiar?"

"For fuck's sake Zander. He kept me in a torture room, shared me with strangers, charged admission. Does it get any more bizarre than that?" She looked at him with pleading eyes, her internal struggle evident.

"Wait. There is something. When he left for more than a few days, he'd come back pale and sickly. The color would come back to his face after he'd touch me." Violent shivers wracked her body. "Those were the best days. When he was gone on business. I would be locked in my room and left alone. Servants would bring me food. I begged for help once..." Grayce stopped. The shimmer of tears told him all he needed to know. He didn't urge her to continue.

"Firecracker, there's something extra special about you. Tyr and Stephen can't get their fill. Shit, I even noticed at the bar. Men are drawn to you. It's not just physical. It's chemical, like you're a walking bottle of pheromones."

"Talk about a cluster fuck of DNA," Grayce huffed. "Why isn't Nikolas attracted to me then?"

Zander ran a hand through his hair. Thank God Nikolas wasn't attracted to her. It was bad enough that he had to compete with a six-year-old for her attention. "Maybe because he already has Chelsea. Stephen and Tyr, they haven't bonded yet."

Grayce gasped. "Oh shit. What if Tyr finds his mate? How powerful would he be?" She trembled.

Zander loosened his grip on Grayce, hoping to hide his own sharp shiver. "Let's hope we never find out."

"So we're going to do this. We're going to find him, right?" Hope lit up her face like a spring sunrise. "When can we start?" She tried to crawl away.

Zander pulled her back to his chest. "I told you, we'll start tomorrow. Right now, I need to make love to you again. Soft and slow this time."

Chapter 9

"Insatiable fiend. Let me eat first." Grayce pried Zander's fingers from her hip bone and stormed toward the door. Sure, she wanted round four every bit as much as he did, but come on, a girl needed to recharge and rehydrate. "Fuel. I need fuel." As she stepped through the threshold, she entered a lush green jungle. The air hung heavy and wet. Bird calls echoed through the foliage and a monkey screamed somewhere in the distance.

"What the hell?" Grayce stumbled back into Zander's embrace. Her head bounced against his chest as he laughed.

"Where are you my friend?" Zander called out. With a sweeping motion, he moved his arm in front of him and the jungle swirled in a rainbow of colors. "This is some of your best work yet." He chuckled. "Sound effects are new."

Grayce hadn't realized she was frozen until he nudged her to move forward through the illusion. It shimmied and misted around them showing hallway, then jungle, then hallway again.

"Can you please tell me what the hell is going on?" Anger fizzled before it could manifest into more. The scene was so beautiful, so real, the only thing missing was a coconut bra and a palm leaf sarong.

"You've frightened my lady, Marcus. I might have to give you a beat down for that."

In an instant, the jungle lifted and disappeared into the ceiling, leaving behind the hallway and a beast of a man. He rested, shoulder against the wall, chiseled arms crossed over a massive chest, head held in a playful tilt.

"Did you just say lady?" Marcus headed straight for her, ignored Zander and pinned Grayce with a smoldering gaze.

He offered a muscular hand. "I've been waiting a long time to meet you. Marcus Lothario, treasure hunter, master illusionist and sexy mother fucker, at your service." His eyes widened and his nostrils flared when she grabbed his hand and gave it one good shake before letting go.

"A beacon," he whispered so only Grayce could hear. "How wonderful."

She recoiled. Oh shit. Was he drawn to her too?

"I'm Grayce. Are you mated?" she asked with a nervous quake to her voice. Zander's arm tightened around her shoulder.

Marcus' lips quivered. "No."

She huffed. "Just my fucking luck."

Marcus took a step back and held her gaze with haunting hazel eyes, dangerous and seductive with a hint of playfulness. It pissed her off beyond measure that she couldn't stop the natural urge to study the fine male specimen standing before her. Deep brown hair hung just below broad shoulders in natural waves. An unkempt goatee graced his angular face framing a pair of full lips. Thick brows formed a deep angle over his eyes giving him a downright dangerous appearance. His black t-shirt clung to his muscular body like a second skin. No way in hell would she let her eyes wander any lower. His shape brought to mind an ancient warrior and a shiver made its way across her skin. He was death waiting to strike. A beautiful yet savage beast. A shudder rocked her body at the thought of another powerful man being in the house.

"Z, my man!" Marcus continued to hold Grayce's gaze. "Looks like we've got some catching up to do."

Zander released Grayce and trapped his friend in a hearty embrace. They clapped each other's shoulders.

"We've got a lot to talk about." Zander gestured for them to walk. "I've missed you. It's been way too long. Let's go find Nikolas. I'm sure Chelsea already knows you're here."

Zander grabbed Grayce's hand and started toward the kitchen. "Marcus lives here with us when he's not hunting."

"Hunting?" Grayce asked. Yeah, she could picture him with big ass guns and knives.

"Treasure hunting. We have Marcus to thank for most of what we know about our race. He's collected artifacts from all over the world." Zander chuckled. "Bastard gets himself in trouble more often than not. But he always comes home with a killer story and another piece of the puzzle."

Marcus walked a few steps ahead. Comparable in height to Zander, he wasn't as wide, but carried solid muscle over his long limbs and lean midsection. His gait was every bit, if not more confident and cocky as Zander's.

Marcus turned and pulled up beside them. "Enough about me. Let's talk about this gorgeous lady of yours first." He punched Zander in the shoulder. "Damn, boy. You found yourself one hot *tamale*." Marcus winked at Grayce and she couldn't help but laugh out loud.

Zander grunted. "You have no idea."

* * * *

The blond toy lay limp across the wooden table. No need for wrist restraints, for much to his displeasure, she passed out over an hour ago. Too bad, things had just started to get fun. Tyr threw a blanket across her naked form and huffed out of the room, locking it from the outside.

He loathed the dank, musty smell of the mining tunnels. Unfortunately, in this small sleepy town, hiding places were limited. Funding and resources were not an issue. He could make it livable, for a while anyway. Grayce's apartment was no longer an option due to increased police activity. He had no choice but to find a new place to stay. To play. Set up his new playroom. Nobody would think of searching the long abandoned and mostly forgotten mine for the missing girls. Or Grayce, when he reclaimed her.

He'd been staying in Grayce's apartment for some time between detective visits, being able to teleport in and out as he so desired. It was there her essence, her addictive energy was the strongest. But he needed his playthings and he couldn't keep them in her abandoned home. So, he made a temporary abode deep underground, in a mountain that absorbed their screams.

And thank his lucky stars, the land the mine belonged to had come up for sale, the previous proprietor having died a sudden and unexplainable death. Along with the land came a modest but livable hunting cabin located near one of the tunnel entrances, complete with a wood burning stove and a dog. A convenient coincidence? Tyr didn't believe in happenstance. He designed his own destiny.

The time had come to put Houghton to use again. The convict had failed him miserably, but remained an important pawn in the game.

Rules had changed slightly.

Confident he'd be able to lure Grayce out of hiding, he headed for the hospital. Having just fueled himself with his blond toy, he'd be able to transport a few times before being drained physically, but he chose to drive. Gave him more time to contemplate Grayce.

Behind the wheel of his Porsche he was young again. Elated. And the women, all the pathetic females, fell like Jezebels at his feet when they discovered he was the owner of the beauty. God, they were so easy to manipulate.

He waited patiently down the hall until visiting hours were over and the reporters and detectives retired for the evening. After the security guards at Houghton's door nodded off, which they did frequently, Tyr transported into the prisoner's room. It was a short trip so didn't require much effort.

The paunchy man stared out the window. "What the fuck are you doing here? You gonna kill me?" Houghton refused to look at Tyr, a clear indication that he was either scared to death of his punishment or just didn't give a shit anymore. Tyr guessed it was the latter.

Punishment was coming. It was inevitable. No one failed Tyr without facing his wrath.

"Make it quick, will you. This catheter is a motherfucker." The man struggled to reach his dick but padded handcuffs had his arms restrained to the bed, inches out of reach.

Tyr stepped into Houghton's line of sight. It disgusted him how ugly this man was. His oily balding head and fat bulbous nose made Tyr grateful for the genes he'd been blessed with. "I'm not going to kill you."

Not yet anyway.

"We still have work to do."

* * * *

Zander's chest brimmed with pride for the family that surrounded him and the overflowing table of food. He was seated next to Grayce in his usual manner, with his body pressed firm against hers wherever possible. Thigh, shoulder, elbow. Hell. He'd have her in his lap if it was appropriate lunchtime behavior.

Stephen claimed the spot on Grayce's other side. He too, had his chair scooted as close to her as possible. Although they weren't touching, he was noticeably more relaxed next to Grayce.

Nikolas, the patriarch of the family, sat at the head of the table where he belonged, and struggled with a bottle of wine. After he muttered a few curse words under his breath, he gave up on the bottle opener and uncorked it with his mind. So much for being suave. He rarely used his telekinesis, but since Stephen's arrival, he pulled out his mad mind skills more often to get a giggle out of the boy.

Marcus, whom he loved as a brother, sat next to Chelsea, and hadn't stopped talking since they sat down.

Everyone, except for Grayce, listened intently to the stories Marcus told of his latest adventures. She sat, stiff and quiet, no doubt battling the demons that had her convinced all men were bad, and each and every one of them was out to get her. But she was trying. And that was progress. She pretended to listen. Zander kept a careful eye on her, ready to spring into action at the slightest mood shift.

"Marcus, please say you're going to stay for awhile." Chelsea begged, holding his hand to her chest. "We've missed you so much."

"I've got no immediate plans." Eyeing the last turkey and Swiss, he hit Stephen with a challenging smile. "Anyone wanna fight me for that sandwich?" Stephen's eyes lit up as he shook his head and rubbed his stomach.

"It's mine then." Marcus snatched the sandwich from the tray. "So, you two gonna tell me how you met?"

Zander and Grayce exchanged a quick glance. The mood in the room darkened.

"That's a conversation for later, my friend." Zander glanced sideways to Stephen and tilted his head.

"So Stephen, I hear you have the gift." Marcus considered everyone's powers a gift. Complete opposite view to Zander, who'd always regarded his powers as a curse.

"I have lightning." Stephen beamed. "Do you want to see? I'll show you after lunch."

"That would be awesome." Marcus downed the sandwich in three bites and chased it with half a glass of Barolo.

"What can you do?" No sooner did the question leave the boys lips when the kitchen turned into a dense jungle. Stephen reached out to grab a giant leaf and laughed when it misted around his arm. "That's hella dope."

Chelsea cleared her throat. "Marcus, I hear you brought something home. Where is it? I can't wait to see what you found us this time."

"Nikolas quarantined it until we figure out exactly what it is. Right now it looks like a large clump of dirt. I excavated it from a tomb in the northern part of Sudan." Marcus brushed crumbs off the table and shot Grayce a nervous glance.

"So, Grayce is a beacon. Does that mean we're staying put for a while?"

The room fell silent, except for the loud ding as Nikolas' spoon dropped to the floor.

"A beacon!" Nikolas shouted. "How did I not figure that out?"

Grayce's red glow had already seeped from her skin. "What the fu—I mean, what the heck is a beacon?" Grayce glanced at Stephen and mouthed a "sorry" to him.

Zander jumped in. "Firecracker, you give unmated males power. That's why Stephen is so strong around you, and that's why men horde you at the bar. It's why..." He shook his head and couldn't continue.

Nikolas finished his sentence. "It's why Tyr won't leave you alone. He can't leave you alone. He's addicted to you."

Zander fisted his napkin in his lap. "You probably gave him his power."

"But there's more," Chelsea chimed in. "Our kind will be drawn to you. Unfortunately, the dark warriors will be drawn to you as well as the light, which means—"

"The war is coming," Stephen interrupted.

For the second time, the room fell silent. Zander stared at the fragile boy. How could he know anything about a war? He was too young.

"What did you just say?" Marcus asked.

Stephen shrugged his shoulders "What? Am I in trouble?"

"No, Stephen, it's just that—"

Chelsea jumped from the table. "We are finished with this conversation for now."

With that, Marcus changed the topic of conversation back to himself and his latest acquisition.

* * * *

Grayce watched the interactions play out in front of her with a heart yearning for the kinship they shared. Why was it so hard for her to like these men? Why couldn't she relax and join the conversation?

Every muscle, every fiber of her being wanted to recoil, slip into the dark corners of her mind. She had to keep reminding herself that Zander was her safe place now, not the black shadows of her soul she'd been forced to escape to for so many years.

Now they're telling her she's a beacon, attracting more males? What kind of cruel joke were the fates playing on her? Shit.

She overflowed with guilt, knowing that she'd never be able to love, not the way these people loved each other.

Chelsea pressed into her thoughts. *"Honey, would you like to take a walk with me?"* Glancing across the table, she nodded yes.

"Zander, I'm going to kidnap Grayce for a while." Panic bulged his eyes and Chelsea giggled. "Don't worry, we won't go far enough away for you to miss her." She stood, planted a peck on Marcus' cheek and turned to give Nikolas a real kiss. Every face in the room blushed at their show of affection.

"You boys clean up." Chelsea sauntered around the table, clasped Grayce's hand and led her out the door.

They walked in silence. Too many words crowded her brain. When they reached the thick underbrush, Grayce stopped and plopped herself on a mossy tree stump. The tranquil scenery did help to quiet the chaos in her mind.

Her head slumped between her shoulders. "I'll never be able to love him, you know." Wow, she said it out loud. To an actual person. This sharing stuff wasn't so horrible. "I'll never be able to love at all."

"Oh, sweetie." Chelsea knelt to face her, pine needles and twigs crackling under her legs. "I can't begin to imagine what you've been through." With motherly endearment, she blotted a tear from Grayce's face. "You have to know that we already love you. All of us. If you can't love us back, that's okay. We're going to keep on loving you anyway."

Chelsea stood, cupped Grayce's hands and continued her pep talk. "You're an amazing, charismatic woman. You have love inside you. I can feel it. You've buried it so deep, it seems impossible to get back. You had to protect yourself. I know that. You've trapped yourself behind an impenetrable field." Tears flowed heavy between them. "It's going to take a long time, but you'll find a way to trust again. That needs to come first. Love will follow." She chuckled. "Zander's an exceptionally patient man. He'll wait forever."

Grayce choked on the lump in her throat. "Zander. This is unfair to him. How can he want to be with me? I'm damaged. I'm broken. I'll never love him, not like he deserves." Sun peaked through the tops of the pines. Grayce imagined herself light as a feather, floating upwards until the heat burned away the anger and pain.

"And Chelsea, he's gorgeous. I mean out of this world, knock-you-on-your-ass perfect. Like he's not real. And look at me." She raised her shirt, exposed the evidence of her abuse. "I'm hideous."

"Let me tell you something about Zander." Chelsea's angry voice boomed. Fists to hips. A mother scolding a child. "That man has loved you since the day he laid eyes on you. He loved you the moment he knew you existed. He came home after seeing you the first time and I'd never seen him so happy. So alive. He told me you were the most beautiful creature he'd ever laid eyes on. And this was before he knew for sure that you were the one. He wanted it to be you. It was all he talked about."

She pointed an angry finger at Grayce. "It took all his will power not to grab you that day and drag you here. And believe me, that man had his choice of women. They swoon over him. You know what? He's turned every one of them away. You know why?" Chelsea didn't let Grayce answer. "Because he knew you were out there. He saved himself for you. You're the only woman worthy of that man's love. You're the only woman he's ever loved."

"Chelsea." Grayce kept her tone low.

"Wait a minute, I'm not finished." Chelsea held up her palm to stop Grayce from continuing.

"For fuck's sake, don't move." Grayce gripped Chelsea's forearms and squeezed hard to get her full attention. "Shut up."

Holy Fuck was the first thought that came to mind. Get Chelsea out of the way was the second. Without a moment's hesitation, Grayce shoved herself in between Chelsea and the imminent threat.

"Get behind the stump," she ordered.

The grizzly stood no more than twenty-five feet away. Shit. Now what? Don't panic.

Act like prey, they'll treat you like prey.

She remembered hearing that once. Probably on a reality series where no one was ever in any real danger.

Chelsea spoke slow and calm. "Don't move Grayce."

The stare-down lasted mere seconds, but seemed an eternity. Her bones rattled so hard it was likely a few of them had fractured.

Where was the damned fire when she needed it?

She closed her eyes and concentrated on the painful rhythm pounding against her breast. The heat swelled. From gut to heart, then through her arms. Her fingers tingled with the need to release. Arms trembling, she threw her fire toward the majestic creature.

It grazed the grizzly's head. The bear shook ferociously, stood on hind legs and exposed large, terrifying fangs and claws.

Fear tightened her bosom and squeezed the air from her lungs. Blood pounded through her ears louder than a college drum line. Pulling another blast of heat from deep within, she aimed at the roundest spot on his exposed belly.

The shot would've hit dead center. It should've sent the creature on a dead run to the next county. Talk about bad timing. Zander appeared out of nowhere, caught the blast and flew straight into the creature. Man and beast tumbled in a ball of dirt, fur and flesh.

The earth stopped spinning. Air fell silent. Grayce stood horrified as Zander rose from the chaos. Unsteady. Shaken. Bloody.

Holy shit.

The grizzly scrambled to its feet and swiped a deadly paw.

Zander stumbled backwards, regained his balance, and assumed the stance of a warrior ready to strike the final blow.

God he was a sight to behold.

Fangs bared, the bear charged.

Zander shifted his weight, leaned forward and caught the animal at his chest. It was thrown, flailing, into a small pine. The tree bent and snapped as the grizzly fell to the earth with a thud. A flock of birds soared to the sky and screamed in protest. A mound of dusty, matted fur shook wildly and retreated into the thick of trees.

* * * *

His knees hit the dirt. His legs no longer able to bear weight. Warm liquid spurted over his thighs forming a dark, glistening puddle around him. Three open lacerations stretched from his left shoulder to his navel. "Grayce."

"Chelsea, help!" Grayce peeled off her shirt as she ran. The cotton tank she applied to his bloodied torso might have been a square of tissue for all the good it did. "Zander, you have to get yourself to the house. Can you get up?"

"Are you hurt?" He whispered. She looked unscathed. It was hard to be sure through the dark shadows crossing his line of sight.

"No. Oh my God. No." Her hands trembled as she pressed the useless rag tighter to his wounds. Her breath came in hitches, like it did when they made love. "Zander, you need to get back to the house. Can you do that?"

He examined the damage.

So much blood. She shouldn't have to see him weak and vulnerable.

"Zander, please. We can't carry you. You have to get up." Her fingers were ice against his raw flesh. The flow of crimson refused to slow.

Zander thanked the heavens it was him bleeding out, not her. Grayce was strong. A fighter if he'd ever seen one. She would survive the grieving process.

Chelsea's voice was faint behind him. "Nikolas and Marcus are coming as fast as they can." She grunted then applied pressure to his stomach. "Please, please get up," Chelsea cried.

He wanted to move. God did he want the strength to will his body up and out of the pool of blood. Into Grayce's arms.

Looking into the eyes of his love, Zander for the first time in his crazy long existence on earth, felt mortal. Shit, she was beautiful. Even with her face contorted in anger. She cried. For him. Made his heart swoon.

Grizzly? Well, first time for everything, right?

The spinning nauseated him. Fuck, he needed to wrap his arms around her and hold on for dear life. Grayce screamed at him. He couldn't register her words, but didn't doubt most of them started with the letter F. Rage burned in her eyes. He needed to kiss the fury away. If only he could reach her. If only he could move.

A dark fog clouded his brain, narrowed his vision.

Oh fuck, this was bad.

"Grayce." He swallowed hard, choked on the taste of blood. "My Grayce..." He searched for her face through the darkness. "I love you." Raising his hand, he found her tear soaked eyes. "Don't cry, baby. Don't cry," Zander whispered, cursing himself for letting her down again.

Fragile.

Broken.

Tempestuous.

His Firecracker, who hid behind the facade of anger and aloofness, just needed unconditional love. Someone stronger, to help her heal, to guide her out of the private hell she'd been living. It was his job. His fucking duty. His privilege.

Grayce's lips found his, and damn she tasted sweet. He cupped the back of her head and crushed her to his mouth. He kissed her. Deep. Desperate. All of his being, his love, his emotion were poured into that one kiss. If this was the end, he'd make damned sure she would feel him on her lips for the rest of eternity. He held tight. Drank her. Bruised her. Loved her until the darkness stole her away.

Zander watched from above the tree tops. Lighter than a feather, he ascended toward a brilliant white light when a scream bellowed dark and fierce from below. "You're not leaving me you son of a bitch."

Deadly eyes flashed to Chelsea, hazel retinas had been replaced with flaming red. A guttural warning escaped her lips. "Chelsea. Run."

Zander hovered.

"Grayce, he's not gone, I can still feel him. Please try not to lose control." Chelsea made a feeble attempt to calm her friend.

With a heated flash, Chelsea was thrown back onto her rear.

"Please run, Chelsea. Run!" Grayce cried.

Chelsea jumped to her feet and sprinted toward the open path that led back to the mansion.

Zander ached with need to calm her. His ghostly form wouldn't allow it. "Firecracker. Be strong, you'll get through this," he whispered.

Fear and sadness didn't exist in the realm he entered. Heart and soul, he was saturated with light, peace and pure joy.

A deep boom echoed through the sky above him. A voice, familiar and strong. "It's not your time, son. Love her well."

* * * *

With bare hands splayed across the open wounds, Grayce squeezed her eyes closed and prayed for control. Begged. Pleaded to a God she'd never before acknowledged.

Chelsea needed time to get away.

Grayce prayed for Chelsea, prayed for Zander. Prayed they wouldn't die because of her.

Her wits slipped away. Raw emotion drove her actions now. Blood covered her arms. Her lips throbbed with the remnants of his kiss. A kiss that felt like goodbye. He couldn't die. The primal need to protect him overwhelmed her senses.

"Take me," she implored. "Take me instead."

Hell's own fire coursed through her veins. Savage. Brutal. Pissed off.

She would've sold her soul at that moment to keep him alive. Zander didn't deserve this. She did.

Earth and grass swirled and gyrated, turned to ash around her. Her small fingers stretched across his bloodied and shredded skin. Her insides boiled. Her skin bubbled and vibrated with indignant protest.

He said her loved her, now he was dying. What the fuck? What kind of cruel fucking joke was this, anyway? Violent trembles overtook her as an earthquake made its way through her body from the inside out.

"I will not let you die. This isn't right."

She forced the trembles into her arms. Excruciating pain ripped through her muscles.

"I'm not ready to let you go." Eyes screwed shut, she directed the tremors down through her hands. It hurt so fucking bad. Her fire had never been this unbearable. Every cell in her body exploded with nuclear wrath.

She was going to die.

Another scream tore from her soul. White fire blasted from her fingertips. Spasms forced her back to arch and her head to fall back against her spine. A blinding white light enveloped their bodies and lifted them off the ground.

Time stood still.

Then nothing. No sound. No air.

Only light.

* * * *

Stephen woke with a throbbing pain at the base of his skull. Ouch. He rubbed the back of his neck. Super ouch.

"Hey, little man." Marcus burst through the door with a plate full of donuts and a glass of milk. "Time to get up." He planted his butt next to Stephen. The chair wiggled and made a funny squeak.

Stephen wiped goo from his eyes and looked around the room. Grayce and Zander hadn't woken up yet, but at least they'd been moving in their sleep.

He hadn't left their side since Nikolas gave him the okay to go in. Man, they'd been asleep for a long time. Nikolas said they were going to be just fine but they needed to rest and recharge their batteries. Stephen insisted he needed to be next to them and he wasn't going to leave until they woke up. Thank goodness the doctor didn't argue. He was a little old for temper tantrums, but if that's what it took to stay with Grayce, he would've done it.

"Thanks, Marcus." He managed a quick smile before devouring a maple bar. Man, he loved the food around here. Someday, after he was strong enough, he'd bring his mom here so she could have this yummy food too. Maybe she'd get better and be able to take care of him again.

He had a dream last night. Shayde again. This time, he was fighting on a mountain. Marcus and Zander were helping him. The girl was in the dream again too. She was pretty, as far as girls go, especially her red hair. Anyway, in this dream, he wasn't scared. He was mad. He was mad because Shayde was trying to hurt the girl.

"Fucker," Stephen whispered under his breath.

"What was that?" Marcus raised his eyebrows.

"I'm sorry." Stephen smiled.

"Don't let the ladies hear you talk like that," Marcus scolded.

Stephen laughed. "Ladies? Grayce talks like that every day."

"I know, right?" Marcus punched Stephens shoulder. It hurt. Not too bad, though. "That girl cusses more than a trucker." Milk sprayed across the floor and Stephen doubled over with laughter.

"Hey, Stephen." Marcus grabbed the now empty plate. "Chelsea wants you to come and eat a decent breakfast. Afterward, I thought the two of us could go outside. You can show me what you've got."

Marcus posed, flexing his chest muscles. Stephen's pulse raced, eager for the day he'd look like that.

"Show off." Stephen giggled as he glanced back to the sleeping couple. Leaving was the last thing he wanted to do, but Chelsea would come and drag him to the kitchen if he didn't go on his own.

"They'll be here when we get back, don't worry." Marcus headed through the door. Stephen didn't want to leave, but he followed, running to keep up with the warrior's strides.

* * * *

The room came into focus one blink at a time. Window, bathroom door, dresser. Everything was right where it was supposed to be. The scent came next. Skin and sun. Zander's heady smell. Then the heat, pressed warm and hard against her backside. The musk that invaded her senses lit a fire that shot a swelling desire straight to her sex.

Wait. He died.

Grayce rolled over and buried her nose in his chest. An erection pressed against her overheated skin. Maybe they were both dead. Was this a dream? Didn't matter. She needed him inside of her, fantasy or not.

She slid her foot up his thigh, wrapped her leg around his bare ass and pulled him tighter against her hips.

They were naked, but how they got that way, she didn't know. Sure as hell didn't care. Saved her some time and effort. With a slight shift, she positioned her body until his smooth, heated sex pressed against her folds. Three rolls of her hips and his hardened flesh was slick with her moisture.

A sensual groan vibrated through his chest. Oh fuck, she ached with desire. Warmth spread up her legs, through her abdomen, continued upward and burned a blush into her cheeks. As she pressed kisses across his chest, his heart pounded a primal rhythm under his pecs.

"Good God, firecracker. I love you." Zander kissed the top of her head.

He loved me.

Kiss. Lick. Nibble. Damn he tasted good.

A sharp hiss plucked her from her fantasy. "Careful love, that's tender."

What?

With one fluid motion Zander grabbed her waist, flipped to his back and lowered her onto his over eager erection. Sweet agony filled her from the inside out. An orgasm already threatened to destroy her. Damn. This power he had over her body was infuriating.

"Oh. My. Fucking. Hell." Grayce's eyes filled with tears as she caught glimpse of his pale, heaving body. Three large scars marred his torso. Covering her face, she peeked through her fingers. What the fuck? He shouldn't be here. He died in her arms. "Am I dreaming?"

With a sharp thrust of his hips, Zander drove his sex deeper into her. Grayce threw her head up and arched her back.

"Does this feel like a dream, baby?"

No. God no. She leaned forward and traced the scars across and back. "How can they be healed already?"

"You healed me."

Zander's name escaped her lips when he gripped her hips and thrust again.

"I don't remember what happened."

"You. Healed. Me." Each word came through gritted teeth. Every force of his hips validation that he was very much alive.

In an attempt to slow the torture, Grayce squeezed her thighs together.

For a moment, Zander relaxed beneath her. "Nikolas thinks your red energy hit the bear and me at the same time. Either gave the grizzly incredible strength or stripped me of mine. That's how its claws were able to pierce my skin."

He sat. Pulled her legs around his waist. Drove his cock deeper.

Her insides coiled then exploded in a painful series of convulsion and sweet, agonizing release. Grayce screamed his name and buried her face in his neck as she rode out the soul-shattering orgasm.

When able to lift her head, he brushed her lips with feather light kisses.

"You saved my life." He breathed against her mouth. "You're my superhero now." Claiming her lips again he pulled her harder over his erection, wrapped his arms around her waist, then flipped and pinned her underneath him. "I need to properly thank you."

Grayce whimpered when he pulled out of her and traced her abdominal scar with his tongue, leaving a trail of fire along the path.

"We match now." He nibbled her hip bone. "Matching scars. How cool is that?" Another nibble. Her hips jerked up to him. "Firecracker." His lips blazed a trail from her hip to her clit, kissing and biting along the way. So soft and gentle.

Grayce appreciated his tender touch. His tongue pierced her folds. Brain and libido jumped into hyperdrive. He stroked up and down her slickness, applied just the right pressure in all the right places.

Sucked. Licked. Bit. Then stopped on the brink of another release. One finger, then two pushed inside. Rubbed. Caressed. He pulled them out halfway, then plunged again. Grayce rocked her hips to meet him as his fingers worked their magic inside and his mouth drove her insane on the outside.

How in heaven's name could she survive another orgasm? There hadn't been time to recover from the last. "Zander," she cried, grabbing his head and swiveling her hips back and forth against his hungry lips. "Fuck." Grayce bucked, wild and wanton, under his head. "Oh fuck!"

Pain and pleasure tore through her from the inside out. Each shiver left her gasping, every tremor melted her muscle and bone until there was nothing left inside her skin but warm liquid.

Grayce's muscles continued to clench with aftershocks. Zander crawled up the length of her body, eased his cock between her legs, filled and stretched her to the limit. She pulled his face to hers, bit his chin and licked her moisture from his lips.

"My love." He reached his release, collapsed at her side, and locked their bodies together. Within seconds, he was out cold.

Physical exhaustion wasn't enough to whisk her away to dreamland. Her brain wasn't ready to shut down, not with all the nagging questions mud wrestling inside her head. She saved him? How was that possible? Why her? Why give her the power to both destroy and heal? If this fallen angel, warrior, soul mate mumbo-jumbo was true, why did she have to battle these demons? Something dark dwelled in her; it had always been there. But for the first time in her life, there was something light too, something...good? Maybe she was just crazy like her mother.

Great. Would she start hearing voices in her head soon? The thought brought on an unpleasant shudder.

Zander moaned in his sleep and gave Grayce a squeeze. Face pressed against his chest, she breathed deep and let his scent and warmth settle the unease. Concentrating on him alone, to block the bullshit bombarding her brain, she drifted to sleep.

Chapter 10

Every jaw in the room hung open as Nikolas read the words printed on the front page of the Chastain Inquisitor. "John Houghton, escaped convict, claims he is the father of Grayce Smith. Miss Smith is wanted for questioning in the murders of two local women and the disappearance of another."

Nikolas continued reading. Grayce pulled her knees to her chest and hid her face behind trembling fingers. When Zander offered an arm for comfort, she batted him away.

He heard the drag of breath as she pulled oxygen into her lungs, deep and slow, trying to stay calm. Good girl.

With a frustrated sigh, Nikolas looked up from the paper. "Did you know your father?" All eyes turned to Grayce.

With a sigh, she raised her head and lowered her hands. "No. My mother never talked about him." The room temperature rose a few degrees in a matter of seconds. Zander shot her a worried glance.

"I've got it under control," she barked at him, then continued with the deep breathing.

Damn, he was proud of her. He watched as her glow hovered then disappeared into her skin.

"What if he is her father?" Chelsea asked and grabbed her husband's arm. "We have to get to that man."

"They're transferring him back to prison soon as he's stable enough to be moved," Zander interjected. He, too, was drawing deep breaths in effort to contain his dangerous and foul mood.

Chelsea turned toward her husband and placed a hand on his thigh. "Nikolas, my love. Will you take me to the hospital with you tomorrow?" Her hand slid closer to his crotch.

Oh crap, Zander thought. Chelsea was pulling out the big guns. Nikolas was in for a fight.

The twinkle in Nikolas' eye couldn't have been missed from a mile away. "What are you thinking sweetheart?" His words flowed like molasses.

Zander's mood wasn't so foul anymore. This was gonna be a good show. He relaxed into the couch, crossed his arms and nudged Grayce. He didn't want her to miss this. She'd yet to be witness to a tiff between the Comptons.

"I'm thinking we can get close enough so I can read him. We need to find out what's going on." Emerald eyes flashed big and bright. Damned those big beauties. No one had ever been able to say no to them.

Tearing his gaze away, Nikolas swallowed hard. "Darling, I love you. It's a brilliant idea. But you know as well as I, there's not a chance in hell I'd let you get anywhere near that man." His chin jetting in protest, Nikolas folded the paper and placed it on the floor next to his chair.

Her tone darkened. "We don't have a choice." The hand on Nikolas' thigh clenched. The gesture was meant to be inconspicuous, but Zander had been watching and waiting. Her fingernails dug into his thigh, no doubt sending blood to the one place Nikolas didn't want it to go, and the precise spot Chelsea had intended.

She leaned closer to her husband. "This is Grayce's life we're talking about. If he's connected to Tyr, perhaps I can find out where that monster is hiding."

"No Chelsea. You're asking me to put you in harm's way knowing full well I'll never let that happen." Nikolas shifted in his chair.

Poor bastard. He'd already lost the battle. Chelsea never played fair.

In a move so sly only a trained eye could see, Chelsea brushed a finger across the bulge in Nikolas pants before raising her hand to his chest. "Lover. Please. Marcus and Zander can come. There's no way I'll be in danger with the three of you. Besides, I've made up my mind. You can take me and make it easy, or I'll go myself and find another way to get near him." The hard-headed hottie stood, straightened her skirt and sauntered to the kitchen.

Zander exchanged glances with his friend.

Shoulders deflated, cock...not so much, Nikolas rose from the chair and followed his wife.

Grayce pounded the couch cushion. "Fuck. Stop arguing about it. I don't care if the asshole is my sperm donor. I don't want to know. Bastard can die for all I care."

Nikolas turned to her wearing a warm smile. "Oh, we're not fighting dear. She's won this round. Once she's left the room, her mind is made up. Nothing I can do to change it now." He rubbed his bald head and continued after Chelsea.

"Was that a fight?" Grayce asked, bewilderment contorting her face.

"Yeah. That was a fight." Zander pulled Grayce into his lap.

She snuggled against him. "Where are they going?"

He laughed. "To make up."

* * * *

Monsters came in many different forms. In Stephen's opinion, Shayde was the scariest monster of them all. To most people, Shayde looked like a normal human being. Stephen knew better. Evil lived in Shayde and it wanted out.

His jet black hair, dark eyes and pointy nose haunted Stephen's dreams almost every night before his mom sent him away. The way he looked at Stephen made his bones rattle. The few times Shayde spoke to him, Stephen was certain he saw evil spirits dancing around in his dark retinas. The spirits called out to him, like they wanted his soul. Like they wanted to suck him into the blackness.

Stephen's mom tried to keep them separated. It wasn't too hard. Shayde only came to visit at night after Stephen had fallen asleep. Some nights, he'd hear them yelling. His mom would say she didn't know who his father was. Shayde always sounded angry at his mom, always yelled. Called her bad names. If he didn't like her, why did he always come back? Why did she always let him in? He would never understand grown-ups.

They moved a lot. Stephen hated moving. He'd ask why they were leaving again, and his mom would say she was trying to find the perfect home. He knew it was a lie.

Every place they stayed was worse than the last. Most of them had no lights or heat. They almost always smelled bad, like garbage or old people. She would never tell Shayde they were moving away. He would find them, though. When he did, that's when he was the scariest. The last time, it took Shayde a couple of weeks to track them down.

That's the day he tried to kill his mom and the day Stephen found his power and tried to kill Shayde. That's when his mom sent him away. It was the last time he'd seen her. Didn't even get to say goodbye. He missed her so much.

* * * *

Grayce sat on the oversized sofa with arms crossed, legs curled under her. Stephen sat motionless at her side, his head resting on her shoulder. He laughed at some ridiculous cartoon about a yellow dog and a boy that wore a silly white hat.

The close contact drove her to the brink of insanity. With great effort, she held it together for the boy's sake. He needed to be near her, and despite the battle between her brain and body, his needs were much more important than her issues with the male species. After all, it wasn't his fault he was born with a penis, right?

The shrimp was pretty funny. Grayce enjoyed his sense of humor. She couldn't shake that feeling that she'd seen him before though. It irritated the hell out of her.

A bushy head of light brown hair, cut and styled at Salon de La Chelsea shone under the bright lights from the television screen.

Grayce huffed. There was nothing that woman couldn't do.

"I want it cut like Z's." He'd demanded earlier in the day. Chelsea, of course, obliged.

Squeezing her eyes shut and praying he wouldn't freak, Grayce uncrossed her arms and ruffled his hair before wrapping an arm around his shoulder. "I like your new haircut."

"Do I look like Z?" Staring straight ahead, he snuggled closer. Grayce tensed, but didn't pull away. *I can do this. I can do this. He's a boy, he can't hurt me.*

"Yeah, you look like Z. In fact, I think you look better than that big lug."

His tiny shoulders shook with a giggle.

"You look like my mom," Stephen whispered.

"I do?"

"Yeah, except her hair is yellow." He looked up, studied her and pressed a sticky finger to the tip of her nose. The lingering scent of hot fudge sauce filled her nostrils. She fought the urge to turn away.

"Your noses are the same. Your eyes are the same too."

Grayce's heart skipped a beat. No. Impossible. She examined the boy's features. Oh my fucking hell. Same big hazel eyes. Same button nose. Same high cheekbones.

"Tell me about your mom, Stephen." Her shaky voice caught in her throat.

"My mom was always scared. She pretended not to be. We played under a blanket with the flashlight every night."

Grayce gasped. No, no, no.

Stephen continued staring at the television. "She used to forget about me at school. But it's okay. The principal was nice and let me stay at her house a lot. The other kids hated the principal. But I liked her. She made the best chocolate chip cookies. Well, except for Chelsea's."

"Stephen, what's your mom's name?" Heart in her throat, she braced for the answer she didn't want to hear.

He looked around the room as if checking for spies. "Her name is Dawn." A click of the remote and the television went black. Turning toward Grayce, he propped himself on his knees. "Can I tell you a secret?"

Gulping, Grayce nodded her head.

"She used to have a lot of names. I'm the only one who knows her real name. She told everyone else her name was Monica or Melissa or some other stupid ones I can't remember. I got in trouble once because I almost told one of her boyfriends her real name."

Her lungs deflated, then stuck. A tear sprung free in spite of her efforts to hold it back. She scrunched her face. Tried to stop the dam that was about to burst.

Oh fuck it.

She cupped Stephen's cheeks, gazed into his big, beautiful, innocent eyes and let her tears fall.

"Why are you crying?" His worried expression opened a new fissure in her heart. How did she not see this before? "Did I make you sad?" he asked.

"Where is your mom now?"

"I don't know. But I'm going to find her as soon as I'm bigger." Mimicking Grayce, he cupped her cheeks and squeezed. "Why are you crying?"

Did she tell him? She hadn't given her mother a second thought for years. Wrote her off the day she refused to help Grayce hide. The bitch had handed her over to Tyr once. She'd do it again. Was she angry? No.

Downright pissed.

Did she miss her mom? The idea of a mother, sure. Dawn? No.

Could she blame her? She wanted to. But the reality was, Dawn was a little off her rocker. A lot off her rocker. Bat shit crazy.

Stephen was better off without her.

Grayce decided it best not to say anything to Stephen. Not until she talked to the others anyway.

"I'm crying because you made me think about my mom, too." Wow, a brother. A fucking baby brother. A beautiful, bratty, perfect brother.

Stephen laughed and squished her cheeks, rolling them between his palms. "You look funny." Pushing them in and out, he mocked Grayce with a girlie voice. "Hi." Squish, squish. "I'm Grayce." Squish. "I'm sad."

He pulled her cheeks down to form a frown and laughed. He wrapped his arms around his stomach and rolled back on the couch in hysterics.

Grayce grabbed a yellow throw pillow and hit him over the head. "I don't sound like that."

She hit him again. Stephen grabbed a bigger blue pillow and hit her back. For the first time in her life, she had a pillow fight. And for the first time in many years, Grayce was having fun.

* * * *

Passerby's either stopped dead in their tracks or did a double take before they scurried away from the waiting room. The funk of agitated testosterone hung thick in the air and made for one hell of a do not disturb sign. Zander paced with a nervous twitch while Marcus did his best to stay out of the way.

"I need coffee." Marcus sulked. "You want anything?"

Zander shook his arms, cracked his neck and continued to forge a zig-zag pattern across the checkered tiles. "Fucking withdrawals."

Marcus clapped his shoulder. "Hang tight. This will be over soon. Come with me. It'll take your mind off the misery."

Like hell. He felt as if he'd been dipped in a barrel of honey then rolled through a field of fire ants. A jolly stroll through the hospital would do little to ease that torment. It would however, lessen the chance that he'd tear the fucking walls down while waiting for the Comptons to arrive.

As they waited for the elevator, several men turned in a quick, comical fashion and headed the opposite direction the moment they caught sight of him and his buddy. Opportunity for Zander and Marcus to appear in public together didn't present itself often, which by the looks on passing faces, was a good thing. Zander did his best to smile and appear friendly.

Marcus on the other hand, liked to play. On not so rare occasion, he'd flash his trademark evil eye to scare the shit out of people, just for fun. His high arched eyebrows were intimidating enough, but when cocked just right, not even Jason or Freddie Kruger would mess with him. Marcus prided himself the prankster and loved to make people squirm.

The down arrow above the doors flashed green. After the familiar yet annoying ding, they glided open. A tall woman with platinum blonde hair and porcelain glowing skin stepped off and entered the foyer, oblivious to the two giants standing less than three feet in front of her. With her nose planted in a book, she turned and glided down the hallway.

Zander waited for a crude remark from Marcus or detailed description of what he'd do to the woman if he ever got her alone. When it didn't come, he turned to find his friend slumped against the wall and holding his chest.

"What the hell happened to you?" He laughed. "See a smoking hot woman, you faint now?"

Marcus stared down the corridor with a dumb ass smile on his face.

"Oh shit." Zander knew that look. It was pathetic as fuck.

It was official. Marcus was off the market. The woman who'd just floated off the elevator, swept him off his feet and flat-out ignored him, was Marcus' soul mate. He could hear the collective shattering of hearts from women across the globe. This was a day Zander would mark on his calendar.

When it came to women, he and Marcus were polar opposites. Marcus loved women and lived for the hunt. He chewed 'em up, spit 'em out, moved on to the next one. As a man who broke hearts on a daily basis with playful enthusiasm, he never cared too much about finding his significant other. He used to tell Zander. "It'll happen when it happens. For now, I'm enjoying the ride." And he did.

Marcus shook his head and pushed himself from the wall. "I have to follow her."

Zander grabbed his arm and held him still. "It knocks you on your ass, doesn't it?" He embraced his friend and offered a congratulations before breaking the bad news. "You can't follow her. Not now. But hey, she was wearing a doctor's coat. Nikolas will know who she is."

Marcus growled. "I know. We're here for Grayce today." He punched his fist into his palm. "Let's do this thing and do it fast. I have a woman to claim."

Nikolas led Chelsea around the corner, arm in arm. When he caught sight of Chelsea's grim expression, a new knot formed in his gut. "Zander. I want to try something."

He glanced at Nikolas who nodded in approval.

"Okay Chelsea, what is it?" he asked, rubbing his arms brisk and hard. God he needed to get home.

"When we get close enough to Houghton, I'm going to open my mind to you. You'll see and feel what I do as it happens. It will overwhelm you at first. I'll filter people and shut them out as quick as I can. When we find him, I'll zero in." She grabbed his hands and squeezed. "Two minds are better than one. You may be able to pick up on something that I can't."

"I'm game. I'll try anything that'll get us closer to stopping that maniac."

"Good." She turned to Marcus. "Stay close to him in case it's too much." She hooked her arm back through Nikolas' and led the way.

The trip through the corridors of Mercy Mountain Medical Center proved difficult. The entire hospital staff respected and adored Nikolas and his wife. Friendly "hellos" and "good afternoons" came from every direction. A three minute walk turned into ten, but they made their way to the wing one floor below Houghton's room.

Chelsea held Zander's hand and blinked up with compassionate eyes. "Are you okay?"

He nodded. Aside from wanting to peel his own skin off, he was just peachy.

"Here goes."

An onslaught of thoughts and emotions flooded his brain and threw him off balance. Like a pussy, he grabbed Marcus to steady himself. Most impressions came at him like unclear photographs, but disappeared before he could process what he'd seen. Chelsea filtered through the insignificant thoughts like she was shuffling a deck of cards. Everything was a blur. Zander was forced to close his eyes. Marcus continued to hold him steady.

A piercing shiver shot up his spine and landed at the base of his skull. Everything froze.

For a moment, Zander floated on a cloud, surrounded by hazy, blurred images. He'd never used a drug in his life, but he imagined this was what it'd feel like.

"I think we found him," Chelsea whispered. "He's too drugged. We won't be able to get anything."

"Keep trying," Zander pleaded.

"Oh." Chelsea's voice trembled. "There's somebody with him."

As if he were a television, the channel changed and horrifying images invaded his psyche. Blackness, pain and blood inundated his thoughts. Followed by flashes of Grayce. His knees would've hit the floor if it weren't for Marcus.

As fast as they had come, the thoughts were gone. "I'm sorry. I can't do it. Oh God. What was that?" The tremor in her voice reflected the panic shredding his insides.

Fear bogged his brain, his skin prickled with dread. A horrifying black figure shimmied in his thoughts then disappeared.

"Zander. I'm so sorry you had to see that. It's all my fault." She clung to Nikolas.

A deadly, primal rage brewed in his chest, spread through his limbs. His arms and legs trembled with eruptive fury. "Nikolas. Get Chelsea home. Now."

"What the fuck happened?" Marcus released his grip on Zander.

"He's here," Chelsea sobbed.

"Z, don't do anything stu—" A bone chilling snarl cut Nikolas' sentence short.

"Did you just fucking growl?" Marcus snapped.

In a flash, Zander was nose to nose with Marcus. "You didn't see what he did to her." His chest tightened and he couldn't say another word. In that moment, Zander was no longer a civilized man. He was a brutal, barbarian warrior prepared for a bloodbath. His friends understood. They made no attempt to stop him. Grayce was in danger and that was unacceptable. Plain and simple. It's how they were built.

Marcus took a step back and held his hands up in surrender. "Go get him."

Chapter 11

It's inevitable. In everyone's life at one point or another, they find themselves at a crossroads where their souls are on the line. Decisions must be made that will not only have a profound effect on their future, but could also determine their eternal fate.

Zander faced that crossroads. Instinct told him Tyr must die. Instinct told him Houghton must die. Conscience told him taking a human life was wrong. Society told him murder was wrong.

He'd never given a shit what society thought.

What would Grayce think? He'd have to answer to her alone. Her opinion would be the one that mattered above all others.

His brief look into Tyr's memories burned horrifying, gut wrenching images into his mind. As those images stood forefront in his brain, he knew the right decision, the one proper course of action would be to strike those bastards from the face of the earth. He'd live with the consequences.

From the other end of the hall, he sized up the officers seated outside Houghton's door. The tall one slouched in his metal chair. One hand rested on his holster, the other scratched at his crotch. His partner, a stalky, balding older man, nodded off behind the pages of his hotrod magazine.

Although Zander was able to move fast enough to avoid detection by the cameras, even these two fuckups would be able to feel something if he rushed past. He needed nothing more than a few moments inside, but couldn't risk having the guards come in to check on their prisoner.

Fuck it.

Zander flew past, and knocked them each on the head. In the same heartbeat, he was in Houghton's room.

* * * *

Unease sat like a cement brick in Tyr's gut. Apprehension was an unacceptable character trait. It darkened his already sinister mood. If all went according to plan, Houghton's announcement to the media would draw his little dove from hiding.

The story was only broadcast a few short hours ago, but really, he had nothing better to do than wait. He wouldn't miss another opportunity to get her back. The current toy no longer gave him the buzz he needed and he'd grown extremely dissatisfied. She'd become a zombie right before his eyes. No longer showed fear. He would dispose of the useless bitch by day's end.

The greasy fat man in the bed mumbled something inaudible in his unconscious state then pulled at his restraints. His face contorted as if haunted by a dream.

A moment later, Tyr felt a prickle in his brain. A probing sensation. Odd.

Sitting with arms crossed and head held high, he recalled his play sessions with his little dove. What was it about her? He'd never been able to pinpoint it. What he did know was that she made him feel more alive. More powerful. Indestructible.

Memories of Grayce flooded his thoughts and gave birth to an erection. His ability to teleport surfaced after the first time he had his way with her. It took him weeks to understand that she alone was the trigger. The spark that started it all. The charge that kept his battery juiced. And that made him hate her all the more.

A whoosh of air snatched him from his reverie and before he could blink twice, the giant man from the gym was standing in the room. Even more spectacular up close, Tyr thought. Oh my, if only his playroom were ready, he'd drag the beast there right now. His imagination ran wild with possibilities.

The giant glanced at Houghton, who enjoyed a drug induced slumber, then back to Tyr. Blazing blue eyes promised a shit storm of wrath and fury.

"Today, you die." A crushing grip choked him as he was lifted off the floor. The beast had one hand around his neck, the other holding his belt.

Tyr rolled his eyes in mach disgust. It was obvious this gargantuan thing in front of him could do serious damage. He wasn't afraid. Fear was for the lesser. He drew his power from fear.

Words gargled up his trachea. "I can smell her all over you. She tastes exquisite, doesn't she? Like a fine wine."

Breathing was difficult but he feigned indifference. "Imagine what a team the three of us would make."

The hand at his throat constricted.

"This is for Grayce." The man with fierce blue eyes tensed his fingers with slow, torturous intent, and crushed his windpipe.

Tyr was no match for such physical strength. He would accept defeat, this time.

But never again.

When next they met, he'd be prepared. With the minuscule reserve of strength he had left, Tyr transported himself out of the death grip and into the safety of the tunnels. He was out cold the moment he hit the ground.

* * * *

Zander stood empty handed and dumbfounded.

What the fuck just happened?

Why didn't he snap the bastard's neck the second he entered the room? Why did he give the fucker a chance to speak?

He turned to the freak on the bed.

His fists clenched and unclenched, then clenched again. It was so unfair. He laid there, pumped full of drugs in peaceful slumber. Where was the justice in that?

Nikolas' words reverberated through his skull. "Don't do anything stupid." God, he wanted to kill this man. Rip him to shreds for what he was putting Grayce through.

Withdrawals wreaked havoc on his body, so intense he struggled to focus. He needed to get this over with and get back to Grayce.

Could he take somebody's life? Was that the man he wanted to be?

"Fuck!" Zander punched the wall and left a hole large enough to fit a basketball through. A gust of fresh air burst into the room.

With no concern for the man's comfort, Zander ripped Houghton's arms free of the cuffs. He didn't bother to remove his catheter or IV's. That was a kindness he didn't deserve.

He threw the convict over his shoulder, bare ass hanging out. In a matter of seconds, he dropped Houghton face down in the center of the prison recreation yard, naked as a jaybird and passed out cold.

Let the other inmates take care of the pile of shit.

His conscience was clear.

* * * *

Each time the pain reached intolerable on the "how much can she take" scale, Grayce brought her fire to the surface of her skin, let it hover long enough to burn away the withdrawals, then drew it back in again. Stephen slept warm and peaceful at her side, unaware of the torment she suffered.

"Grayce." Chelsea tiptoed into her line of sight.

"Holy shit." Pillows flew and Stephen twitched. "You scared the crap out of me."

"Lost in thought?" Chelsea giggled and looked at the mess. "You two have fun?"

Grayce nodded and rubbed the lingering tears from her face. Not quick enough to hide the evidence from Chelsea.

"What happened? Is everything all right?"

Grayce slumped.

Nikolas trailed in behind his wife and scooped the sleeping boy into his arms. "I'll take him to his room." With a kiss and a wink to his wife, he headed down the hall.

"I'll be there shortly, my love." The smile she flashed her husband brought a blush to Grayce's cheeks. Chelsea patted his firm ass when he passed, then replaced the vacant spot where Stephen had been curled up with her own rump. A loving arm wrapped Grayce's shoulder."You want to go first, or shall I?"

Laying a hand over Chelsea's, Grayce released a drawn out sigh. "You go first."

Chelsea proceeded to fill Grayce in on the happenings at the hospital. Listening with great difficulty, she tried to push the effects of her withdrawals to the back of her mind. She'd managed not to go insane yet, but if Zander didn't return soon, she might have to jump off a tall building.

"So that's it? You left and you don't know what happened?"

Oh fuck. This was bad.

"He wouldn't try to kill Tyr, would he?" Grayce wanted Tyr dead.

Duh.

But that burden shouldn't fall on Zander's shoulders. He represented what was good in this world. What would taking a human life do to him?

"I don't know. His rage was palpable, Grayce. There was no talking to him."

"Can you read him?" Grayce leaned her head into Chelsea's, wondering if this is what her mother's arms would have felt like, if she'd ever been able to offer comfort the way a mother should.

"No, he's too far away. As fast as he travels, he'll be here before I can read him anyway. He was a mess, from withdrawals I mean. I'm sure whatever he's doing, it's fast so he can get back to you." Chelsea paused and kissed Grayce's cheek. "Your turn."

"Oh Chelsea, I don't even know what to say." Clapping her hands to her face, Grayce sunk deeper into the couch cushion that she'd occupied for most of the afternoon. "Can you just read me?"

"I already have, but sometimes it helps to say it out loud." Chelsea snatched a pillow from the floor and fluffed it in her lap.

"He's my little brother. I have a brother."

"Nikolas tested his blood. We had our suspicions, but we didn't want to say anything until we knew for sure."

"What do we do? Do we tell him?"

"Let's discuss this with the men after they get back. It might be better to wait until some of this blows over."

"Chelsea, I still feel like I'm stuck in one big, crazy fever dream. I want to wake up."

Warm solid flesh enveloped her. Hot air caressed her skin. Faster than her heart could palpitate, Grayce was transported to the bedroom and pinned against the wall.

Plush lips brushed the sensitive spot behind her left ear and worked their way up her chin to her mouth. Eager hands were hard at work unbuttoning her jean shorts. As they slid down her hips and fell to her feet, a fevered ache pounded between her legs.

Powerful fingers made their way under her shirt and hunted down her breasts. As he thumbed her hard nipples, soft spasms danced in her abdomen.

Shit. Two seconds with Zander's hands on her and she was ready to come. The soft cotton of her baby-doll tank was no match for his determination to get her naked.

"That was my favorite shirt." She pouted.

"You say that about everything you wear. Can I just apologize now, for all the future clothing I'll shred? I need to be inside you." His lips traveled to her breasts. His rough tongue flicked across her hard nipple. He pulled it into his mouth and sucked until it was a taut peak. Grayce's knees buckled.

In a blink, she was sprawled across the bed. Zander stood to remove his shirt and for the first time, looked her in the eye.

"Firecracker. You've been crying. What happened? What's wrong?" Climbing over her naked body, he pressed a gentle kiss on her lips. "Tell me."

"Did you kill him?" Her trembling hands pressed against his heated abdomen.

His head sagged on his shoulders. "No. I wanted to...but...wait, is that why you were crying? You thought I killed him?"

"No, fuck no." The monster deserved to die. She'd never shed a tear for him.

"Why, then?" His worried eyes caught her gaze and reignited her desire.

"Can we talk about it after you make me come? At least twice?" Grayce faked a smile, hoping to ease his discomfort.

"You want to make love, baby?"

"No. I want you inside me, now. Fast. Hard. After that, do whatever the hell you want."

It took Zander two-seconds to remove the rest of his clothing and drive his sex deep. After the day she'd had, hard and fast was precisely what she needed. It was obvious by the force in which he pounded, that he needed it too.

That's exactly what he did, over and over, hard, deep, unrelenting. She came within minutes. So hard, her contractions drew him to the brink. He shuddered and froze, let her pull, squeeze and draw out every heated drop of his release.

As she relaxed, he pulled her close, rolled to his back and nestled her head between his pecs.

His heartbeat slowed, quieting her soul as it beat through her ear down to her heart. She'd take the soothing rise and fall of his chest over a rocking chair anytime. With the warmth of his skin, comfort of his chest and the lullaby of his heartbeat, Grayce drifted into dreamland.

Zander chuckled, then whispered. "Sleep, baby. There will be plenty of time for orgasm number two later."

Chapter 12

Blood pounded fierce and hard. With each throb, pain pierced his brain like a rail spike through the skull. A warm, sticky goo dripped from his chin as he lifted his face from the floor.

He'd never been in so much pain. Neck, throat, head. Felt like he'd been run over by a road roller. The darkness made it impossible to gauge his location. A ray of light peaked from under what he assumed was a door. Tyr waited patient and breathless for his vision to come into focus.

As his eyes adjusted, the table next to him took form.

The playroom. Perfect.

Standing took a considerable amount of concentration. Tyr grasped the wooden legs and struggled to gain his balance. The distance separating him from the light switch seemed insurmountable. His shoes stuck, then tore away from the mucky floor with nauseating resonance.

Tyr swayed and grabbed the wall to hold steady as he surveyed the room.

She was gone.

Impossible.

Blood dripped from the table, puddled on the floor and now seeped into the fibers of his Brioni suit. A trail of smeared footprints led out the door.

How did she get free? He'd left her on the fringe of death and tethered to the wall. He had thought he'd be coming back to a quick clean up and disposal job. With the amount of blood spilled, she couldn't have made it far.

His hook hung bloodied and filthy at the end of the table. A tingle rippled across his scalp. Resourceful little nugget, wasn't she? Must have ripped her skin to shreds trying to cut loose with that thing.

He'd underestimated his toy. Great little actress, that one, playing zombie like she did.

Fueled by adrenaline, Tyr stomped to the door and headed down the tunnel. The trail of spilt blood would make her easy to find. It was going to be fun punishing the bitch.

Punish her for the audacity at attempting escape.

Punish her for ruining his suit.

* * * *

Bones cracked and muscles protested as Grayce stretched under the weight of Zander's arm. Wow, sore would be an understatement. Who knew sex was a better workout than going to the gym?

Zander slept like a baby and didn't budge when she wiggled herself free.

A long steamy shower soothed her aches. She studied herself in the full length mirror as she toweled off.

Tracing the scars that zigzagged across her breasts, Grayce scrutinized her form. She'd never made a habit of looking at herself naked. In fact, that last time she'd done so was after her second visit to the emergency room. The stitches hadn't been removed and Frankenstein's Monster would have looked like Sophia Loren next to her. Grayce had made a vow never to look again.

Today, however, due to the afterglow of mind-blowing sex with a man too beautiful to be real, she found the courage to examine the body she'd spent so much time ignoring.

Breasts sat high and firm. Stomach tight, six pack tight. Arms and legs were lean and muscular, but still feminine. And her ass, holy shit it looked great. She'd never been partial to her backside. Until now.

Maybe, just maybe, there was something to this soul mates bullshit. Or perhaps she'd been hit by a car and was lying in a coma somewhere. Made more sense.

She grabbed the hairbrush from the shelf and pulled it through her hair. The tendrils fell in soft waves over her shoulders. It was pretty and the red highlights brightened her eyes. She'd never considered herself attractive before, especially not her hair.

Zander sauntered through the door naked and glorious. Planting a kiss on her head, he positioned himself behind her, took the brush from her hand and groomed her with long sleepy strokes.

Grayce froze. "Zander stop."

"What?" Eyes heavy with exhaustion met hers through the mirror.

"*He* used to brush my hair. Please, let me do it." It was an intimate act she wasn't ready to share. Baby steps, right?

"I'm sorry, love." He handed the brush back. "Can I watch?"

"Yes."

Hurt burned behind his sleepy gaze.

"Please don't take it personally." Time for a subject change. She turned to place the brush on the counter. Her breast pressed against his arm as she reached around and liquid heat churned in her abdomen.

"Do I look different?" Turning to face the mirror, she rubbed her rear with strategic precision against his steel frame.

"What do you mean?" His breath caught and he grasped her hips. Purple flashed through his retinas.

"Why do your eyes do that?" She tried to face him, but he held her in place.

"Do what?"

"They change. Turn purple. It's the second time that's happened."

He didn't answer. Instead his fingers dug into her hips and pulled her against a swelling erection that tickled her backside as it rose. His left hand splayed across her abdomen, holding her close, while the other slid up her torso and cupped her left breast.

"You haven't answered my question." She met his gaze again in the mirror. Hot damn he was sexy towering behind her, framing her pale body with his golden mass of muscle and skin.

He nipped her shoulder then trailed kisses to her neck, sending pleasure shivers straight to her nipples. "No. I haven't answered your question." His dimples came out to play.

Moisture spread between her legs.

When he rolled a hardened peak between his thumb and forefinger, her thighs clenched to absorb the spasms that pumped a swell of heated blood to her womb.

"What was the question?" His tongue traced the outer edge of her ear.

Fuck. Who could remember? "My body is changing, isn't it?"

"It's a perk. We get stronger when we bond. Healthier." His left hand slid lower and a finger-probed her moist folds. "Your stomach is tighter. Not that it wasn't perfect before."

She glared at his reflection. He was just trying to get laid now. Didn't he know he could have her without kissing ass? "We need to talk about yesterday."

"Now?" Warm, wet lips brushed against her cheek as he ground his hips against her backside.

"Yes," Grayce commanded and attempted to pull away.

"Shit baby, you're torturing me right now, you know that?" Shoulders slumped, he released her and let his arms drop to his sides.

With a huff, she stepped into the shower, turned on the double heads and side jets, and gestured for him to join her. Who cared if she'd showered already, they needed to do this.

His eyes twinkled with delight. "Are you going to wash me?"

"I'll wash if you talk." Standing at the shower door, she pointed for him to get in.

Craving skin to skin contact, she ditched the bath sponge and poured vanilla scented bath gel directly into her hands. Beginning with his chest, she massaged the heavenly scented soap into his perfect body.

"Talk."

* * * *

Zander found it challenging to form a sentence while Grayce's fingers worked their magic.

She covered every inch of his body with her delicate hands. Every touch, stroke, soft brush of her fingers sent a new ripple of life-giving energy through his flesh.

Somehow, he managed to spit out a detailed account of what happened at the hospital. She deserved the whole truth. He gave it. Even the internal struggle he fought about killing the fuckers.

"Grayce. I was going to kill them both. I was. For you, I was going to kill them. If that bastard hadn't vanished into thin air when he did, he'd be dead right now. If I hadn't hesitated... I shouldn't have hesitated—"

A soapy hand smacked his face and shocked him into silence. "Don't fucking talk like that." She doubled over and massaged her hand. "Ow. Will I ever learn?" Her red glow danced across her skin and spread through the shower stall.

"You slapped me."

"Yes, dammit." With a thrust and a grunt, she pushed at his chest. He didn't budge, but it warmed his heart that she kept trying.

"You are not a murderer Zander. Do you hear me? You are not a fucking cold-blooded killer." The burning fury in her eyes had his blood pumping hotter than humanly possible.

"Sit down." Grayce pointed to the shower floor.

"Here? Right here?" Disappointed at the turn in her demeanor, he shook his head.

"Yes," she snapped.

Bossy Grayce was kinda hot. He sat and leaned against the black slate.

"That's better." Her confidence seemed to grow tenfold now that she looked down at him rather than up. "You are the only good man I have ever known. If you kill somebody, even for me, it will change who you are forever. Guilt will eat you alive and then you won't be a good man anymore. You will be exactly like those fucking sick pricks. You couldn't live with it. I sure as hell couldn't live with it."

He tried to interrupt. "Grayce, listen. I—"

She was on a roll. Hell bent on releasing the words she needed to say. Determination gleamed in her fiery eyes. She held up a warning finger.

"You are a good man. I need you to stay good and sane and beautiful, because you're the only person in my life that's ever been that way. If you change, there's no hope for me. Do you understand? I'm broken. I'm damaged. You can't be. I need you to—" She threw her hands in the air. "Oh fuck it. Zander. I need you. Just you. Just the way you are."

Arms crossed, breath heavy, she waited for his response.

"You need me." He'd never heard sweeter words. "Grayce. Come here."

With a sigh, she knelt before him and rested her hands on his thighs. "You can't kill him. Please. I'm begging you. It would destroy any chance we have."

"Grayce. We have to stop him. You know that better than anyone. With his ability, a prison won't hold him. We don't know the full extent of his power yet."

"There is a way. There has to be. Promise me you won't do it. If he needs to die..." Grayce paused, her eyes glazed over, then drifted to the floor. After a long deep breath, she nodded and met him square in the eye.

"I need to be the one. It has to be me."

"What? No. No way in hell." He didn't doubt that Grayce was powerful enough and she certainly had just cause. But he'd burn in hell for eternity to protect her from that pain. "I'll be damned before I let you get anywhere near him."

"Zander, think about it. I'm damaged beyond repair. Because of him. It wouldn't be murder. It would be justice." Grayce's tone took a frightening turn. Her conviction burned through Zander like a blowtorch. In that moment, he realized, it was the only way she'd ever truly feel free.

"No. It's not an option. Absolutely not. We'll find a different way to stop him. Nikolas is the most brilliant man I know. He'll help us come up with something. We're done talking." The thought of her being anywhere near that monster made his soul swell with a dark, deadly rage, one he wouldn't be able to control.

Brushing hair from his face, he released an exasperated sigh. Excruciating seconds ticked by before he lifted his head and captured her heated glare.

"You've been naked in front of me for too long. If I don't make love to you right now, I might self combust." He pulled her up into his lap and brushed his lips against hers. "You need me. Sweetest words I've ever heard."

"Don't let it go to your head." Grayce lifted her hips and centered herself over his swollen cock. "This conversation isn't over."

Cupping her round, firm ass, he leisurely lowered her down his shaft allowing her body time to stretch and form a perfect grip. Oh shit, it was mind blowing, sweet torture.

"I love you, firecracker."

He knew all too well she wasn't able to offer a verbal reciprocation. He said it anyway. He loved her. She needed to know.

"I love you," he repeated. With a kiss, he silenced her response. The last thing he wanted was to make her feel pressured to speak those three life-altering words back to him. She wasn't ready. He was okay with that. Did it hurt him? No. What she couldn't communicate with words, over time she would reveal through actions.

They kissed with feral hunger as she swayed her hips back and forth, up and down. He supported her weight while she rode his entire erection.

Fuck she was warm. Slick. Tight. Heaven. Grayce wrapped her arms around his neck and pulled at his hair. Soft moans set his emotions into overdrive as she unraveled him bit by glorious bit. His head spun and blood pounded in his ears so fierce, it drowned out the thunder of the water. Her skin glowed brighter and hotter with each thrust. Her petite body threw off so much heat, the water turned to steam before it hit the floor.

Holding her tighter, he thrust his hips and drove deeper inside her. He'd never be deep enough, couldn't possibly get enough of the glorious creature.

As his release built, he cupped her face and forced her to look at him. She cried. She tried to look away, to hide her tears.

"Look at me Grayce." He needed the connection. Needed to see into her soul when she came.

"Grayce, come for me. I'm about to explode." This time, it was him lost in her hazel gaze, mesmerized by the shimmer. Something shifted, danced across her retinas, then Grayce cried out his name and her body tightened and spasmed around his sex. He let go. They climaxed together, becoming one. In that suspended moment, he saw her wholly and completely. Every detail from birth to the present was downloaded into his brain. Her memories became his, the good, the godforsaken.

Her red glow burst into a brilliant white light and shattered the glass shower wall. They both collapsed, panting and depleted of any will to move or speak.

It was then that Zander let his tears fall.

* * * *

"Stevie," the redheaded girl yelled from behind the door, "come outside and play."

Knock. Knock.

"Come on. Let's play."

Stephen concentrated hard on tying his shoes. "I can't right now. I have to train." He stood, placed his feet together and compared laces on each foot.

"Please, come outside and play with me. I have to show you something." She knocked again, a bit softer than before.

"No. Not now. Shayde is coming. I have to practice." Jeez. Didn't she get it? Duh. No time to play. Busy trying to save everyone. Girls were such a pain.

"Maybe later?" Her voice saddened.

Oh great. She's gonna cry now. "Yeah, maybe later." After he tucked his blue shirt with the red superman symbol into his jeans, he puffed his chest.

That's how Marcus did it.

Muscles flexed, he turned from side to side and admired the view in the hallway mirror. Yeah, just wait. He'd be bigger than him in no time.

"Ok. I'll come back later," the girl shouted. He watched through the window as she skipped across the lawn. Red pigtails bounced behind her. Before crossing the street, she stopped, turned to him and flashed a joyful grin.

Stephen's heart stopped beating when a black cloud rose from the street behind her. With all his might, he pounded his fists on the window. "Wait! Come back."

The mist crept over her feet, twisted its way up her legs, over her shoulders and around her neck.

"Come back! Run!" Stephen screamed.

She couldn't hear him.

Before it engulfed her, it smiled at him with grotesque rows of teeth. And just like that, she was gone.

"No."

Stephen jumped, pillow clutched to his chest. His heart pounded like a drum and his pajamas were sticky from sweat. These dreams were not fun. Not. At. All.

He tiptoed to the kitchen for a drink. To his surprise, Marcus and Nikolas were sitting at the table playing a game of cards. "Hi." He rubbed his eyes. The bright light forced him to squint. "I need a drink."

Marcus beamed at him. "What's up dude? Can't sleep?" He jumped up to grab a glass. Stephen shook his head no.

"We can't either."

"Marcus has his mind on a lady. That's why he can't sleep." Nikolas chimed in. "I can't sleep because Marcus won't shut up about it." Pulling a chair out, he gestured for Stephen to sit. "What's going on with you, little man?"

"I'm dreaming about Shayde again." Stephen hated admitting to the men he was having bad dreams. But at least they'd understand why he needed to keep training.

"I think I'm supposed to stop him. I think that's why I keep having the dreams." He cocked his head to meet Nikolas in the eye. The doctor had an answer for everything. He'd know what to do.

"Well..." Nikolas rubbed his chin. "Can you tell me more about your dreams?"

"One time I was in a coffee store with Chelsea. We were drinking hot chocolate and he came through the floor. One time, I was in the park. This time, I was in a house. Shayde comes. But he's not a man. He's like a big black, drippy cloud. And he sucks everybody in. And they disappear. Then he gets bigger." He stopped to inhale. "The red girl is always there—"

"Whoa, whoa, whoa." Marcus threw his hands in the air. "What red girl? What do you mean?"

"She has super long red hair. And I think she's my friend. She always wants to play. And she's always smiling at me." He scrunched his nose in disgust. "Her red hair is so cool. Like fire. But gross, she's a girl. I don't have time to play with girls."

The men laughed. He wasn't trying to be funny, but, whatever.

"Stephen, let me think about these dreams of yours. We can talk more about it tomorrow." Nikolas gave him a firm pat on the shoulder.

"Please, do tell us more about the girl, though." Marcus winked.

"I don't want to talk about girls." Stephen took one last gulp of water and hopped from his chair. He made sure to puff his chest as he passed Marcus. "Good night."

"Hey, Stephen. We're going to town tomorrow. You want to come along?"

"Yes." He yawned.

"Good. We'll go after breakfast." Marcus gave him a knuckle tap.

Nikolas cocked his head and glared at Marcus. "That's low, brother," he said, shaking his head, "using a child to woo your woman."

"I don't know what you're talking about." Marcus laughed. "The little guy needs to get out of here for a while. Don't worry, he'll be safe. And just for the record, I don't need any help when it comes to the wooing."

"I won't argue with you on that one. Unless you use the word woo in front of her. You sound like a pussy." Nikolas cleared glasses from the table.

Marcus lipped the words "fuck you" to Nikolas. Stephen laughed and shook his head. "I saw that." Grayce's potty mouth seemed to be rubbing off on everyone.

"Sorry, little man." Marcus messed Stephen's hair. He batted his hand away. "Come on, I'll walk you back to your room."

"Goodnight boys, I gotta go woo Chelsea." Nikolas headed in the opposite direction.

"Hey, Marcus." Stephen had to run to keep up.

"Yeah, buddy."

"What's a pussy?"

* * * *

Zander settled next to Grayce in bed.

Damn. Even snoring like an angry warthog she was sexier than sin. As he kissed the top of her head and pulled her snug, he fought to block the tormenting images from her past. Not only did he see her memories, he felt every emotion.

How could anyone live through that? What Tyr did was beyond abuse, beyond control, beyond sadism.

Evil personified.

No, evil was too gentle a word. The psychopath pawned her to the highest bidder. Leveraged her to build his empire. Drew pleasure from her pain. Flourished in her fear. A shiver wracked Zander to the very depths of his soul.

He would avenge her. If it meant she'd never forgive him, he'd find a way to live with that. The hell she'd suffered through—fuck. No wonder she was a ball of raw nerves.

He considered and appreciated the fortitude it took her to get through a day, let alone years. The resolve and courage it took to stay here with him, with his extended family. He couldn't fathom how she'd held it together. How she'd stayed sane.

She had strength in spades. No lesser human could've survived. Hell, he couldn't have survived. Grayce possessed something special. There was a higher purpose for his lady, that was for damned sure.

He pulled her tighter against his chest, closed his eyes but didn't sleep. It would be a long while before he'd be able to erase the images from his mind. It'd be even longer before he'd feel peace enough to slumber.

He'd thought the spontaneous bout of bawling that struck him in the shower would've cleared some of the shit from his head. Turned out, it only made him feel worse.

He hated feeling vulnerable. Hated that he cried like a pussy in front of Grayce, that he couldn't bear the weight of her pain even for the brief exchange.

She held him, didn't say a word, didn't tell him everything would be all right. She hugged him tight and let him cry. When it was over, when the tremors stopped, she left him shriveled and depleted on the shower floor and went to bed.

Knowing her, she was pissed to no end that he now knew every gory detail of her past. To talk about it would hurt worse than rubbing a shitload of salt into unhealed wounds.

He was okay with never talking about it.

* * * *

Mountains of pancakes, gallons of maple syrup, stacks of bacon and heaps of scrambled eggs lasted all of ten minutes at the breakfast table. Stephen worked with vigor on his third helping in his quest to keep up with the men. He'd already outgrown the clothes Chelsea bought him a few days ago.

Grayce watched him mimic Zander as he swigged his second glass of orange juice, glanced at Chelsea to make sure she wasn't looking, then wiped his mouth with the back of his hand. It was unbelievable how much he'd changed in a matter of days. His skin was brighter, face fuller, and he'd grown at least an inch taller.

Clearing her throat to get the attention of the adults in the room, Grayce fiddled with her fork. "Stephen, you finished?"

"Yeah." The boy rubbed his stomach and pushed his half empty plate away from him. "I'm too full."

Nikolas shot her a nervous glance. She offered a nod of encouragement.

"We need to have a talk." He gestured around the room. "Grayce and I have something very important to tell you."

Stephen fidgeted in his chair, eyes wide, mouth crinkled at the corners.

"Okay." Stephen straightened his shoulders.

"The other night you told Grayce about your mom? Do you remember?" Nikolas asked.

"Um, yes." Stephen's face paled.

"Well, Grayce realized then that you were describing her mom as well." Nikolas paused, giving the boy a moment to respond. When he got nothing but a blank stare, he continued. "I've done blood tests on both of you. You know, when you were in the hospital downstairs?"

"Yes." Stephen rubbed a worried look from his face.

"Come on, enough beating around the bush." Grayce pushed her chair from the table and turned toward Stephen. "You are my little brother. Your mom is my mom. We're family. Do you understand what I'm saying? I'm your big sister." Glancing at Zander and then Nikolas, she flashed a smug smile. "There, that was easy enough."

Stephen stared at Grayce, blinked once, twice. She imagined giant gears in his brain ticking and grinding as he processed the information. He looked back to Marcus, then to Zander and back again to Grayce.

"Did my mom send you away too? Is that why you didn't live with us?" Stephen looked anguished, but not for himself, for her. Her heart sunk.

"Well, yes, sort of," Grayce lied. No need for Stephen to know the truth about why she left. That was her cross to bear, not his.

"Do you miss her?" Laying his hand on her forearm, his hazel eyes bore right through her hardened exterior and found a soft mushy spot dead center in her chest.

"Yes. I do," she lied again.

Stephen slouched in his chair, strummed his fingers on his knees and swung his legs back and forth underneath him. Uncomfortable silence consumed the room. All eyes were on the boy.

With head lowered, he raised his gaze to Nikolas. "Why did you test our blood?"

Nikolas paused before answering and studied the boy's face. He looked as awestricken as Grayce felt. What a smart child. "Well Stephen, I study blood. Mostly of people like us. When we found you outside and brought you here, I took some of yours to study. So I could learn more about you. I noticed you and Grayce had similar traits right away, but at that time, I wasn't sure why. Now we know. It's because she's your sister."

"But there's more, isn't there." His tone and demeanor changed to that of a person well beyond the maturity of Stephen's meager six years.

Nikolas folded his hands on the table and cocked his head to the side. "What do you mean?"

"There's more about our blood. It's different, right? We're special. I've heard you talk about it."

"Yes. We know that you both have healing qualities. We know that Grayce has a special affect on males. I would like to run more tests, if that's all right with you and Grayce, of course."

"Yes, I like the lab. Superheroes always have secret laboratories." And with that, Stephen was back to the little boy with big dreams.

"Yes they do, don't they?" Nikolas' mouth twisted at the corner.

The boy continued his questioning. "Are there a lot more of us?"

"We know a few others."

Stephen leaned toward Nikolas, to make sure he was paying attention. "You should call them. You should invite them over right now."

"Stephen, why the urgency?"

Stephens eyes widened. "The bad guys are coming."

At that comment, Chelsea stood to clear the dishes. "That's enough for today. Help me clear this mess so you boys can head to the hospital."

"Yes ma'am." Marcus jumped up like a stick of dynamite was lit under his ass. "Hospital. It's about freakin' time."

"Yes ma'am." Stephen popped out of his chair, grabbed his plate and glass and plopped them in the double stainless steel sink. He ran to Grayce, threw himself into her lap and wrapped his arms around her neck. "I'm happy you're my sister." His cheeks flushed and he jumped down. "I'll go put my shoes on. Don't leave without me," he shouted as he skidded down the hallway.

"I think that went well," Chelsea declared after Stephen was clear of earshot. "Honey, you need to buy him some new clothes while you're out today. He's growing so fast."

"What now?" Grayce whispered. "What about our mother? He's hell bent on finding her."

"Do you know where she is?" Zander rested his chin on his clasped hands.

"No. Honestly, with her lifestyle, I thought she'd be six feet under by now." Grayce hadn't given her mother any thought in years. She sure as shit wasn't keen on the idea of starting now.

"Do you think we can find her?" Chelsea chimed in.

"I don't want to find her," Grayce snapped, folding her arms over her chest. She didn't want Stephen to find her either. Stephen belonged with them.

"If we don't, Stephen will. He'll try on his own." Zander was right. The boy was all about saving his Mom. He talked about it day and night. Like it was his sole purpose for being.

"I know, you're right." Grayce slouched. "I left her in California. We used to move. All the fucking time. She could be anywhere. Dead for all we know." Shaking her head, she tried to imagine what her brother's life must have been like, watching his mother jump from man to man, crappy home to crappy home. "It's a miracle that Stephen found us. A boy his age left to fend for himself—"

Marcus interjected. "No not a miracle. He was drawn to us, just like we were drawn to you, Grayce. I think the little guy is right when he says the bad guys are coming. A storm is brewing. It's drawing us together. You can feel it Chelsea, can't you? That's why you cut him off."

Chelsea sighed deep and slow, her cheerful countenance morphing to a scowl. "Yes. I've sensed something. Something dark. It's not just Tyr Collins. I have a feeling this is only the beginning."

Chapter 13

The grass was soft and wet under Grayce's backside, the cool moisture a balm on her heated skin. She'd enjoyed her morning traipse near the newly relocated lake with Zander and Stephen. Would even venture to say she'd had fun. Upon their return, the boys, as usual, made a beeline for the kitchen. Grayce stole the opportunity to stretch in her favorite patch of lawn and enjoy some testosterone free time.

Emotion churned through her in rolling waves of contradiction as she pondered the past few weeks. Rage. Contentment. Fear. Apathy. Lust.

It was amazing her head hadn't exploded yet. Yeah, super glue and duct tape had nothing on her when it came to holding shit together, the few bouts of nearly burning everyone alive excluded.

In the past week, no more women had been found dead or reported missing. John Houghton was no longer making national headlines. Maybe Zander scared Tyr off.

Okay. So she wasn't one hundred percent convinced that was the case. Too easy.

Regardless, she'd had more time to process the turn of events in her life. First, there was her power, which would be freaking awesome if she could control the urge to incinerate everyone who pissed her off. And hey, she could be helpful if they ever ran out of matches in the house. Then there was Stephen. An innocent child who escaped an incapable mother only to land in the hands of an unqualified sister. Thank God for Chelsea. She was like the mother of all mothers. Stern when she needed to be, adoring and encouraging every other second of the day. Third, a new home filled with every amenity imaginable and came stocked with an instant family. That was still blowing her mind.

Last, and definitely not least, Zander.

What would she do about Zander? He was a good man. He loved her. At least he thought he did.

Was she even capable of that emotion? Zander was getting the raw end of the deal in that department. He needed to be with someone who could love him back, right?

Soul mates—there was that too. Eternity was a long fucking time to be stuck with someone. Seemed a bit unfair. What if her un-repairable, screwed up psyche wasn't capable of hanging with a man for that long? Would she die from withdrawals if she left? Would it kill Zander?

She uprooted a fistful of grass and tossed it in the air. Maybe she should leave and never look back. Disappear for Zander's sake. He needed, no deserved, so much more than she could offer. Surrounded by friends and family, he beamed with genuine happiness. And he was so amazing with Stephen, a natural father.

The man was born to breed.

Tyr made sure that Grayce would never bear children. That alone should be enough to make Zander reconsider their eternity together.

No, he was far too honorable to let her infertility be an issue.

Tyr wasn't gone. He lurked in the dark shadows and bided his time.

Zander wouldn't let her kill the black beast, but she sure as hell wouldn't let the burden fall on his shoulders. She'd have to disappear. It was the best option. Tyr would follow her, then everyone in Chastain would be out of danger. With her new found power, there wasn't a doubt in her mind she could take him down.

Could she put Zander through that kind of pain? Not just emotional, but physical? She could bear the withdrawals. They had nothing on the pain she'd suffered. But was it fair to inflict that pain on Zander?

If it meant no more Tyr, hell yeah, it was fair.

Stephen? Everyone loved the hell out of him and would lay down their own lives for his safety. The funny little brat completed their makeshift family, like he'd been part of it all along.

Was she capable of offering him all he needed?

No.

Besides, if he stayed, he'd grow up learning how to be a decent man like Zander. Grayce couldn't teach him how to be a man. Hell, chances were she'd screw up his brain with her fuckedupness. Her hatred of men would, without doubt, have an effect on their relationship. Food on the table? Safe place to sleep? Nah, wasn't gonna happen. The boy was far better off without her.

There had to be a way around this.

What was Nikolas' theory on the mated connection? Blood? Yes, that was it. *It has something to do with our blood, although we haven't been able to pin it down.* He had explained in dummied-down terms for her one day in the lab when she had complained about the withdrawals.

Oh shit. It couldn't be that easy, could it?

Her blood.

That settled it. Grayce jumped from the spongy grass and headed back inside.

* * * *

After clearing the lunch mess, Stephen challenged Zander to some Mario Kart Racing. With his devilish, sexy grin, Zander invited Grayce to join them. Pretending to be put off, she rolled her eyes and waved them off. "Go have fun. I'm going to take a nap."

"I'm taking you down this time, little man." Zander threw Stephen over his shoulder and jogged toward the game room. "I'll see you soon, Firecracker," he shouted. Stephen giggled and waved as he bounced away.

Well, that was easy.

Grayce waited until they were out of sight, then snuck down the back stairs to the lab. Thank God she'd been programmed into the security system last week. She searched the stark white walls trying to remember which panel held the vials of blood.

Bingo.

Four was the magic number.

Keeping one eye on the door, she searched the labels for her name and grabbed the vial with the most recent date. She tucked the little glass bottle into her pocket with a shaky hand. A bead of sweat tickled her brow. Heat and electricity pounded against her insides. Begged to be released. Fuck. This had to be quick.

The distance to the bedroom seemed like miles. Heart pounding, throat tight, she dug through Zander's drawers. Because of the ferocious tremble in her hands, it took eons to find what she was looking for.

A gold, heart-shaped locket. Zander showed it to Grayce a few days ago after a marathon sex session. He must have been feeling sentimental. Inside was a picture of Zander's parents taken on their wedding day. His father had given it to his mother on their tenth anniversary. The one item of his mother's he'd kept after they were killed.

Grayce had told him it was sappy, but deep down she was jealous of his cherished memories. She removed the photo and tucked it in the back of the drawer. It was the picture he held dear, not the jewelry.

The bathroom shrunk around her as she locked herself in. "Please forgive me," she whispered under her breath. It took a tender touch to pry the vial open without breaking it. The blood dripped slow and thick into one half of the heart shape. After it was filled to her satisfaction, she closed the locket and laid it on the tile.

The red energy took several long moments to conjure. When it boiled through her veins and churned in anticipation, she took a practice run and traced the outer edge of the locket. She traced the rim again, allowing a zap of heat to escape through her fingertip. Slow and steady she dragged it around the seam, melting the gold and sealing it tight.

There, that should do it. The half empty bottle of blood was wrapped in toilet tissue and placed in the trashcan. A pang of guilt squeezed her chest.

No time for cheesy emotions.

This was best for everyone, she reminded herself. She undressed, placed the locket under her pillow and waited. Zander would be along soon. He couldn't leave her side for too long. Her body was already flushed and warm with the thought of making love—no, no, no—fucking him. Her gut clenched with a violent twist. This was going to be their last time. She rubbed away the threatening tears.

Leaving was the right thing to do. She was a disaster and he was perfect. He needed somebody equally flawless. She imagined him with a wife, kid and a ridiculous dog. Labradoodle perhaps. His bitch of a wife would be tall and blond. They'd picnic. He'd have a young, blue-eyed boy sitting on his lap. Happy and laughing. That's how it should be. He deserved that life.

Tyr would follow her, no more women would die, and she'd kill him. Simple.

Grayce jumped when the door slammed and before she turned to look, Zander was sprawled naked by her side.

"Firecracker, had I'd known you'd be here like this, I would've cut my gaming session short." He trailed his finger down the length of her scar and back up. Prickles of burning heat followed its path.

"Do you like dogs?" She rubbed his scar. He quivered under her touch.

"Not particularly fond of them, why?" He chuckled. "You want a dog, baby?"

"Hell no. Just curious."

* * * *

Zander had wrapped a protective arm and leg around Grayce and succumbed to a deep sleep. She waited. And waited.

When his soft shallow breaths became deep and steady and the weight of his body melted into the mattress, she inched her way out from under his heavy arm.

She retrieved the necklace from under the pillow and wrapped it twice around his wrist before clasping it. Her fingers lingered over the thick veins of his wrist. A pounding ache swelled in her chest as her heart beat in time with the pulse beneath her fingertips. Only when she'd memorized the rhythm of blood flow drumming through the blue vessels beneath his skin did she release him.

The letter was harder to let go. She'd pained over it earlier, and now clutched it to her chest like a precious gem. Would it matter? She was leaving. Would her words matter when she'd all but ripped his heart out of his chest, chewed and spit it out like a wad of gum?

Not in the slightest. But he deserved an explanation, pathetic as it may be.

She laid it on the dresser, put her clothes on in a frenzy and threw her backpack over her shoulder.

She stole one last look at his naked physique. His shoulders spanned half the bed and caramel skin stretched over mounds of fierce, commanding, indestructible power. Unlike Tyr, Zander chose not to exploit his gift for his own gain. Instead, it was used to protect and worship her.

She was walking away.

"I'm sorry," she whispered and closed the door behind her. Her legs didn't move until she once again convinced herself that she was doing this for him.

* * * *

Grayce trekked through the forest, confident she was headed in the right direction. Well, at least fifty percent sure. Her immediate goal was to put as much distance as possible between her and the house. Sure, she could've taken one of their vehicles and driven away, but it was safe to assume they were equipped with high tech tracking devices. A chance she wasn't willing to take.

If her theory was correct, the blood she'd left with Zander would prevent him from waking from withdrawals. He was sleeping like a baby when she left, wearing a shit-eating grin, thank-you-very-much. There should be plenty of time to either hike or thumb a ride far enough away that it would be impossible for Zander to find her.

Needle in a haystack.

If she did make it to town, her hot wiring skills were rusty, but she should be able to procure a vehicle and get herself the hell out of Dodge easy enough.

Fuck, he was going to be mad.

Her heart wrenched at the thought of causing him pain.

He loves me. She shook the thought from her head. Grayce didn't do love. This was the best thing she could do for him and for Stephen.

She put her headphones on, hoping the music would drown the voices in her head. Bastards were trying to change her mind.

The feeling she was being followed turned into a nag, then a relentless pounding rhythm between her ears. She needed to get further away. Her jog morphed into a full on sprint.

It was only a matter of time until withdrawals kicked in. Although she deserved to suffer, with luck, she'd be able to push through them. The running should help. Concentrating on the music, she tried to keep pace with the tempo and ignore the branches that whipped her face and legs.

Keep going, keep going.

Eminem's "Shake That" played on repeat to remind her how much she hated men and to push her harder. Running full force, Grayce wasn't out of breath or the slightest bit fatigued. She looked down.

Holy shit.

Her body glowed and the ground passed under her feet in a blur. She couldn't fathom how she traveled so fast, but who was she to question the gift?

At this rate, she'd be in another state before Zander woke up. Hopefully, tracking your lover wasn't a perk of being bonded. That would suck for her. Up ahead, she spotted a hunting cabin. It was small, weathered and judging by its dilapidated appearance, abandoned. She screeched to a halt before tripping over a shorthaired pointer stretched on his back with paws in the air. The dog jumped to attention and pounced toward her with tail wagging and tongue flopping.

"Hi there fella." Grayce squatted and held out a hand, palm up, toward the creature. A quick sniff and lick, then he pushed his hind quarters into her thigh, begging for a good rub.

The snap of a twig had her hairs standing on end. Jerking around, she fell on her ass. The pooch, unconcerned about the sound, made quick work of licking her wherever he could find bare skin.

"Stop." The harder she pushed him away, the more determined he became to climb in her lap. After managing to push herself up, she scoured the tree line. Someone or something was coming her way.

Zander. Seriously? How did he find her? Her thighs coiled to run.

"Grayce." A small voice called out. "Grayce, wait."

Shit.

Straightening her back, she looked over her shoulder. Stephen huffed and puffed. "Where are you going?" Heartbreak riddled his dirty little face.

"What are you doing here?" she asked. As he approached, she dropped to her knees and grabbed his arms. "Did you follow me?"

He nodded, still gasping for air.

"From the house? You followed me from the house?"

He nodded, mouth open wide to draw oxygen.

"How in the hell did you keep up?"

"I don't know. I saw you leave and I wanted to go with you. I was calling you, but you didn't hear me." Tears bubbled over, forging streaks through the dirt on his skin. "I thought you were running away. You kept going faster so I kept going faster."

Grayce dropped to her ass in the dirt and pulled him next to her. The happy fleabag licked Stephen's face and plopped down at his side.

"Well, this sure screws up my plans." She picked up a rock and threw it at the cabin.

"Where are you going?" By the intensity of his tears, Grayce was certain he already knew the answer.

No use trying to hide the truth. Maybe it was better he heard it from her than anybody else. "I'm leaving, Stephen. I can't stay here." Can't stay anywhere for that matter.

He sniffed and wiped his nose with the back of his hand. "I'll come with you."

"No." Grayce shook her head. "I can't promise you'll be safe. I can't feed you or give you a home to live in." It would be even worse with her than it had been with their mother. He was so young. How could she make him understand?

"But I can keep you safe," he stated. "Zander said it's our job to keep you and Chelsea safe. I'm your brother. I should go with you." He gazed at her as a father would his child, with imploring wisdom, like his was the only acceptable truth.

Her eyes blurred with the sting of his words. Of course he would see it that way. He'd been learning from the best. She pulled him into her arms. "You are such an amazing little man. Don't ever change. Promise me." She kissed his sweaty head and they sat like that until Stephen's sobs slowed.

Now what? How was she going to get out of this one? Her phone buzzed against her left butt cheek. Great, that will be Zander, she thought. The buzzing stopped and the ringing started.

Knowing the opportunity for escape had passed, she groaned and stood to pull the phone from her back pocket. Stephen snatched her free hand and held it tight. She squeezed back to let him know she wasn't going to bolt again.

With trembling hands she pushed the accept button. "Hi."

"Fucking hell, Grayce. Where are you? What the hell were you thinking?" His tone was fierce, deadly even, with the slightest undertone of fear. How did he know? She'd been gone for what? Maybe twenty minutes?

She sighed in defeat.

"You're scaring the shit out of me right now. Where are you?" he asked with a growl.

Her skin prickled, not from fear but with shame for what she'd done. That, and embarrassment for not getting away with it.

"I'm sorry, Zander."

* * * *

Sweat beaded his forehead. Tremors of rage made it difficult to hold the phone without reducing it to dust. Zander grabbed the bedpost with his free hand and snapped it like a twig.

Well, that didn't help.

He hurled the entire bed through the window, out across the lawn. A blast of fresh air blew across his skin.

That was more like it.

"Fuck the apologies right now. Where are you?" He paced the room, ready to dash as soon as she told him which way to go. Looking down, he realized he hadn't dressed yet. Shit. He grabbed his boxers off the floor and pulled them on, trying not to fall over.

"We're by a hunting cabin. East. I travelled east, I think." Her voice quivered. Good.

"Wait, what do you mean, we?" He heard a child's scream on the other end of the receiver. "Grayce. Grayce." There was a crumpling sound, followed by scratching.

"Zander!" Stephen's scream echoed through his ear. Then, dead silence.

"Stephen! Grayce!" In seconds, Zander stood half naked in front of the cabin. Her cell lay in pieces on the ground at his feet. A dog whimpered and cowered toward him with head down and tail tucked tight between his legs.

His heart stopped beating. "Grayce!" he called, cupping his mouth with both hands. "Stephen!" His voice boomed so ferocious it sent the dog running in the opposite direction. Eyes and ears on high alert, he turned circles and forced the air back into his lungs. He made kindling of the door as he entered the log home. It was empty, but hadn't been for long. The scent of expensive cologne collided with the fetor of must and aging pine.

"Mother. Fucker." Zander stormed back outside and gave the doorframe a punch as he passed through. He was home before the old, tired bones of the shack had crumbled to the ground, reduced to dust and rubble.

Chapter 14

"My little dove. Welcome home. I'm so pleased to have you back where you belong." The words slithered off his tongue and violated her ears.

Every muscle spasmed in unison.

No, please, no.

Her first response was to retreat to the dark corner in her mind where she used to ride out the sessions in the playroom. To hide inside herself, blanket her soul with the darkness, until the bad part was over.

She knew better than to pull at the leather cuffs binding her wrists and ankles to the wall.

The room hadn't changed in the three years she'd been gone. Except for the smell. That was different. Mold and dirt. Odd. Tyr had always been a clean freak.

She sucked in a deep breath and started her mantra, *"you are stronger than the pain, you are stronger than the pain."*

A child's scream pulled her from a relapse into the darkness. Her heart beat violent punches against her chest and dread pooled in her gut. No, he wouldn't. He couldn't. Breaking the first rule of the playroom, she looked Tyr straight in the eyes. Unable to find her voice, she mouthed the word *no.*

His face twisted into a horrifying grimace, like he wanted to smile but didn't know how. He retracted his arm and with the slightest flick of his wrist, slashed the whip across her breasts.

"Eyes down." The threat in his voice terrified her more than the bite of the scourge. Shivers of pain bit through her flesh. On a sharp inhale, her gaze dropped to the floor. The lingering sting from the strike disappeared as her fire emerged. Melted the pain. Caressed her aching body and spirit.

"Good girl." Stepping forward, the monster bit her ear lobe, not hard enough to draw blood, but enough to make her wince. "Next time, I'll remove those eyes." A slender forefinger traced the top of her left brow. "If you're blind, you won't be able to escape."

Another bellow came from outside the room. "Oh my little dove. It appears I'm being called away."

Grayce watched his feet as they crossed the room to the closet. Recognition flared with the familiar click as he hung the whip back into its clip.

"I'll be back very, very soon." He headed for the door. "It appears you have yet another man in your life. Spirited little pest, this one. I might just let him watch once he's been tamed." Grayce looked up as the door closed behind Tyr. The hallway wasn't the same as she remembered. This wasn't the same house. He'd moved his torture chamber.

A churning, rolling heat swelled deep in her nucleus. A sensation she no longer feared. With a bravery that surprised her, she willed it through blood and bones and begged it to hurry.

* * * *

Zander stormed into the living room. His anger, amplified through his footsteps, rattled the walls. "Fuck. How did this happen? What on earth was she thinking?" A trail of curse words followed the path his mindless pacing created.

"You want to find her?" Chelsea yelled at him. "You need to calm yourself down. I can't concentrate with you hovering." She planted fisted hands on her hips and growled up at him. "Your emotions are too raw and overpowering right now. Give me some space." She rubbed her temples and closed her eyes.

Shocked at Chelsea's outburst, Zander planted his half naked form on the couch. Head hung low, he studied the necklace Grayce had fastened around his wrist. She tried to leave him. Did he do this? Did he drive her away?

"I shouldn't have told her I loved her. She needed more time." The pendant shimmied in the light as he twisted it between his fingers. What's with the necklace? Was she trying to tell him something?

"What the fuck is taking Nikolas so long to get here?" He glanced at the clock. "It's been over an hour. I have to get back out there. I have to keep looking..."

Chelsea snapped her eyes open. "An hour? Already?" With a deep breath she crossed the room and sat next to him on the sofa. "Zander, you don't seem to be having withdrawals yet." Her delicate touch offered no consolation as she rubbed his arm.

"Shit. I didn't think about that." He should've been writhing in pain by now, agitated out of his mind. "No. I'm not having withdrawals." Fear gripped his chest, squeezed hard, and wrung the blood and life out of his heart like a wet towel.

Nikolas and Marcus stormed into the room chests heaving, eyes wild with worry. Nikolas at once had Chelsea trapped in a loving embrace. "Lover, what happened?"

"Oh, Nikolas. We're not sure. Grayce left. Stephen was with her. They were there one second, then they were gone. I can't feel them. I can't pick up on them."

Marcus wrapped a solid arm over Zander's shoulder. "How you holding up, my man? You must be in misery right now."

"I'm not having withdrawals. What does that mean? Does that mean she's dead?" A panic worse than he'd known possible burned like acid through his sanity.

Nikolas' green eyes darkened with unspoken anguish. "Doesn't make any sense. If she were dea—gone, you would feel it. The pain would be unbearable. No. She's not gone. She's not." He shook his head as if that action alone would make his words truth.

"I need to get back out there. I've circled town twice, the mountain too, but maybe I missed something. I'll take Chelsea, start at the hunting cabin again. We'll work our way south and go slow, maybe she'll be able to pick up on something."

"Dude." Marcus crossed his arms and gave Zander a once over with a smirk plastering his face, his eyebrow raised in trademark Marcus style.

"What?" Now wasn't the time to fuck around.

"You gonna get dressed first?" He rolled his eyes. "I mean, you're sexy as hell and all, but come on."

Zander looked down at himself.

"Right." He was in his room in a flash. Throwing on the first shirt he found, he sat to put on his jeans and shoes. The letter was crumpled at his feet. He picked it up to read again.

You deserve so much more than what I can offer. So does Stephen. Please don't try to find me. I trust you'll see to it that my little brother has everything he needs. You've shown me what love looks like. Thank you. I'm so sorry I'll never be able to do the same for you.
Grayce

He walked to the bathroom, stood in the doorway and stared into the shower. Last time they were in this room she had bared her soul to him. Their conversation played on a continual loop in his head. She said she needed him. Why would she try to leave?

Crushing the letter, he threw it across the room, claiming the wastebasket as a victim. A vial rolled across the floor and landed at his feet.

"Holy shit." Grayce's name was printed on the label. "What the?" He ripped the necklace from his wrist, laid it on the counter and ran to the other side of the estate. Halfway there, his skin started to crawl. The insatiable itch and burn consumed him within seconds. He hightailed it back to the bathroom and retrieved the heart.

"She's a fucking genius." Zander slammed the locket on the table and held the vial in the palm of his hand. "This is why I'm not having withdrawals. She filled the thing with her blood."

He would've been proud of her, if he wasn't so pissed.

Nikolas stood, mouth agape and twisted the glass bottle in the light. "Zander, I think I'm in love with that little firecracker of yours. Your right. Fucking. Genius." His eyes glazed over, the first indication that his brain was kicking into high gear. If Zander didn't pull the brakes immediately, Nikolas would be lost for days.

"Get a grip, man. You can mull over this later. We need to go. Now."

"Yeah. Sorry." Nikolas blinked away the lost expression. "Put that locket back on and go get Grayce." He shoved the vial in his pocket. "I've been called to the hospital. One of the missing women was found alive. I'll take Marcus with me. If she's able to talk, perhaps we can find out where she was being held. We'll meet up with you there."

* * * *

Stephen hung from shackles looped over a beam in the ceiling. How did that man catch him? He was so fast. Not as fast as Zander, but super fast.

He tried to throw his lightning but his palms were pressed together and bound too tight. He'd burn a hole through his own skin. He wiggled, squirmed, screamed in anger. The binds pulled tighter. He stiffened as the door creaked behind him.

"Boy. Stop fighting. It will only insure that you become more uncomfortable." Footsteps drew close behind him and an arm encircled his waist. "Now listen carefully to me." The arm squeezed and lifted enough to allow a little slack in the rope. "Would you like to come down from here?"

Stephen fought back tears. He was a man. He would not cry.

He lowered his voice trying to sound brave, hoping to hide the nervous tremble. "Yes."

"Good. I'm going to let you down, but you have to promise to be a good little pet." The man released him from the hook and his arms fell in an agonizing thud against his groin. A painful tingle rushed through his veins as the blood returned to his limbs. As Stephen turned to face the man, a scream of terror escaped his lips.

"No." He slammed his lids shut. It was his imagination. It couldn't be him. It couldn't be Shayde. A sharp sting to his cheek forced his eyes open.

"Boy, look at me." Stephen eyed the man up and down. This time, a tear did manage to sneak down his face. Not a tear of sadness or fear, but a tear of relief. It wasn't him. Holy cow, he sure looked like Shayde. Same eyes. Same narrow, pointy nose.

"Who are you, boy?" The man grabbed his shoulders and spun him around. "I said, who are you?"

"I'm—I'm Stephen," he sputtered.

"Stephen who? Where do you come from?" Stephen liked that the creep seemed confused. Wow, he looked so much like Shayde. They could be twins...almost.

Another smack to the face. "Dammit, boy. Answer me." He was shaken so hard he thought his head was going to snap off and fly across the room. He sure was as mean as Shayde.

"I don't know. I don't know!" he screamed. A metallic taste filled his mouth.

The man pushed him to the ground and kicked his thigh. "Don't know who you are, or don't know where you come from?" He kicked again and paced to the other side of the room. Stephen scanned the area for some means of escape or maybe a weapon. The room was empty except for a metal chair.

With his hands tied together, he couldn't get to his feet quick enough to make a run for it. "I don't know who I am." He glared up at the monster. "I don't know where I come from."

Something in his shoulder popped when he was jerked up by his arms and shoved into the chair. He bit his tongue to hold back the scream.

"Boy, I have a game I like to play. I think you might like it too." Stephen's skin tingled as the man caressed his sore cheek. "It's a game I like to play with Grayce. You like Grayce, don't you?" Stephen fought to get up as the man grabbed his face and forced him to make eye contact.

A flash of red jetted across his retinas. Stephen had seen that before in Shayde's eyes, right before he tried to kill him.

"Does she make you feel good, boy?" Stephen nodded again. Why was he asking about Grayce? There was no way his sister liked playing games with this man. She didn't play. Ever. "Grayce makes me feel good, too." A smile that didn't look right showed large, straight teeth. "Why were you following her?"

Stephen blinked. "I was protecting her." He spat blood in anger and waited for the man to laugh. The laugh didn't come. Just a hard stare going right down to his insides and reading his thoughts.

He didn't want to talk to this man anymore.

* * * *

Zander set Chelsea on her feet and braced her shoulder until she found her balance. Shame riddled his spirit. He'd never experienced such a feeling of helplessness. They'd made four rounds on the outskirts of town and found nothing. Mental and physical exhaustion claimed Chelsea. It killed him to stop, but she needed a recharge.

"I'm sorry, Zander." Utter dread filled her eyes.

He cupped her face. "It's not your fault and we're not finished. We'll find them."

Failure wasn't an option. Nor was quitting. Chelsea needed to recoup, but he didn't.

"I'll leave you here to rest awhile. Find your husband, give him a squeeze, you'll be good to go in no time." They stood at the hospital entrance. Zander grabbed her hand and led her inside.

"Come with me. We'll see if Nikolas has any information." Chelsea took a few steps, then froze. "Nikolas is near her room. He can't get in. The detectives are with her, but she's conscious."

They started to jog. Hope and relief swelled in Zander's gut. Adrenaline surged through his veins. When they rounded the final corner, he skidded to avoid bowling down a crowd of doctors, police and reporters. The hall buzzed with excitement.

"We're not getting any closer than this." He held Chelsea to his side. "Can you read her thoughts through all of this? Are there too many people?"

"It'll take me a minute." Chelsea grabbed his arm for support and closed her eyes.

Zander scanned the crowd in search of Marcus or Nikolas. Not like either one of them would be hard to find. In the center of the chaos, Nikolas appeared to be consulting with a few other doctors. Marcus pushed his way through the crowd toward them, clearing a path with little effort.

"Any news?" Zander asked when Marcus drew near.

"She can't talk. Dislocated jaw, shattered bones in her face and skull." Marcus' head hung low on his shoulders. "Hunters found her, hidden in the bushes. Said they would've walked right by if the buck they'd been chasing hadn't trampled her. They heard her scream. God, the poor girl."

Chelsea's eyes snapped open and she grabbed Zander's arm. "She escaped from the mining tunnels." Her knees buckled. She fell so fast he missed her waist and caught her around the bosom. "Oh, dear Lord. The things he did..."

"Stop, Chelsea. We have enough." He choked down the thick lump in his throat. "Chelsea, you saved her today. You found her when I couldn't. I owe you my life." He planted a kiss on her forehead. "Stay here with Marcus."

He didn't give them time to answer. Marcus would've insisted on helping, but would have slowed him down. While he didn't mind carrying the ladies or a child while engaging light speed, he had no desire to get that up close and personal with his tall, dark and deadly friend.

Mining tunnels? Shit. He thought those had been closed down for decades. He cursed himself for the oversight then headed for the hills.

* * * *

Grayce hung on the wall, arms above her head, legs sprawled, naked but no longer afraid.

Not afraid of Tyr, anyway.

The darkness beckoned, promised safe haven from whatever fate the monster had in store. She could see now, that the security and comfort if offered was a lie. It wanted her soul, the same as the monster.

She had her fire, and Zander. The darkness had nothing on them. It was no longer welcome in her world. Like Tyr and the control he once wielded, it was her past. Zander was her future.

She no longer feared Tyr. She feared losing the one thing in her life that offered her true grace.

Zander.

The man offered unconditional love, physical and emotional protection, and never asked for one goddamned thing in return.

Like an idiot, she had tried to run away from him. What the fuck was she thinking?

How did she end up like this again? How did Tyr find them in the middle of nowhere? She'd been on the phone and he'd just walked out of the hunting cabin like he was going out for a stroll. By the look on his face, he had been every bit as shocked to see her as she'd been to see him. Everything after that was a blur.

Fire rose. Flames of anger licked the reopened wounds of her psyche. She hoped that when Zander found her it would at least be after Tyr had played and let her down. The thought of him seeing her tethered to the wall angered her beyond reason.

Zander would tear down the town, the surrounding mountains, and anyone who dared get in his way until he found her. He would find her. There wasn't a doubt in her mind.

Grayce pulled against her restraints and peered down at herself. Fuck no. She'd kill herself before letting Zander see her strung up like a puppet. He'd caught a glimpse of her lowest moments and it broke something inside him. He'd never see her weak and frail again. She'd make sure of it.

Summoning the tempest she'd been holding at bay, she forced it through her arms and legs, concentrating on her wrists and ankles until the binds smoldered. The glow engulfed her, then expanded and billowed through the room.

Focus and control was vital. Stephen was close. She couldn't risk hurting him just to watch Tyr burn. In agonizing slow motion, the binds turned to ash and fell from her skin, releasing her naked body from the wall.

Her body trembled with need to let loose the fury. Grayce quelled the inferno. It danced, swirled, taunted and begged to be unleashed, but she held it at bay.

It wasn't time. Not yet.

She turned her thoughts to Zander, her refuge. She imagined him wrapped around her as she swam in those mystical eyes of his. As she relaxed, the energy dissipated and receded back into her skin. Her clothing was nowhere to be found.

Fuck it. If she had to do this naked, so be it.

Chapter 15

Zander's anger swelled, pushing the limits of his sanity. The pitch black tunnels made it impossible, even for someone with his superior senses, to travel any faster than a turtles pace.

The deeper he wandered, the more treacherous the terrain, the more complex the web of corridors. He would've skipped to the end and brought the whole mountain down on top of Tyr and himself if his Grayce hadn't been trapped inside.

It was an endless network of passages. One opened to two. They opened to two or three more. There were so many. Like a labyrinth. The monster hid Grayce and Stephen in a fucking labyrinth. It was the perfect place to hide. Or to hide somebody.

A child's scream echoed through the dark corridors drawing his attention to the left. A smaller passage he would've otherwise passed held the faintest illumination. One a normal human eye wouldn't have registered.

With a huff and a shove, he reduced the ominous heavy wooden door at the end of the trail to splinters. Energy flooded his veins. His strength increased. Heart rate, too. Grayce was close.

So help him, he would tear the psychopath limb from limb without a moment's hesitation this time.

He entered an empty room lighted with a small bulb hung over a ceiling beam. At the far end, a door hung ajar. Stephen's scent and the stench of sulfur filled the air, the remnants of his lightning.

With savage fury he tore through the open door leaving rusted hinges in his wake. Fuck. Another tunnel. This shaft was lit with several dim LED lamps spaced every five feet. Several more doors lined the dirt walls.

The first was ajar and revealed an empty cave. Door number two led him to a makeshift bathroom. Bloody rags lay on the floor in the corner.

His rage spiked, beating through his ears like the hoof beats of a thousand stallions marching off to war, carrying armor clad warriors upon their backs.

He walked straight through the next door with not so much as a flinch. Zander stopped dead in his tracks and pressed his palms to his temples to stop his brain from exploding with rage. He stood in an exact replica of the room Grayce had been tortured in for years.

Burnt ropes lay on the ground at his feet. Good girl. She was fighting.

He turned to leave and a searing heat struck his head and threw him back through the doorway. Dirt and rocks exploded around him as his body made a permanent impression in the wall behind him. The earth rumbled, bits of the ceiling fell, black air filled his lungs.

Zander didn't bother to wipe the dirt from his eyes.

Attack. Kill.

Full blown rage consumed his thoughts, his actions, switching his brain to hard-core combat mode.

No thinking. Just doing.

He pushed himself from the gouge in the wall and charged. Blinded by dirt and dust, he slammed the attacker to the ground, wrapped both hands around his neck and prepared to detach it from the shoulders. A deep ancient battle cry escaped his lips, so fierce the walls trembled.

"Zander?" A soft voice pierced his scream.

What the fuck?

Blinking the grime from his eyes, he looked down to see Grayce underneath him, naked and beautiful, her red glow a protective shield. "Shit. Zander I'm sorry. I thought you were—"

His lips were on hers before she finished. Hunger, need and desperate gratitude rushed through him. He chewed her lips, savored the flavor, then moved to her neck.

"Grayce, baby. I'm so sorry. Thank God, you're alive."

She trembled under his touch, covering her breasts as he performed a thorough examination of her body. Scratches and bruises, but nothing life threatening. " Did he hurt you?"

"No. I'm fine. He didn't touch me." The quiver in her voice was faint, but enough so that her lie was obvious. Zander took his shirt off and pulled it over her head. His breath caught when he spied the gash across her chest.

She glared and shook her head in warning. "Not now. We have to get Stephen. He's here somewhere." The panic in her eyes set his blood aflame.

"Fuck that."

He carried her through several long corridors before Grayce found her voice. "Zander. What are you doing? Put me down." Pounding his chest and arms with useless abandon, she tried to free herself from his embrace. "We have to get Stephen."

"I'm getting you the hell away from here first. I'll come back for Stephen." He searched the darkness, trying to remember which way to go. The absence of light and sound played tricks on his senses.

"No!" She punched at him harder. "No Zander. We get him now. Together. Don't fucking do this to me."

The growl that rumbled deep in his chest and throat surprised even him. Grayce froze. "Don't fight me right now, love. I can't think straight until I know you're safe."

"No. I can help. Please." In a display worthy of an Oscar, Grayce hugged his neck, buried her face in his shoulder and begged. "Don't leave me alone. Don't leave me."

Oh God, this was not in her character and pathetic as hell. He may have laughed at her audacity if the situation weren't so dire.

"Zander. I need you, I'm scared. Let me stay with you," she whimpered against his neck.

"For fuck's sake. Grayce. You're killing me." He lowered her to the ground. "I'm not an idiot. I know what you're doing."

She pulled his shirt over her bare ass. "Sucker. Don't be mad. I can help." He watched with pride as a warm, red glow illuminated the tunnel. "See?"

With a deep sigh, he shook his head. She was right. "Damn, Grayce. Fine." He wrapped his arm around her and guided her back through the dark maze. When they were back in front of the playroom, Grayce paused.

"Give me a sec." Placing her hand on his abdomen to block his entrance, she lifted her chin, rolled her shoulders and entered. Standing in the doorway, his heart damn near burst in his chest as he watched his woman raise her arms, and with complete control disintegrate the entire contents of the room, right down to the paint. It bubbled and blistered on the walls until there was nothing but ash. It was necessary. He understood. It was healing, soul cleansing. She turned and pushed her way past him. Mouth sealed tight, he watched her wipe a tear from her cheek and carry herself with a new found confidence.

"They went this way." Grayce stormed through the door to the left. Her glow cut through the dark better than a flashlight. Barefoot and half naked, Grayce led the way, her determination stronger than the cuts and blisters on her feet.

God he loved this woman.

* * * *

The man yanked Stephen through a dark tunnel into the fresh air. He glanced around at his surroundings. Above the entrance, which hid behind large boulders, the mountain towered in a steep stretch toward the sky. Around him, tall grass and smaller trees spread down a small hill. He tried to decide which would be the safest direction to run. But if he ran, he couldn't save his sister. No way was he going to leave her alone.

"Come here, boy." Long fingers stretched in front of him. Fingers that hurt people. Fingers far too pretty for a man.

Stephen backed up one tiny step at a time, careful not to take his eyes off the creep in front of him. The ropes binding his wrists loosened as he wiggled his arms, frantic to free himself.

"We're going to have fun together."

What would Marcus do? Marcus would fight.

Zander would smash.

Still struggling to free his arms, he ignored the blood that formed around the binds. Stephen jetted toward the man with girl hands and kicked him in the shins with ferocious strikes.

"Where's Grayce?" He charged again, shoved his shoulder into the man's thigh, bounced off and tripped over a large rock. "Asshole! Where's Grayce? Take me to her." He leapt to his feet and gave the man the most threatening glare he could muster.

"Boy. Maybe we got off to a bad start." The man tapped his chin with his long finger, folded his arms over his chest and backed away.

Stephen bit at the ropes on his wrists. He had to save Grayce.

"That isn't going to do you any good. You could chew on those for a week and you wouldn't be free."

Stephen spat at the man. His blood boiled and a hundred different ways to kill the black-eyed beast flashed through his mind. Anger pounded and beat against his temples. He was angry for getting captured. Mad he couldn't get himself loose. Most of all, furious he hadn't protected Grayce.

"I'll untie you, but hear me child. If you run, I'll catch you. The punishment will be severe." The man slanted his head and looked Stephen up and down. "You're a fighter, boy. I like that about you." In one stride, the man had a grip on Stephen's arm and swiped at his feet, knocking him to the ground. "Don't try to escape. I'm tired and not in the mood for playing chase." He straddled Stephen's thighs and unknotted the rope. "Now boy, you are going to help me—"

The moment his wrists were free, Stephen sent a blue bolt straight at the man's heart. The force threw the man backwards and he landed with a thud against a tree trunk. Stephen's lightning danced playful and free around the man's body as he looked down at a charred wound in the center of his chest. "You shouldn't have done that."

Before Stephen could stand, the man's skinny hands were wrapped around his throat.

"What was that, boy?" Evil spirits danced in the man's eyes. The same demons he used to see in Shayde's glare.

If he didn't get away, he was going to die.

Death by girlie fingers.

No. Not gonna happen.

Stephen struck again, but the man disappeared. A fearsome chuckle gave away his location behind a nearby tree.

"Where's Grayce?" Stephen screamed. Another shot hit the tree dead center. Sparks and sticks flew. The tree snapped at the point of contact.

The man stood and looked down at the hole just below his chest. It was a perfect circle and went all the way through.

The scent of burning flesh filled Stephen's nostrils, stinging his eyes. The man laughed. He wore no smile on his face, but he laughed.

"A boy? Bested by a pathetic child?" He cackled. "Impossible." He staggered and balanced himself against the tree stump.

"Boy." The scowl he shot Stephen would be forever burned in his memory. "I'm going to have to kill you now. It's a shame. We could have done—" He stumbled forward and clenched his chest. "We could've done some amazing things, you and I."

Stephen watched in horror as the man staggered toward him. The hole in his body oozed black goo.

He was mesmerized by the wound. Looked like he could fit his arm clean through it. He made that hole. Where was the blood?

Gross.

His knees wobbled. "Where's Grayce?" Stretching his arms toward the man again, Stephen crouched, ready for battle.

The man swayed toward Stephen, reached for him with long trembling arms. "You won't kill me. I'll take you to Grayce. Come here boy. Help me. I'll take you to Grayce."

Bracing to strike again, Stephen nearly jumped out of his skin as a large hand lay across his arms, forcing them down to his sides. "Get behind me Stephen. Now."

For the first time in what felt like hours, Stephen breathed.

Familiar arms pulled him behind Zander and locked him in a tight embrace. "Oh thank God. Are you all right?" Stephen nodded but didn't answer. Relief washed away the crippling fear. She was safe. Grayce was safe.

"Stephen. Listen to me. You need to go back into the tunnel."

He shook his head no. "No way." If there was a fight, he was gonna help.

"Don't argue with me. Just go. We'll be right there." Grayce's eyes were red. Bright, shiny balls of red. He knew better than to argue. Slumping his shoulders, he turned toward the entrance.

* * * *

"My little dove. You're here." Tyr held welcoming hands toward Grayce. A wet cough had blood and black liquid spewing over his chin. "I'm already feeling better. It's amazing, the effect you have on me."

"You've got a bit of a hole in your chest." Grayce stepped out from behind her giant guardian. "Does it hurt much?" Her lips twitched and the coldness in her glare gave him cause to take a step back. Fear no longer existed behind those hazel eyes.

Hatred. Fierce, flaming hatred.

Tyr's body convulsed as he tested his ability to teleport. Too weak still. Perhaps if she came closer he could grab her and disappear.

"You're mine, Grayce."

Dead or alive.

"Remember that." He warned.

"Like hell I am." Raising outstretched palms, she took a confident step toward him.

"Grayce no." The giant commanded and grabbed her arm. She turned with shocking speed and forced a red flaming ball at the blond warrior. He stumbled backwards and fell to the ground.

"This is my fight" She glared with stone cold fury. "Stay the fuck back."

Tyr struggled to maintain his composure along with his balance. What was this? A red glow enveloped Grayce, swelled like a rising tide, expanded and spread toward him. His mind raced with possibilities. How did he not know of this power she possessed?

She moved closer. His body warmed.

That's it, keep coming...just a little closer.

With every step she took toward him, his body strengthened. The pain in his chest subsided, his breathing came easier. She was so close. He just needed to touch her...

* * * *

Time slowed almost to a stop. The familiar snap, pop and buzz of electrified heat swarmed around Grayce's head.

This was it. Her only chance to stop him, to end Tyr. The monster lay on a silver platter. Apple in his mouth. Just for her.

Shit. It was almost as if he begged her—*come and get me.* Was he anxious for the end? He appeared weak and vulnerable. A state she'd never seen him in. The hole in his chest was a pleasant surprise. Gruesome as hell, but amusing to see nonetheless.

"Yes, my little dove. Come to me." Fingers splayed, he reached for Grayce, nodding as if to assure her everything would be fine.

With measured steps she inched toward the monster. Fury swept around her, turning underbrush to embers at her feet. The demon who'd turned her into a shell of a human, who had made sure she'd never love or feel loved, stood powerless before her, yet dared to assume control.

Zander loomed behind. Vibrations of protective rage radiated against the back of her head with each angry breath he released.

Tyr stood straighter, took a step forward, eyes filled with hope. "That's it. Yes. My little dove. My Grayce. Mine."

"Yours, yes yours." Grayce stopped just close enough to envelope Tyr inside her red field of retribution.

"Your pain."

His clothing smoked and charred. Thread by thread it fell away from his body.

"Your suffering."

The deep black hair on his head turned gray and piece by piece blew away, ashes on the wind.

"Your demise."

His perfect skin bubbled and blistered.

He didn't flinch. Didn't scream. Didn't try to get away.

"Mine."

A large hand wrapped around his neck, held him just out of arms reach. Zander lifted Tyr off the ground, an offering to her. A gesture she would hold dear to her heart until her dying breath. A simple act that proved without a doubt his deep love for her. Her mate, her lover offering up a chance for true healing.

"Your angel of death."

Grayce pulled hard from the molten depths of her soul and forced every bit of fury, fear and torment straight at the monster now dangling in Zander's hand.

An unholy scream spilled from Tyr's bloodied lips as his skin charred and peeled away from his body in flakes. His flesh ignited, turned to flame then ash. As Zander released his bones, they hung for a moment, floating and dancing, suspended on a gust of thermal wind.

Grayce screamed as a flaming ball erupted around her. Tyr's bones were carried away, embers glowing through the darkening sky. Zander was thrown back through the trees. Above, the mountain rumbled as rocks tumbled and rolled toward her.

Bone-tired, Grayce fell to her knees and sucked hard to pull oxygen back into her lungs. A boulder missed her head by inches as it skidded and bounced down the mountain.

Oh shit, Stephen.

Grayce forced herself to her feet and ran toward the tunnel opening, dodging falling rocks. A sharp pain bit her shoulder and knocked her backwards. Hot, hard muscle broke her fall and she was whisked deep inside the mine.

Zander and Stephen were at her side. The threesome covered their ears. A thunderous roar echoed through the opening as the entrance was sealed by rocks, dirt and collapsed mountainside.

* * * *

Stephen rubbed at the bandages around his wrists and smiled. They made him look tough, but they'd be so much cooler if they were black. There had to be a magic marker lying around somewhere.

"Stephen, aren't you hungry?" Chelsea asked and leaned her elbows on the table.

He glanced down at his grilled cheese. "Not really."

"Does it taste bad?" She picked up his sandwich, took a bite and chewed. "Nope, no poison. It's safe to eat." Chelsea always made jokes and usually he made them too. Just didn't feel like it today.

"Did I kill him?" He picked up a pickle spear and stabbed it at his fruit salad. "I made a huge hole in him." Disgusting too. Made his stomach sick. But he didn't need to tell Chelsea that. She would worry.

"No Stephen, you didn't kill him. You were so brave. I'm very proud of you." She scooted her chair closer and rubbed his back.

"But he's gone, right?" Zander and Grayce had taken him away so fast, he didn't see what happened. They wouldn't tell him afterward either.

"Yes, he's gone. He'll never hurt you or anyone ever again."

He pushed his plate away and leaned his chin on the table. "But he was bad, so if I killed him, it would've been okay, right?"

"You're right. He was a very bad man. The worst kind. But no, it's not okay to kill people."

He took a deep breath. "Chelsea, I wanted to kill him. I was so mad that he hurt Grayce." Did that make *him* bad? He sure hoped not.

"I know, sweetie." She pulled him toward her and kissed his cheek. He hated lip germs. He didn't want to hurt her feelings, so he didn't wipe his face. "And there is nothing wrong with you feeling that way."

"I'm strong enough, I could've killed him."

"Yes, but being strong doesn't make it okay to hurt people, even when you think it's for the right reason. If you do, you'll be just like him."

"I don't want to be like him. The bad guys never win. I want to be the superhero."

"You will be, Stephen. The best superhero ever." She smiled her big happy smile. He loved it almost as much as her cookies. Maybe Chelsea would help him make a cape. Not red though. It would have to be blue or silver to match his lightning.

"What's for lunch?" Marcus kissed Chelsea on the head, grabbed the chair next to Stephen and started to fill his plate. "Why aren't you eating?"

"Just not hungry." He looked at Marcus and shrugged.

"Too bad. I was hoping for some racing action after lunch. You can't beat me with an empty stomach. I bought two new controllers. I'll be gone for a few weeks. This is my last chance to beat your high score."

Stephen picked up his fork and started in on the fruit. No way was he going to let Marcus beat his high score. No way. "Wait a minute. Gone? Where are you going?"

"I'm taking a vacation." Marcus wiggled his eyebrows and then winked.

Oh yeah. He had some stupid crush on a girl. Yuck.

"Did you find out where she went?" Chelsea asked.

"Yeah. Go figure. Her first vacation in years. Great timing, huh? She's heading to a private island off the coast of Guyana. I swear. The gods are punishing me."

Chelsea giggled. "So you're going to follow her."

"Well, I'm certainly not waiting two more weeks to meet her."

Stephen finished the fruit and picked up his sandwich. Marcus was acting goofy about this woman, all soft and sweet. So not Marcus. It was weird.

Chelsea sighed and rolled her eyes. "Poor girl. She'll never know what hit her."

Nikolas burst through the room. "You're not going to believe this." He rushed to Chelsea's side. Oh no, Stephen thought. They're going to kiss again. He squeezed his eyes shut.

"What darling?" Chelsea pushed her chair back.

Stephen waited for the yucky kissing sound. It didn't happen so he peeked out of one eye first.

Nikolas slapped a picture down on the table. "We found another one. She's six. Her mom brought her in, thought she had a broken arm. It was a fluke that I even saw her. Just happened to be walking by. I knew the moment I looked into her eyes, she's one of us." His voice got higher and his eyes looked funny. Stephen perched himself on his knees to get a look. Hey, he knew that girl.

He grabbed the picture. "That's my friend."

"What?" The grown-ups said at the same time.

The girl in the picture looked like she was smiling just for Stephen and her eyes seemed a brighter green that what he'd noticed in his dreams. Her curly red hair filled up most of the photo. The color made him smile.

He handed the picture back to Nikolas. "She's my friend from my dreams."

"What a looker." Marcus whistled and patted Stephen on the back. "I can see why you'd dream about her."

Chelsea gasped and covered her mouth with her hand.

Nikolas looked like his head was going to explode.

Things sure were getting strange.

* * * *

Zander was angry. But more than that, his heart fucking hurt. He'd spent his whole life searching for her and she didn't want him. Well, he didn't give a shit if she wanted him or not.

This was not how their story would end.

"Why, Grayce?" Back turned to her, he forced the emotion down, choked on it. If she saw the fury on his face, she'd shut down. He needed her to explain. Needed to understand.

Voice meek, she whispered, "I can't love you."

"I don't care." He carried enough love for both of them. His Grayce. God, couldn't she see how amazing she was? What could he do to help her realize her worth?

"I want you to be happy. Loved. It's what you deserve." She paused, and drew a deep breath. "I can't have children. He made sure of that." Grayce cringed. "I'll never be able to give you a family."

Zander unsuccessfully fought back a shiver. Fuck. What he wouldn't give to pull Tyr back from the depths of hell and kill him all over again with torturous, painful precision.

No children. He'd never even thought about having kids. His whole adult life had only been about Grayce. Finding, saving and loving Grayce.

"I don't want children." He glanced over his shoulder, feet frozen in place. Fighting back the images of what Tyr had done to make her barren, it took several deep breaths before he continued. "Why can't you see I only want you?"

Unable to bear the distance between them any longer, he crossed the room and swept her into his arms. "Only you."

Fresh from her shower, hair fell in wet tendrils over her shoulders, dampening her thin cotton shirt. As he pulled her close, her nipples hardened against his bare skin. "I killed a man today."

"No. That thing you killed was a monster, a demon." Zander had wanted to be the one to end the life of the psychopath who tortured his love. "He lost his humanity a long time ago. You saved countless lives today."

"I wasn't thinking of anyone other than myself. I wanted him to suffer." She squeezed his middle. "I'm damaged Zander. Mentally as much as physically. You got the raw end of the deal in this match-up. You deserve so much better." Her wet cheek pressed against him. Tears cascaded down his torso.

"Dammit Grayce. Don't say things like that. I never want to hear those words from you again." He sat her in the chair, knelt between her thighs and clenched her wet face in his hands. "You're beautiful and amazing and I love you. I love you so much it hurts." Her tears fell faster than his thumbs could wipe them away. "Stephen loves you too. We love your bad temper. We love your foul mouth."

"You deserve to be with a woman who can love you wholly. Not just physically." Chin raised, she met his gaze. The wisdom and experience of a thousand lives shimmied behind her tears. "What if I'm never able to? That can't possibly be good enough for you."

"Grayce, let me ask you something."

She nodded, wiping moisture from her lashes.

"If we hadn't met, if I was unable to find you, do you think you would have ever given any man a chance?"

Confused, she shook her head. "Hell no. No fucking way."

Relief coursed through his veins. "I often thought of our withdrawals as a curse. You know, a cruel joke."

A breeze rolled through the broken window carrying the scent of fall into the room.

"Think about it. If we didn't have the withdrawals, if we didn't physically need to be near each other, you would have no reason to stay, right?" He didn't wait for her response. "But because of them, you and I need to be close. We don't have the option of leaving or giving up. We have to make this work."

An exasperated sigh escaped her lips. He held up a finger to stop her from speaking.

"Wait. Before you get mad, hear me out." He sat next to her in the chair. "You can't disappear into your dark place, right? You can't run away. You have to stay here with me. Don't you see? This is a good thing, not because it's taking your free will away, but because in time, you'll see that you can love and be loved. You will learn to love and trust again, because leaving is no longer an option."

* * * *

Grayce remained silent as she pondered his words. She hadn't thought of it that way. Maybe he was on to something.

There was no fucking way she would've let another man get near her. Because of the bond between them, Zander could never physically hurt her. His soul was too good to hurt her emotionally. So there was no reason to be afraid.

Could she love him eventually? Maybe she already did and just couldn't recognize it. Would she be able to love her brother? He'd already burrowed his own little groove into her heart. One thing she knew for sure, being alone sucked. Although it had kept her physically safe all these years, it left a vast hole in her spirit. One that could only be filled by her new family.

"Zander. Where's the bed?" She looked around the room, then toward the green valley through the missing window. The serene view steadied her spinning thoughts.

"You're not the only one with anger issues." He rubbed his fingers up the length of her arm and rested them in her hair. "I was pissed and scared. I didn't know where you were."

Worms danced the jitterbug in her stomach as he played with a curl. "Grayce. Please don't leave me again. It would kill me. Please tell me you'll at least try. Give us a chance."

He may as well have punched a hole in her chest and squeezed her heart with his bare hands. He didn't want to be alone. He was abandoned as a teen. She almost abandoned him again.

For some crazy reason, his need for her was more than physical. Maybe someday she'd understand why. Maybe not. In that moment, what she knew to be true, was in this man's arms, she felt safe and right and free.

Oh my God. She was free. No more running, no more hiding.

He knew everything about her twisted past, fucked up present and the instability the future held. Despite it all, he still wanted to be with her.

Craving the shelter of his arms and the rhythm of his blood flow, she climbed into his lap, straddled his marble hard thighs and nestled her hips against his groin. With hands splayed across his chest, she tried to speak the words he deserved to hear. The three words she wanted to say, but her throat shriveled and closed tight.

"You love me." He pressed a kiss to her nose.

"I can't love." She wanted to. She really did.

"You love me." A knowing smile sat smug and sure between deep dimples.

"Stop saying that."

His hands were hot brands against her butt. "Remember when you asked about my eyes. Why they turn purple?"

"Yes. You never answered me."

"They only do that when we've surrendered ourselves completely to the other. When mind, body and soul we've given ourselves to our mate." He pulled her against his growing arousal.

"I don't understand."

"Love, Grayce. That's love."

"Zander." She didn't want to argue anymore. "I have no doubt that you feel that way. You've proved it time and time again."

"Shut up. Let me finish." He groaned and moved her to the floor, trapped her in a cage of flesh and bone.

"Grayce. You silly, stubborn, hot tempered little fool." He ripped her shirt down the middle. "You love me." He sucked a nipple between his teeth.

"Zander, please—" He silenced her with warm, moist lips. She writhed with lustful need beneath him and worked to free his erection from the evil denim holding it prisoner.

"Your eyes, Grayce. Your eyes turned purple. Right before you blew the shower door to the moon."

He swallowed her gasp with another kiss. "Deny it all you want, but you love me."

Meet the Author

Years ago, while I was shopping, a group of firefighters walked into the store. One man stood head and shoulders above the rest. His blond hair, blue eyes and superhero stature stole my breath. The world slowed. My heart stopped. The entire store went silent, including my screaming children. Every head turned in his direction. That man was the sole inspiration for my first alpha male. While writing Zander's character, I searched relentlessly for a suitable likeness to share with my readers. I'm afraid I've had zero success. We all have a different standard of beauty. The wonderful thing about reading is, no matter how detailed the author's description, our own imaginations paint the portrait of each character we fall in love with.

Grayce is a culmination of women I've known. Some survivors, some broken spirits, all still fighting to find inner peace and a sense of worth. I let Grayce have revenge for all of us who aren't able to find closure, no matter the situation. I hope you enjoyed her journey as much as I did.

Acknowledgements

To my Sexy Boyfriend, thank you for the laptop and the ginormous leap of faith it represents. And of course, for rockin' my world every day in every way.

My babies, who wholeheartedly believe I'll be rich and famous, your imaginations and sense of humor inspire me beyond reason.

Mom and Share-Bear, thank you from the depths of my soul for your beautiful spirits and unwavering faith in me. I love your poochy lips to the moon. We can't kick the asses we need to in real life, so let's do it through stories.

Jen, the greatest storyteller I know, your relentless encouragement means the world to me. It's because of you this book exists. Now it's your turn.

Thank you Lyrical Press, for the YES. Corinne, thank you for holding my hand through this, my first rodeo, and kicking my arse when I needed it. Your comments made me giggle and guided me through the soul-sucking edits with a bit of hair left on my head.

And thank you Jesus, the one true superhero. I've been uplifted, humbled, educated and challenged. This awesome journey is your story, not mine.

Turn the page for a special excerpt of Krissy Daniels's

How to Kill Your Boss - An Erotic Love Story

When Tatum's daydreams of murder become a reality, all fingers point to her.

In Tatum Wood's opinion, murdering her boss on a daily basis within the safety of her thoughts is better than therapy. Until he takes a swan dive off a building and all evidence points to her. Thank goodness she has Franklin Reed. Her mysterious, overprotective and drop-dead gorgeous coworker is all too eager to play hero. With two attacks in her building and her stalker with a penchant for roses, Franklin's injection into her life couldn't have come at a better time.

As Tatum and Franklin scramble to discover who's behind the murder, secrets are unearthed that question his motives...as well as his identity.

On sale now!

Chapter 1

As the blade sliced through the taught flesh of his stretched neck, revenge was not first and foremost on my mind. When his skin spread wide, revealing the muscles and tendons beneath, I didn't squirm, gag, or suffer the slightest queasiness. Warm blood stained his shirt, sprayed across his desk, coated the leafy fern nestled in the sunny corner of his office, yet my thoughts were not filled with twisted delusions of hell yeah, he's getting what he deserves.

No.

Rocky road ice cream called my name.

Mmm. My stomach rumbled. The closest grocery store was what, five minutes away? What time was it? I used the back of his shirt to wipe his blood off my watch. He wouldn't mind. He was dead. Oh good, only nine-thirty. Plenty of time to get to the store before it closed.

When I released my death grip on the over-gelled, wiry hair rooted in Wallace Cruse's head, he slumped and fell with a hard thud against the hickory desk. I cringed, thinking that must hurt, then remembered he couldn't feel a thing.

Before dropping the weapon, I contemplated stabbing him in the back a few times, for dramatic effect. But time was-a-tickin' and I needed my chocolate fix.

"Tatum!" he called out to me with his whiney voice.

What? I killed him. Dead people didn't talk. Raising my arms over my head, I double-fisted the thick handle of the butcher knife, and with all my might pounded into a less-than-spectacular back. His flesh offered no resistance, and at first, I thought I'd missed.

So I did it again.

A pillow stuffed with pudding would've put up a better fight. The blade sunk with no effort right through flesh and bones. Its tip stuck in the edge of the desk.

Interesting. Apparently, his physical form was as weak as his moral character....

"Tatum. Tatum!" A whack to my backside snapped me back to reality. "Stop daydreaming. You gotta see this." Nan looped an arm around mine and guided me down the hall. Stacy, from accounting, shushed us from the opposite side of Wallace's door. Acting the love-sick teen, she wiggled her eyebrows, pointed toward his office, fanned her face, and swooned.

Whoever came to visit had to be hair-curling hot, because Stacy never behaved in such a manner. Maybe Wallace had landed a celebrity client again. Last time that happened, a fresh buzz of excitement chased the doldrums clean out of the place for weeks. We were long overdue for another shot of team spirit adrenaline.

"Tatum!" Wallace screeched with his high-pitched tenor. Thank goodness Nan still held my arm, because I jumped hard enough to hit the ceiling.

I'd yet to ascertain why, when Wallace needed me, he didn't use the phone like everyone else. Nan's office was one door down in the opposite direction, yet he'd never screamed for her. I'd stopped trying to figure him out years ago. Instead of dwelling on the three thousand reasons I hated my boss, I fantasy-killed him at least once a day.

A chill swept over me when I stepped through the threshold. The room, as always, reeked of overpriced hair and hand lotion. Only this time, a familiar scent tickled my nose. Dad's cologne. I choked back the emotion that gelled in my throat. Even though he'd been dead for three years, I still welled with sentiment every time I caught a whiff of the beloved fragrance.

Wallace wore his fake smile and sat, back straight, hands clasped atop his desk. The unnatural gesture wasn't for my benefit, but the person seated across from him.

"Ah, Miss Wood." He lifted his chin to me. "Mr. Reed is joining our team today. Would you make sure Steve's old office is stocked with the essentials?"

Miss Wood? Oh, jeez. Wallace only addressed me with the formal title when he needed to crank the schmooze dial to high for important clients—important meaning filthy, stinking rich. This guy wasn't a client, so why the show?

"Of course." I didn't add "Mr. Cruse" to my reply because I knew it'd knock him down a peg. "I'll be happy to." Although I'd known Wallace my whole life, he insisted I call him Mr. Cruse at work, a request only made after my father passed. Dad would've slapped him silly for being so high-handed with me.

"Anything else?" I asked, sugar-coating my words.

The man seated in front of me turned his head my direction, revealing what had incited the tizzy outside. Yikes! One glance and my heart pitter-pattered. Those eyes. Electric blue, so striking I took a step back. I snapped my attention to Wallace. His ugly I could handle, and it didn't make me drool.

A deep, intoxicating voice rose from the man before me. "Aren't you going to introduce us?" he asked, and turned to face Wallace once again.

My boss' eyebrows crinkled. "Of course. Miss Wood is our receptionist. Tatum, this is Franklin Reed." Wallace cleared his throat, a nervous gesture he'd developed over the years. It only happened when he lied, or as he called it, embellished the truth, to land clients. "I've hired an auditor to tighten up productivity around here."

Franklin rose, lithe and poised, from the chair. He turned toward me and offered a hand. "Pleasure to meet you, Tate."

Tate? Nobody had called me Tate except for my father and the assholes in high school. One-Date Tate. The nickname and the curse followed me like a perpetual shadow through most of my academic career.

I would've corrected him, but when his full mug came into view, my tongue curled up and shriveled. My IQ dropped thirty points. Again, I quickly averted my eyes. I had no choice. They threatened to pop out of my head. There was good looking and there was gorgeous. This man played in a league that put both of them to shame. "Pleasure meeting you," I managed to stutter. With grace comparable to a drunk college freshman, I grasped his hand and gave it one good shake. When I tried to pull away, he squeezed tighter and caressed a thumb across my knuckles.

My girlie parts twitched. No joke. I needed to leave before I left a puddle of desire on the floor between my feet. Holy cow, I'd never been affected in such a way.

"The pleasure is all mine." Franklin tilted his head as if inviting me to admire him.

Nope. No way. I would not look into those eyes again. The way my body reacted, I'd end up sprawled naked across the desk with a rose between my teeth. I reclaimed my hand and jetted through the door.

www.ingramcontent.com/pod-product-compliance
Lightning Source LLC
Chambersburg PA
CBHW031431250626
47155CB00004B/1701